THE SCREAMING LANDS

THOMAS GRAMZA

The Screaming Lands
©2021 Thomas Gramza

All rights reserved. This book or any portion thereof may not be reproduced or used in any manner whatsoever without the express written permission of the publisher except for the use of brief quotations in a book review.

print ISBN: 978-1-09839-597-1
ebook ISBN: 978-1-09839-598-8

CONTENTS

Prelude: Blood in the Frostlands		1
Chapter 1.	Running Late	9
Chapter 2.	The Ash River	15
Chapter 3.	The Apparition	24
Chapter 4.	A Little Errand	28
Chapter 5.	Cloudless Thunder	53
Chapter 6.	Summoned	74
Chapter 7.	The Sacred Vault	79
Chapter 8.	Cinders and Soot	84
Chapter 9.	The Dead Mountain	99
Chapter 10.	The Meeting	106
Chapter 11.	The Coastlands	110
Chapter 12.	Troubled Seas	121
Chapter 13.	Orphans	132
Chapter 14.	The Crossing	143
Chapter 15.	The Dark Circle	167
Chapter 16.	The Jungle	170
Chapter 17.	The Beginning	179
Chapter 18.	Serpents	184
Chapter 19.	The Beastwitch	194
Chapter 20.	Freedom	208
Chapter 21.	Strange Travels	217
Chapter 22.	Dark Siege	225
Chapter 23.	A Shift in the Wind	232
Chapter 24.	War	240
Chapter 25.	The Beginning of the End	252
Chapter 26.	A Prayer in the Darkness	259
Chapter 27.	Flight	264

PRELUDE:

BLOOD IN THE FROSTLANDS

"They're too much for us! Pull back!" The urgent call of Clanlord Gresk rolled over the frozen battlefield. "Clanleaders, grab your weapons and follow me!" At once, several other burly dwarves lifted their axes, hammers, and spears and ran after their commander. None of them could believe what they were seeing.

By the time the first scout had rushed in to report that their beloved homeland was being invaded from the sea, the longboats of the warlock army were already being lowered into the northern bay from two great ships. More disturbing than the encroachment itself were the colors of each ship— one bore the flag and markings of the icelock order while the other bore those of the stormlocks. Even though the dwarves of the Frostlands had heard of the warlock orders uniting to unleash a plague upon Vedris only a year ago, they still could not believe these animals could ever stop killing one another. Yet here they were, united, flooding onto their shores.

With impressive speed the fierce dwarf clans were marshaled, but even they were taken aback to find a legion of reapers, casters, and monsters led by both stormlocks and icelocks advancing toward the cliffs that bordered their homeland. Even before the first arrow was loosed against the vicious horde, Lord Gresk knew that their cause was lost.

"Get your spears on those Tuskers," bellowed Gresk as he charged into battle, "your arrows are all but useless against that hide!" Suddenly, a stormcaster arrow struck the dwarf in his right shoulder, imbedding itself in the blessed iron armor beneath his bearskin cloak. In a grunt of pain he crashed down hard upon the ice. Without hesitation, he gripped the shaft of the arrow with both hands and, ignoring the lightning spell that sent shocking pain through his body, wrenched it out.

"Milord," cried Clanleader Delek, "are you all right?!?"

"I'm fine!" growled the rugged dwarf. "You've known me long enough to know that some blood and sparks aren't enough to keep me down." Wincing in pain, Gresk used his hammer to push himself to his feet. His muscles quivered and refused to obey. "Just give me a breath— those storm-arrows have a nasty sting to them." For a brief second the two old friends looked out over the madness of the shoreline.

Waves of reapers and casters were crashing upon the icy cliffs that the dwarves had set as their point of defense. Even with the advantage of high ground, the numbers and sorcerous weapons of their enemies were forcing the valiant dwarves back. Storm-arrows and ice-arrows filled the sky. Worse still, the massive beasts called 'Tuskers' were slashing through their formations and creating openings for the advancing reapers.

"Come on," called Lord Gresk, "if that Tusker cuts through our archers they can take the left pass and flank us!" Shaking off the effects of the storm-arrow, Gresk led the other clan leaders into the fray.

On the left point of the icy cliffs two squads of archers were fighting desperately for their lives. The Tusker before them had mauled his way through the ground troops and was now clawing into them. Easily ten feet tall, the creature bore huge bone tusks over its back, arms, and head. Amidst its long white fur, now matted with the blood of his victims, the beast had bony plates of armor that repelled any arrow or blade struck against them. Using its unearthly strength and its razor-sharp teeth and claws, it was tearing into the archers who were forced to use their long knives against it in close quarters.

"Bring him down before he can loose his tusks!" ordered Gresk. Frantically, the dwarf archers who did not lie wounded or dead piled upon the monster stabbing furiously hoping to find an opening in the beast's bony plates in order to get in the crucial killing stroke. The creature swiped and flailed with its claws sending dwarves flying in all directions. Two determined archers managed to draw blood from the Tusker, but it was too late.

Hunching over on all fours, the beast began to shake and shudder. Its snarls lifted into a great roar as suddenly all of the sharp tusks upon its back shot out viciously. Screams erupted from the dwarves surrounding the beast as almost a dozen tusks tore into them. Lord Gresk, who had almost reached them now, barely managed to raise his own shield in time. A flying tusk easily pierced his thick iron shield.

"You've taken the life of your last dwarf, Beast!" he shouted. Leaping over the bodies of his fallen archers, Gresk brought his enchanted stone-hammer down hard upon the white monster. As it smashed down, the hammer's enchantments sent thunder through the creature's body. The monster howled in agony as its insides were crushed and its fur and bony armor were ripped apart. The ruined

Tusker struggled to rise and bared its now broken fangs in hatred at the dwarf-lord. "Hah!" spat Gresk as his final blow ended the murderous beast's life.

"Here they come, Milord!" called Delek. The stormreapers and icereapers were upon them. Using the gap opened up by the Tusker, the ground forces of the enemy surged forward. Even in the thick snow they moved up the pass quickly with their wicked blades and spears upraised.

"There are too many of them!" barked Gresk. "We must stop their charge now or be overwhelmed by their numbers." Grasping his hammer with his two strong hands, he struck the side of the icy cliff first to the left and then to the right. Again, the magic of the smoothstone within his hammer sundered even the rock and ice of the cliff walls. A crushing avalanche poured over the attacking reapers, burying them completely. "That will only buy us a moment. We cannot let the other pass fall or our soldiers below will be trapped and our enemies will win the shoreline." Even as he directed his forces into new defensive formations, Gresk's heart burned inside him at the thought of the brave dwarves that had already been lost in this hopeless fight.

Now the two armies sought to master the right pass of the cliff. The last three Tuskers charged forward while the sky rained down a blanket of cruel arrows to aid their advance. Dwarves all around fell in smoke from the lightning-arrows or with parts of their bodies frozen solid from the ice-arrows. "We need to return fire!" ordered Delek. "Archers, push them back!" Set up atop the highest point of the cliff, the surviving archers loosed a deadly volley of their own. The barbed iron arrows dropped dozens of reapers, but they still could not penetrate the Tuskers' hides or slow their advance.

"Delek, have the clerics arrived yet?" asked Gresk.

"Cleric Valos is already preparing her spell. Cleric Nagon is not here yet."

"Hmph! Nagon's still riding that old tiger of his. We'll be lucky if he makes it at all," growled Lord Gresk. "Still, Valos is skilled. We'll have to be ready to follow her enchantment." Immediately, the dwarf lord issued new orders to his clanleaders.

In moments a burst of light erupted from behind the dwarven army. Cleric Valos had done her part. Bounding forward at incredible speed, seven giant wolves made of living ice raced toward the enemy. A roar of triumph went out from the dwarves as this magnificent wolf pack tore into the three Tuskers. Down crashed the behemoths into the snow, a rolling, slashing storm. Three of the wolves piled upon the first Tusker while the last two brutes were trying to fight off two wolves each. Lord Gresk marveled at the ice wolves for not even the strength and claws of the mighty Tuskers nor the weapons of the reapers could even crack the enchanted ice that made up their forms.

As the savage battle continued, the reaper forces readied their shields to repel another deadly hail from the dwarven archers. Suddenly, the wind moved unnaturally and the heavy clouds shifted high above the battlefield. An old voice lifted a prayer from the top of the cliff. Bright sunlight streamed down through the gaps in the grey clouds, but only upon the warlock forces. Reflecting up from the ice and snow, the sunlight seemed to double in brightness and blinded the attacking reapers and casters. Bows, swords, and spears were dropped as the fiends threw their hands to their eyes and screamed in pain.

"Well met, Cleric Nagon!" laughed Gresk. "I guess that old cat of yours is more spry than I thought." With the enemy in disarray the call to attack in force was given. Led by long spears, the ground troops of the dwarves surged into their blinded enemy like an avalanche. The clan leaders and Lord Gresk himself were in the middle of the fray wielding their sacred hammers with a wild ferocity.

In mere moments the invading army was now in full retreat. The vaunted Tuskers had been torn to shreds by the ice wolves and the reapers and casters were rushing and stumbling as fast as they could back to the shore of the icy sea. Leading the chase, Gresk's instincts suddenly stopped him in his tracks. "Hold here!" he cried out with his hammer lifted sideways above his head. Reading this command sign, his dwarves broke off their pursuit. "Stand ready!" he ordered. An uneasy silence settled upon the dwarven army.

"What is it, Milord?" asked Clanleader Ursin.

"Warlocks are never vanquished so easily," replied Lord Gresk, "especially a stormlock and icelock alliance."

"Aye," agreed Ursin, "they're too cunning to have only one plan of attack. And Valos' ice wolves crumbled just now. She and Nagon will be too tired to help for a while."

"The locks want us to rush in closer, I can feel it," said Gresk. "We'd best not press our luck. Traps only kill you if you walk into them. We need to move back and dig in before…" A forcing wind from the ocean interrupted the dwarf lord. Spiraling up from the frigid waters, a monstrous waterspout filled the sky before them. "They've conjured an elemental!" shouted Gresk. "Pull back, pull back!"

The dwarves retreated toward the passage up the cliff as fast as their short legs could move them, but they would not make it. Twisting and cutting forward, the living column of swirling water stopped at the edge of the shore. Now the icelocks played their role.

With blasphemy on their tongues, they weaved their sorceries upon the ice. Great fingers of thick ice clawed up from the frozen shore and into the waterspout. Shattering upon the water and wind, immense chunks of ice shot toward the fleeing dwarves. Like a massive catapult, the water elemental rained death upon the helpless army. Blocks of ice the size of boulders smashed onto the fleeing dwarves, crushing dozens instantly. Even those dwarves who made it to the base of the cliff passage were being crushed for they could not traverse the thick snow fast enough. Lord Gresk looked on in horror as his army was being decimated. Indeed, he was so busy using his enchanted hammer to fend off the savage hailstorm that he did not notice a ghostly form bearing great ethereal wings in the sky behind him. The Lockslayer had arrived.

CHAPTER 1

RUNNING LATE

"That's it, that's it— keep moving forward!" Tolund smiled as he encouraged his young 'opponent.' "Well done, Wade! Keep the point of your sword up and forward and make sure that your feet move with you. Remember that balance is everything here." Dust flew from underneath young Wade's steps and a large grin spread across his face. "Good! Good!" cried Tolund. "Now, let's start again from the center of the arena only this time you will be on defense and I'll be on offen—"

"TOLUND DELLENDER!" Heather's sharp tone froze both 'combatants' in their steps. "Have you lost your mind completely?!?"

Tolund knew he was in trouble. "I'm not that late am I?"

"Of course you're 'that late!' We still have to get across the length of the Bronze Quarter which, being that we'll be crossing it at midday, will be packed. Do you have any idea how angry Mr. Pierce will be with us if we're late on today of all days?!?" Heather's face was so red Tolund thought she might burst into flames straight away. Poor young Wade started putting his wooden sword away, making sure to avoid all eye contact with the irate girl.

"Don't worry, Heather, we can still make it on time," argued Tolund. "We'll just have to move a bit faster."

"Wonderful!" Heather scoffed. "I woke up early after packing last night and spent the last hour looking all over the hold for you and now I have to wear myself out to get to the river on time all because you had to give Wade one last lesson!" The girl looked like she was ready to take her spear and turn it on Tolund right then and there.

"If we use the alleys we can cut past most of the crowd," explained Tolund. "Come on, it won't take that long." Quickly, Tolund called 'farewell' to Wade and gathered up his fighting gear and his travel bag which he had placed on the edge of the practice arena. Knowing he was in too much trouble with her to belabor the point, he rushed past Heather without a backward glance."

Weaving and moving as best they could while carrying their bags and fighting gear, the two friends pushed through the crowd. "We're almost to the first row of alleys," Tolund called.

"Are you sure we should be going this way?" asked Heather. Tolund knew that she was referring to the shadows and secluded parts of the alleyways. Even in midday it was best to avoid them as they often harbored people who did not want to be noticed, particularly by the paladins who patrolled the busy streets. Both of them were also aware that servants of all the warlock orders used these alleys to travel about the city unnoticed.

"It'll be fine. It's a bright day and the streets around are full of people," Tolund answered. "Just keep moving and be glad it's not nighttime." Due to the presence of reapers and other dangerous folk, traveling through the alleys at night was a life-threatening and foolhardy gambit.

"Has Mr. Pierce told you anything else about this trip?" Heather asked as she jogged along.

"Nothing more than what he'd told us before. He said we're two of the four fighters representing Breligh's Hold on some far away competition so we'd better be prepared for new challenges. Oh, did you pack for hot weather like he told you to?"

"I did," answered Heather, "but I brought along some warm clothes just in case."

"Hold up," Tolund ordered as he stopped abruptly. In the shadows just behind a tavern called "Senwell's" a dark form began to move toward them. Once he shuffled out in the light of late morning, they saw a slovenly, portly man wearing a threatening grin.

"A couple of mice who've come out to play, eh?" Reaching behind his back the man brought forth a strange dagger bearing odd runes on the blade that shimmered with a faint green hue. Heather held her breath and felt the pendant around her neck tingle. Tolund set his bags down and stood up straight.

"Oh, I think you'll find this game of yours a bit too costly to play," Tolund warned as he unsheathed his dark blade from its shoulder scabbard. The bilereaper froze as he recognized the famous black sword of the boy who had vanquished the great warlock, Celnumus. Tolund shifted his step into an aggressive fighting stance just as Heather stepped up alongside of him, leveling her spear out in front of her. Mr. Pierce's training was serving them well at this moment.

Nervously, the reaper began to step backward as he held his dagger out in front. His eyes never left the gleaming black edge of Tolund's renowned blade. "Lucky for you it's not my place to teach you a lesson, Boy." The bilereaper began to move back toward the tavern door. "Your day's coming though, just you wait. Your day's coming!" With that last threat the man rushed into the dark tavern, slamming the door behind him.

The two friends let out a long sigh of relief. Tolund could feel his heart beating hard within his chest. "It's been a long time hasn't it?" Heather asked.

"Not long enough," Tolund nodded. Quickly, he sheathed his sword and resumed his path through the alleys. This had been his first real encounter with the enemy since his ordeal over a year ago. He'd received numerous threats through anonymous letters and even shouts from a distance when he'd traveled about the city, but it was clear that the warlocks and their followers were giving him a wide berth. It also helped that the boy spent most of his time in the security of Breyligh's Hold under the watchful eye of Mr. Pierce. Even so, despite the greater confidence that his training and arena experiences gave him, it took a while for his hands to stop shaking.

For her part, Heather was just as scared at first, but the pendant Eli had given her warmed over her and allayed her fears. Somehow it was reassuring her that the fool daring to threaten her was the one in danger. She didn't understand how this pendant was doing this, but she knew to trust it. This was the first time the pendant had been anything more than a lovely bauble around her neck. Heather found herself loving the sudden mystery about the necklace. For the first time since she was next to Eli she felt like she was part of something great and magical. The girl surprised herself at how much she enjoyed the thrill of this new adventure. All of these thoughts she kept to herself as she and Tolund rushed through the winding alleys.

Fortunately, the rest of their hurried trip was uneventful. Heather was both relieved and annoyed that Tolund had been correct about using the alleys. By moving through the Bronze Quarter without having to push through the crowds, they'd made excellent time. When they arrived at the banks of the Ash River they were out of breath and sweaty, but right on time. After catching their breath, they soon spotted Mr. Pierce on the last dock.

"Right at midday. Well done, Fighters!" grinned their favorite trainingmaster. "Now, if that river rat and his pet lizard actually make it on time we can all call this a miraculous start." Tolund and Heather exchanged surprised glances at Mr. Pierce's unusually bright spirits. The tough old dwarf motioned them to follow him down to the edge of the dock where two other arena fighters awaited them. Neither of these apprentice-fighters needed any introduction.

"You remember Bex, don't you?" asked Mr. Pierce. Tolund nodded. Heather drew her hood closer over the scars on her face before she also nodded. Bex was a well-known and well-liked fighter at Breyligh's. A few years older than the two Stonelanders, Bex was a respected axe and shield fighter with a fun-loving personality. His father was a trainingmaster for the protectorate who was forced to move his family all about Vedris as he trained the new soldiers. Because of this Bex got along well with just about anyone and loved to include others in anything that he was a part of. The other thing he'd received from his upbringing was impressive physical strength. Though moderate in height, he was as strong as a young bull. Fighters of all ages soon learned to avoid contests of strength with Bex. Nevertheless, his ferocity and intimidating build belied his happy nature. He had a thunderous belly-laugh which was heard often all around Breyligh's.

Both Tolund and Heather were glad to see that Bex was one of their companions on this odd trip.

Tolund himself was thrilled to see that the other fighter was a girl from the Plainslands named Lindris. She was thin and lithe and lovely. Her pale blond hair was straight and flowing and moved easily with the river breezes. Though quiet, Lindris was far from shy and her eyes of deep green oftentimes spoke more than her few words. She was one of the most celebrated apprentice-fighters from Breyligh's Hold who fought with two short swords. When she fought she always wore her beige hooded cloak and seemed to move like a wraith over the arena sand. Tolund had seen her fight three times and not once was her crest even scratched. The boy smiled clumsily as Mr. Pierce re-introduced them. Heather grinned at her best friend's awkward response to the older girl, but surprised herself to find that she wished Lindris was not going with them. Without reason, Heather felt a hint of resentment at the Plainsland girl who had always been nothing but kind and respectful toward her.

Suddenly, Mr. Pierce's introductions were interrupted by a gruff call from downstream, "Hallo, Y'old Scrapper!" Sailing into view from around a large bank in the river was their 'host.' All of the young fighters were shocked to see a grungy, weathered man gliding in on top of a gigantic riverdragon. Indeed, the beast was so large that a wooden platform and shack had been built upon its back, serving as an odd riverboat of some kind.

"Well, Fighters," said Mr. Pierce in a jovial voice, "allow me to present one of the mangiest water-mongrels that has ever crawled out of the mud, an old bag of leather known to everyone on the rivers as "Scrounger."

CHAPTER 2

THE ASH RIVER

Tolund didn't realize that his mouth was hanging open until Heather's elbow nudged him in the ribs. The huge riverdragon drifted up to the dock in a casual manner completely oblivious to the many people and boats surrounding it. Despite the beast's calm approach, everyone except Mr. Pierce took a nervous step back from the edge of the dock. Both Mr. Pierce and his grungy-looking friend laughed at this. "Don't worry, Fighters," said the dwarf, "if she'd wanted to eat us we'd all be in her gullet by now."

"It's true y'know," added the scratchy voice of the boatman, Scrounger. "This ere's 'Miss Respect.' I call er' that cause if ya don't pay us proper respect ya won't be alive long enough to remember wot yer mistake was!" At this last comment old Scrounger cackled joyfully. The young fighters winced at his rotting teeth and raspy laugh. "Don't ya worry, Young Cubs, if ya respect me and mine it'll be all right— she's as mild as a farm cow unless I order 'er to be otherwise."

"Scrounger's been traveling the rivers for over thirty years like this," said Mr. Pierce. "It's safer and faster than any boat or barge and I can guarantee you'll have some wild tales to tell your children and grandchildren someday. However, you'll learn more about Scrounger and his beast once we're on the river, right now we've a schedule to keep."

The Ash River was one of the most important waterways in all Vedris. Boats and barges from virtually everywhere wound up and down this wide river moving various goods to Ansalion and the many villages along its banks. This wide river was also the fastest, surest way to reach the Coastlands, short of a dragonflight.

Immediately, Tolund saw the advantage of using Scrounger's riverdragon boat on this trip. As soon as they boarded the old weathered platform, Miss Respect surged smoothly with the current, deftly weaving around the numerous boats that clustered around Ansalion's trading docks. Whenever a boat blocked their path the beast's huge jaws would snap up out of the murky water with a loud hissing growl. Each time the rattled crew of the other boat would quickly move over to let them pass. Once, after a bulky merchant barge took a long time to maneuver to one side, Miss Respect slapped the water with her gigantic tail in their direction as she passed by. The wave of water that soaked the crew and almost swamped the barge let everyone know that this river belonged to her.

In no time at all their 'boat' had moved past the crowded waters by the docks and was picking up speed down the middle of the deep river. Heather smiled at Tolund. Her best friend knew exactly what the smile was saying; she was excited to be going off on another adventure. "Does it feel differently this time?" asked Tolund. "You know, different than our first dragon flight?"

"Mostly the same I guess," grinned Heather. "I mean, we're heading off to an unknown place and already this 'boat' of ours has been enough of a surprise, but I feel a little better about things now than I did then."

"What do you mean?"

"Well, after the nightmares we went through, I think we're more aware of what's out there and I think we're able to handle ourselves a little better. Besides, I feel sorry for anyone who would bother us with Mr. Pierce along. He sure is different than Mr. Kessing was."

"I know what you mean," he nodded. "It's like there isn't anything he doesn't know about fighting. And Kessing was always so smooth and full of advice. We should have known he was too good to be true. Mr. Pierce is about as smooth as splintered wood."

"I guess so," laughed Heather. "If you're going to convince people that you're a swan I guess you wouldn't growl like a wolf."

Even as she laughed Tolund noticed how she made sure to carefully hold the hood of her cloak over her face. The boy remembered how, at first, she tried to wear her scars proudly. He was there when she first walked out among the townsfolk in Glendien without a hood. Even though she was surrounded by people who loved and revered her for her heroic deeds, some of them, usually small children, could not hide their shock at her appearance. After a while Heather could not bear those reactions anymore and began to hide under her hood on every occasion. Though Tolund knew that she was inwardly proud of the deed that saved his life on that fateful day in the Boglands, outwardly, she had become extremely sensitive to how others reacted to her. He wondered when, or if, she would ever be comfortable enough with her scars to stop concealing them. Still, he loved his friend and never pressed her on this issue trusting that she would come to terms with it in her own time. Tolund continued their conversation about their new undertaking,

"Heather, I need to talk to you about something important. At least, I think it's important."

"What is it?" Heather could tell that his mood had changed and something serious was bothering him.

"I know we're joking about this new adventure and all, but there's still something that doesn't feel right. The last few nights my dreams have been strange. They all start with something good and then literally become dark."

"What do you mean 'become dark?'"

"Well, take last night's dream, we were having a picnic in the meadow just past the waterfalls above Glendien. Mom was setting all of my favorite foods out while I was spreading the blankets out on the grass. We were laughing at you and Emilyse, who was years older than she is now, because you were trying to braid her hair but she was trying to catch the autumn leaves that were moving in the wind. You were telling her to stand still and she was just giggling and running away from you, which made you even more frustrated. It was pretty funny."

"So how did the dream get darker?" asked a puzzled Heather.

"That's the strange part," answered Tolund in an unsettled voice, "everything began to dim. The sky, the sun, the grass… everything. First things went grey, then darker, and then black. We were all happy and then we started getting scared, and then when everything was pitch black we were calling out to each other, but no one could find anyone else…that's when I woke up."

"So you just had a bad dream, so what?"

"Heather, that's just it, I've been having the same thing happen for the last three nights," Tolund said seriously. "Something good is always smothered up in darkness. I can't help but think about Celnumus and what happened in the Boglands last year; it feels exactly the same." At the mention of that terrifying name and that terrifying time, Heather began to take Tolund's concerns more seriously.

"Could it all have been warning you about the reaper in the alley?" she asked.

"I don't know," he said shakily. "I hope that's what it was or that it meant nothing at all. Either way, I'm still not too sure about heading out into the unknown again, we both know what happened the last time we did that. Mr. Kessing and Jareg seemed to be as trustworthy as Mr. Pierce and these others, but I never saw their betrayal coming. And even if they all turn out to be on our side, what about the evil that exists out there? What about all of the new enemies we've made after our triumph in the Boglands? I'm just not sure who or what to trust now. Nothing feels safe anymore."

As young as she was, Heather knew that it was not a good thing for this trip to start off with such frightening thoughts. She quickly decided to lighten the mood. "Do you know what I think is causing these weird dreams?"

"What?"

"I don't think you've been washing your feet enough so when you take off your socks at night the smell gets into your dreams and turns them sour," she said with a good-natured laugh. "Think about it, Tolund, a person's mind can only take so much!"

"Oh really?!?" he laughed. "Is that what your dizzy little head came up with? Well then, maybe we just need to give that empty head of yours a good soaking to clear things up for you!" Grabbing his friend with both arms, Tolund playfully threatened to throw her over the side of the platform rail and into the river. Heather's ploy had worked and they were soon laughing and talking about brighter things. Still, knowing how strong Tolund's dreams could be, each of them held a shadow of a doubt in the back of their minds. The adventure had only just begun and their moods had already been shaken.

As Miss Respect moved quietly through the waters, everyone settled into the trip. Mr. Pierce and Scrounger sat in two chairs within the old shack and talked and laughed over mugs of ale. Tolund could hear them talk about days gone by and old acquaintances and once every so often one of them would lower to a whisper which was always followed by another burst of laughter. The four young fighters surmised that these two had been friends for quite some time as they spent all of the lazy afternoon revisiting old memories.

Bex and Lindris spent most of their time up toward the front of the platform, leaning against the rails and talking. Heather and Tolund held to the back end of the platform, talking about the scenery and watching the banks of the river rush by. In the growing warmth of early spring the woods along the Ash River were coming into their full beauty. New wildflowers blanketed the thick green of the riverbanks making the view along the swift waters enthralling.

Tolund took in some deep breaths, enjoying the new scents and sights. This was a nice change from his strict training regimen at Breyligh's Hold. Suddenly, Bex's loud voice broke the moment, "Dellender, let's play some 'Switch' to start our trip off right. Heather, you can play too, if you'd like."

Tolund smiled. Bex was famous at Breyligh's for getting bored quickly. "I'll get my sword and shield," he answered.

"I'll get my spear," added Heather.

As they retrieved their wooden arena weapons, Lindris and Bex moved their bags and cloaks to the back platform, freeing up just enough room on the forward platform for their game. Once they were ready, they chose to play boys against girls. This was one of the most popular training games at their hold. The trick here was to try and gain a point by tagging your opponent with a light tap of your weapon. Hard strikes were not allowed outside of the arena circles as there would be no enchantment preventing injuries. Once a point was scored against you, your partner would have to switch places with you and try their luck. This would continue until one team reached the score of twenty points.

"Ahh, Lindris," smiled Bex, "I think this is my lucky day!"

The quiet girl smiled back, "Then why don't you and I start the match?"

Bex feinted quickly with his short-axe, but Lindris remained still and calm. Her green eyes narrowed as she held her swords across one another in a defensive stance. Tolund loved to watch her movement when she fought—she reminded him of one of the great cats in the way she flowed and moved. Instantly, her left sword swiped down only to be blocked by Bex's shield. "Point!" she called out. Bex grunted in protest at his left ankle. The flat edge of her other sword had struck his ankle almost at the same time he had blocked her left sword.

"You're in, Dellender!" Bex grumbled.

Even though it was only a tapping game, Tolund was nervous. He didn't want to be embarrassed, even by a fighter as talented as Lindris. "Point!" she called out almost immediately. It happened so fast that Tolund barely felt her left sword tap the top of his head. Bex and Heather laughed out loud as Tolund stepped back to the side rubbing his head.

Lindris scored the next five points almost as easily as the first two. Heather was now sitting cross-legged on the deck with her hands propping up her chin. She wondered if she was ever going to get a turn. Bex was both frustrated and excited as he loved a good challenge, almost as much as he loved overcoming a good challenge. As Tolund moved to take his turn, he noticed now that Mr. Pierce and Scrounger had joined them on the front deck to watch the game.

A thought flashed through the boy's mind, "How would Mr. Pierce beat her?" Before taking his stance he remembered his last lessons with his trainingmaster. Mr. Pierce had been teaching him to find ways to take away an opponent's best asset. Lindris' advantage was obvious, she simply moved too quickly and struck too accurately to avoid her on this small deck. The boy smiled as he realized what he had to do.

"Promise you won't get mad at me?" he asked her wryly.

"Oh, I promise." Lindris answered sarcastically with one eyebrow lifted up.

As soon as both of them settled into their stances, Tolund shocked everyone by throwing his shield at the tall girl's face. As she instinctively blocked the hurtling shield with both swords, Tolund kicked her hard in the stomach sending her backward over the platform rail and into the river. Quickly, Scrounger ordered his riverdragon to halt as Bex and Mr. Pierce reached over the side to pull Lindris up. As the girl's head lifted up from the cold water she felt Tolund's sword tap her once upon her wet scalp. "Point!" he called out triumphantly. It took a full minute for Lindris to join in everyone else's laughter, but Tolund was relieved that she chose to laugh along with them instead of killing him.

"That was a wicked trick, Tol," taunted Lindris. "Don't plan on getting away with that again."

"I won't," he smiled. Tolund was pleased to hear the grudging respect in her voice.

As Lindris took time to dry herself off, Heather was given the chance to finish their game. Although she had made great strides in recent months, she was still very much a novice fighter and, without Lindris, she proved to be no match for the more experienced boys who won the game convincingly. For his part, Tolund was quite proud of himself for besting Lindris and was doing a poor job of hiding it.

"Pay attention to this one 'ere, Old Dwarf," Scrounger said to Mr. Pierce, nodding in Tolund 's direction. "You've got a crafty one on yer hands, I'm thinkin."

"Indeed I might," answered Mr. Pierce, allowing himself a slight smile, "indeed I might."

CHAPTER 3

THE APPARITION

Lord Gresk could not understand what his eyes were telling him. As he squinted through the fierce wind he saw the massive blocks of ice exploding in mid-air. Faintly, the dwarf-lord could make out the sound of metal striking ice, but in the howling air he could not be sure. The screams of two icelocks rang out in agony. "How in the Abyss?" Gresk wondered aloud.

The shining blue blood of the two dead icelocks flowed out onto the snow at the feet of the elemental. The one on the left was impaled by a sleek silver spear while the one on the right had a double-bladed short axe lodged in its chest. One of the dwarf soldiers cried out, "Over there, at the top of the spout."

At the wide mouth of the sorcerous waterspout, a flash of silver and white dashed into the heart of the elemental. A haunting roar echoed from the vortex which suddenly was drawn inward and then exploded outward, knocking everyone within a league to their feet. Even the longboats of the warlock army were nearly upended. As the water from the ruined elemental rained upon them, the dwarves let out shouts of triumph. Lord Gresk, though thoroughly baffled by this instant change in fortune, joined in their relief and sudden joy.

A few moments later, another celebration erupted from Gresk's army for the invaders had all hastily returned to their ships and those ships were turning about and retreating as fast as their sails could take them. No one could make sense of how everything changed so quickly—how certain death had become clear victory with the enemy holding every advantage.

As he turned now to check on his men, Lord Gresk's right arm was yanked up and his feet left the ground. Before he knew how he'd left the ground, his body slowed and floated within a thick, grey cloud. He became aware now of the strong grip that held his right forearm. Instinctively, the mystic hammer in Gresk's left arm smashed upward.

"No," spoke a deep voice above Gresk as something halted his hammer in mid-swing. "I really don't think you would have me release you from this height, Milord."

Gresk squinted up at the voice above him. He heard beating wings, but saw no wings, only shimmering movement. A large strange form that looked like storm clouds reflected in a mirror was speaking to him. "Who…what are you?" asked Gresk.

"I am the one who hunts all warlocks and their ilk."

Gresk's thick eyebrows curved up upon his forehead. "You mean…you're the…the Warlockslayer?" he whispered as if it were a forbidden curse.

"Yes," answered the apparition. "Now, Dwarf, listen carefully because time is less than you know." Lord Gresk's heartbeat thumped faster within his chest. The dwarf was long-renowned as one of the mightiest dwarves in the Frostlands, both in strength and battle prowess, but this legendary creature held him aloft in the clouds as a hawk might bear a feather. It was most unnerving for a warrior of his stature.

"I'm...I'm listening," stammered the dwarf.

"Good," Eli continued. "This invasion was a ruse. It was all a great distraction to draw your forces to the shore. If they wiped you out so much the better for them, but even if they didn't their true raiding party would have a swifter path inland. Word came to the White Council that the warlocks are on a quest in your lands. As I rushed to your aid my senses revealed two trails of dark magic."

Gresk's eyes narrowed and his jaw squared, "Two trails?"

"Two trails. The one nearest you leads out into the ocean and the other leads further north and inland. Both of these trails tell me that warlocks, not casters mind you, but warlocks are seeking out sources of great power, power steeped in darkness."

"Of the trail upon the waters I know nothing, but I fear I know exactly where the northern trail leads. It's a secret my kin have guarded for generations. I'm not sure that I can reveal…"

"I've no time for secrets!" snapped the Lockslayer.

"All right, all right," answered Gresk. "I suppose you've already proven your trust by saving us today or at least that you've no love for that army of filth. In the north there is a treasure room of unbelievable wealth and power. The very reason we live in these frozen lands is to safeguard this cache. Should the enemy ever possess this it could very well shift the balance of this war strongly in their favor. We cannot let that happen."

"Here's what we will do," commanded Eli, "I will pursue the northern warlocks that slipped by your army. Their dragons are swift, but I believe I can catch them before they reach this treasure. You will regroup and muster your forces for an assault on the ocean trail."

"We've boats enough, but we'll have to gather more of our clerics to track the locks." Gresk felt strange planning with an ally he could not clearly see. "Do you have any idea what we'll be chasing?"

"All I know is that it bears dark power and that power is growing. Evil grows best in secret. . .which is something a warrior of your experience should know. Also, I sense that it is moving, but only very slowly. It may be resting upon a large ship or barge." Eli drew the dwarf-lord closer to his faceplate. "You must stop this army. Deliberate invasions like this mean careful planning on their part and since the dark orders have united they are more deadly than ever. This is the hour that Vedris may rely upon the courage of the dwarves." Lord Gresk's only answer was an eager, savage grin.

In a breath Gresk was dropped lightly upon the snow just beyond the blood-stained cliffs. As two invisible wings slashed above a mirrored form, the dwarf-lord called out to the living ghost through the wind, "Good hunting!"

CHAPTER 4

A LITTLE ERRAND

Once the sun finally set on their first day along the river, Scrounger announced that it was time to stop and make camp for the night. Miss Respect settled easily onto a large sandy bank. Scrounger ordered Tolund and Bex to gather firewood while he saw to Miss Respect's needs.

It was time for the great riverdragon to have a little freedom. First, with the help of Mr. Pierce, Scrounger saw to unhitching the great harness that strapped the wooden platform to the beast's back. As she had done daily for most of her life, Miss Respect helped ease the platform onto the small beach area with great care so that not even a cup or plate in the little shack so much as rattled. Large posts hinged at the corners of the platform's base bent outward like legs on a giant table and were fastened together with rope to help stabilize the entire structure. Once free of the harness, the great lizard instantly slipped into the river and rolled end over end and splashed about happily. Lindris and Heather were enjoying this spectacle almost as much as Miss Respect . Standing with their bare feet in the water with the waves from the behemoth's thrashing rushing over their legs, the girls giggled and laughed out loud. "Hah!" Scrounger called out to them. "Don't see that in that stuffy old city, do ya?"

"Well, now," the old traveler continued, "once she's done playin' it'll be time to fill that gigantic belly of hers!" Smiling proudly, the waterman produced a glittering emerald fishing net from his shack. "This ere's one of the greatest gifts wot's ever been gived to me," he grinned. "I got it from an old conjuror in the Coastlands for a great favor she owed me. Ere now, I'll show ya the magic of it."

Wading in up to his knees, Scrounger carefully dipped one corner of the net into the water. "Don't blink or you'll miss it!" he cackled. As the net touched the surface of the river a single ripple that glowed a lovely green spread out over the water. Instantly, dozens of splashes erupted from bank to bank and veered in the direction of old Scrounger. On the sandy bank Miss Respect hissed in anticipation, thumping her tail expectantly. "Patience, ya Big Lump! I'll ave' it in a minute!" called Scrounger. Now, with one smooth motion, he drew the entire net into the water, which Heather now noticed looked more like a sack than a traditional fishing net, and pulled it from right to left. Grunting from the weight of it, Scrounger pulled the net back toward the shore. As it cleared the water, the girls were impressed to find that the net was full of dozens of large fish somehow mesmerized by its magic.

"Amazing!" exclaimed Lindris. "Is that from a smoothstone enchantment?"

"Don't know, Young Missy," answered Scrounger, "never figured its workins, but it's been workin' like this for more'n seven years." Choosing six large trout for their own supper, Scrounger happily fed the rest to Miss Respect. Once she had finished gulping down the last of the fish, the great riverdragon fell asleep— her deep contented breaths caused the sand on the beach to swirl and billow.

Soon the boys returned with the firewood, the fish were swiftly roasted upon the cooking brazier, and everyone reclined upon the deck to enjoy the music of the frogs and crickets while they marveled at the glittering stars that had come out above them. Tolund and Heather each stretched out upon the deck with their hands cupped behind their heads. Bex sat cross-legged upon the deck while Lindris pulled up one of the rough wooden chairs alongside Scrounger and Mr. Pierce.

Mr. Pierce, standing tall while stretching his arms to the sky with a groan of contentment, addressed the group, "Now it's time, I think, for a time-honored tradition of my people." All of the young ones looked at each other with bemused expressions. Their trainingmaster continued, "The first night of any quest cannot be spent in silence. If we're to work together on this trip, and we will, we'd best get to know one another a little better. I'll start with the oldest of you. Bex, the question of the night is 'why do you train and fight?' What prompts you to undertake an adventure of this kind?"

Bex, once he'd overcome his surprise at this sudden questioning, sat up straighter and squared his shoulders, "Duty, I suppose." The other three instinctively glanced at their mentor to see if he showed any approval of this quick answer. The gruff dwarf's face showed no sign of either approval or disapproval.

"Please elaborate," Mr. Pierce responded. "What do you mean when you say, 'duty?' Duty to Breyligh's Hold? Duty to your comrades? Duty to Vedris?"

"All of those and one more, I believe," Bex said without flinching. "I owe all of those my very best efforts, as my family has taught me.

My father is Sergeant Commander Longfield of the Protectorate. His father was a Protectorate commander as was his father and his father before him, along with my great-great grandmother. We Longfields are a family dedicated to protecting Vedris from all threats by raising up new generations of warriors."

"And is that to be your future as well?" asked Mr. Pierce.

"Of course," answered Bex with a confident grin. "I will be the greatest of the line. I'm already more formidable at my age than any of my family. I know my mother, may she rest in peace, would have been proud of me and my father, tough as he is, will also be proud of me…in time."

"Wot happened to yer mum, Lad?" Scrounger asked gently.

"She died giving birth to me, I'm afraid," Bex replied. "I was an unusually large infant and the birth did not go well. Still, my father raised me well until I was old enough for Breyligh's, before that we traveled a lot as he worked for the Protectorate. My father was tough on me, but also really good to me over the years. I've had a good life so far, better than most, I think. I've no complaints."

"Very good, Son," Mr. Pierce said with a nod. "All right, then… Lindris, what set you on this path?"

"Well…," As she began to respond Tolund noticed that she still sat in a casual, relaxed fashion without the intense bearing that Bex had demonstrated. "Unlike Bex, and many other fighters, there's nothing really remarkable about my upbringing. I come from a simple town with a simple family. There's no shame in that, I know, but I'd always wanted to do something more than just live day-to-day."

"So you just decided to become an arena fighter?" asked Tolund, who seemed to be hanging on the lovely girl's every word.

"Not quite," Lindris smiled. "Our village was so small that we were only assigned one paladin. Her name was 'Renna' and everyone was very fond of her. She was brave and wise and always kind to the townsfolk. As a little girl, my friends and I would follow her around and pester her for stories of the great city or of some faraway adventures. Renna told us many tales, even some that she admitted were great exaggerations, but the ones I loved the most were of her days at Breyligh's Hold. She used to act out her battles strike-by-strike, block-by-block against the haystacks and her face would light up with joy as she recounted her arena battles to us. Renna would also make it a point to always remind us of how honorable her station was as a paladin. Even her assignment in little 'Longburrow,' was sacred to her. I remember her saying, 'no duty is small or insignificant, for safeguarding one life is as important as safeguarding many.' I always loved it when she said that."

"So you want to become a village paladin like her?" asked Bex.

"Not especially," replied Lindris. "Once I'd arrived at Breyligh's on Renna's recommendation, I discovered something about myself when I began training and fighting as a novice."

"Which was…?"

"That I liked winning. And even more, I liked improving." Tolund noticed her slight grin as she said these words. "Gaining a new skill or maneuver was what I dreamed about every night. So I got better and better each month and that's when I decided that I'm going to be the best arena fighter the fireshows have ever seen— not for fame or wealth, but just because I will know that I improved more and climbed higher than everyone else. Anything less will mean that I failed myself."

"Hmph," grunted Mr. Pierce, "I suppose we'll have to wait and see how that turns out for you." Now their mentor turned to Heather. "What about you, Lass? What prompted you to stop being an assistant and step into the arena yourself?"

Heather looked around at everyone else as they waited for her reply. She was afraid that Mr. Pierce was going to call on her next, but she knew that he would have eventually. "I…I wasn't really interested in learning to fight when I first came to Breyligh's. I was happy enough when I was helping Tolund, but after all of that madness in the Boglands I realized that things were never going to be the same for me. Like it or not …, and I don't, I'll never be a normal girl living a normal life. As long as there's a chance that the evil folk might come after me, there's a chance I'll have to fight for my own life. Threats and danger have become a part of my life now. My parents and I decided that preparation was better than desperation…or helplessness, so here I am. That's why I'm learning to fight."

"I've some dark news for ya,' Young Missy," interrupted Scrounger. "Threats n'danger are a part of everyone's life. From the moment yer born ta the moment yer buried, don't no one really live a 'safe' life. Ya may as well toughen yerself up fer it. If'n ya don't never need it, ya don't never need it, but it's good ta have…just in case."

He said this last bit with a wide grin, displaying his horrid teeth in the nicest way possible. In spite of the ghastly looking smile, Heather appreciated his kind advice.

Mr. Pierce now turned his gaze toward Tolund. "Tol? How about you?"

"It's easy enough to answer," the boy replied calmly. "After the ghastly time with Celnumus I received some good advice from someone in Glendien. He encouraged me to use my strength to help others. I decided that he was right and that I needed to get even stronger. So that's why I fight in the arena, that's why I'm on this training mission. I'm not sure how strong I really am or really could be, but I want to become as skilled as I possibly can so I can do something good for others with what I've learned." After he finished speaking, Tolund glanced up at the gruff Mr. Pierce to see if he was approving of his answer.

Stroking his beard as a slight smile emerged, their trainingmaster let out a short laugh, "Ha! I daresay I'm pleased with all of your answers, different as they may be from one another. I, myself, am looking forward to putting all of you to the test to see what happens. With any luck, we'll all be pleasantly surprised by what we find!"

The last bit of sharing was done by Old Scrounger who explained how he found and bonded with Miss Respect. Apparently, the great riverdragon's egg was discovered by the good-hearted conjuror that Scrounger had referred to earlier. She had come upon it after a huge rainstorm flooded the river. Miss Respect's egg must have been swept away from her mother's nest and into the surging currents. Owing Scrounger a great debt for some unexplained favor, the conjuror cast a spell of bonding over the unhatched egg that gave Scrounger a unique friendship with the hatchling. Once Miss Respect cracked open the shell of her egg, she saw Old Scrounger as her own parent and has remained a faithful and loyal family member of his ever since. Mr. Pierce added, with a chuckle, that it was a fortunate blessing for Old Scrounger that he had Miss Respect for company because no one else could stand to be around the river-rat for so long. Again, the camp enjoyed the friendly banter and laughter of the two old friends.

"Anyway," announced Mr. Pierce, "it is getting late and we've a long trek ahead of us. Get some sleep and be ready for a full day of drills and sparring tomorrow."

With that, Mr. Pierce excused himself and set up his sleeping area near the back of the platform. Old Scrounger said 'goodnight' and retired to his shack. Reading their trainingmaster's intent, the four fighters whispered some quick 'goodnights' to one another. The two boys stretched out their own cloaks upon the wooden deck near Mr. Pierce and quieted down immediately while the girls set up toward the very front of the platform. Enjoying the light of the stars overhead and the sound of the river flowing by, Tolund thanked the High King for this adventure and prayed for his family, friends, and for the days ahead. With a smile he drifted happily off to sleep.

In the days that followed the little band of travelers continued to get to know one another and enjoy the sights, smells, and sounds of their time upon the river. The new routine of breakfast followed by morning training, a midday meal, and afternoon training that led up to their evening camp and time of rest soon became familiar.

As these days eased along pleasantly, Tolund and Heather, as well as Lindris and Bex, were relieved to find that the man called Scrounger seemed genuinely happy to have them along on the journey. Eager to befriend the young ones with his gregarious nature, the riverman talked almost constantly and asked them a multitude of questions about their homes and experiences. Though it was clear that Mr. Pierce was Scrounger's old true friend, the leather-skinned old man was obviously working quite hard to make new friends out of his young guests. Tolund also figured that this man has led a mostly solitary life and, therefore, was happy to have the extra company that this trip afforded.

Tolund was also pleased that he was getting to know his fellow fighters a little better. With the two older fighters training and competing at the 'Apprentice-class' level, he and Heather did not have many opportunities to socialize with them. The boy soon learned that Bex spoke and shared freely while Lindris really only spoke up when she was asked a direct question. The tall girl clearly wasn't shy or intimidated by things, she just seemed content to listen more than she spoke. Bex was cut from a much different cloth.

The wide-shouldered, thick-muscled boy loved to joke and tease with just about everyone. Tolund had sensed that Bex wanted to join in with the back and forth banter of Mr. Pierce and Scrounger, but it was apparent that Bex's strict upbringing as the son of a protectorate officer demanded that he knew his place in respect to his elders. This, of course, did not apply to Heather, Lindris, and himself so Bex made the most of every opportunity to keep the conversations playful and lively with his peers. With Bex's quick wit and laughter leading the way, they all became fairly comfortable with one another in no time at all.

Mr. Pierce, in keeping with his rigorous expectations at Breyligh's Hold, seemed grudgingly content with the efforts of his young charges. As they practiced and refined their form and techniques in the morning, the stern trainingmaster was pleased to find that the fighters were eager to outdo the others. This was also true in the afternoon sparring matches and even the tests of endurance and flexibility. The boys did not want to be outshone by the girls, nor did the girls want the boys to win the day. However, even with the demands of the hard work and their own expectations pressed upon them. Mr. Pierce was glad to see that the morale was not threatened and that friends remained friends at the end of each day.

On the fifth day of travel, at Scrounger's urging, Mr. Pierce gave them a break from their afternoon training for a bit of fun. For a number of days Old Scrounger had been bragging about something called 'tail-whipping.' This was some kind of game that he'd invented that involved Miss Respect and he was adamant that all of the young fighters should give it a try. He also explained that today was the perfect opportunity for some fun on the river due to the warm sunshine and the calm wide stretch of water that they found themselves on.

To start things off Scrounger ordered his riverdragon to move to the middle of the wide river. Next, he instructed all of the young ones to get into the water and swim directly behind Miss Respect's massive tail. Tolund, Bex, and Lindris happily obliged while Heather, as usual, chose to remain on the deck and watch as swimming would require her to remove her hooded cloak. Even after all of this time the poor girl could not bring herself to show her scarred face and scalp to anyone except her own family and Tolund's family. After allowing a few moments to get used to the cool water, Scrounger announced that it was time to begin.

"Now," he called out with a huge grin on his face, "if yer all brave enough fer this just swim up to the old girl's tail and get a good grip. Heh! You'll all need it!"

As instructed, they each used both arms to grab on to the gigantic tail of Miss Respect. Tolund shook his head in astonishment as he grasped the leathery tail that was as thick and as solid as the trunk of a great tree. Lindris held on just a few feet behind Tolund and Bex was just behind her.

"I'll pay a shiny coin to whichever one of you that can hold on fer four swipes!" challenged Scrounger playfully. Tolund shot a nervous, but excited glance at Lindris and Bex who both smiled back in anticipation. "All right, Darlin'," the old man called out to his beloved riverdragon as he gave her a quick slap on the side, "give em' a spin!"

It began with a slow, strong surge. The three 'passengers' laughed with surprise and delight as the great tail curved toward the left side of the river. Tolund felt his legs and body pull in the same direction as the cool water rolled over his shoulders and neck, almost covering his head. Even on the first easy curve of her huge tail, holding on was already a strain on the boy's wiry muscles.

Once her tail moved all the way to one side, it suddenly churned the waters and the young swimmers' bodies all swept back in the opposite direction. Tolund could hear the other two laughing out loud behind him. He was also laughing hard from the exhilaration of this ride until he caught a mouthful of water and had to cough it out. "That's one!" Scrounger proclaimed loudly. "Better hold tight, Pups!"

Now, after a slight pause, the tail began to move back to the left again. Tolund could hear Mr. Pierce and Heather laughing from the platform above until his head was suddenly covered by rushing water. The second drag of the tail was twice as powerful as the first. Tolund was successfully clenching his arms and handholds so he could hold firmly to the tail, but it was far from easy. With the great rush of water pushing over him, the boy had to hold his breath underwater even as he angled his head downward to keep the water from rushing up his nose.

Again, Miss Respect's tail paused to reverse direction. Tolund quickly shot his head above the surface of the frothing water for a gulp of air. He heard Heather shouting something, but he couldn't make out what she was saying over the splashing waters.

Back the tail went at about the same speed. Tolund's head and body went underwater once more, but he still maintained a frantic grip upon the leathery scales. Even holding his breath under the river's surface, he couldn't help but smile with his body now stretched out sideways from the force of the dragging tail. He felt like he was falling, diving, and flying all at the same time.

From the platform Mr. Pierce, Scrounger, and Heather shook with heavy laughter as they watched the three clinging bodies all get swallowed up by the swirling waters. The second tail whip gave the riders another chance for a quick breath. Even with the water white and frothing about them, the three young ones could hear one another laughing from the excitement of it all.

"And back again!" called Scrounger as he slapped Miss Respect's side twice. Now the tail doubled again in power and speed. Suddenly, Tolund's arms were fully extended as he held on to the tail's ridges by his fingertips. His thin body stayed underwater as he fought to hold on against the rushing current. Now his hands and forearms burned from the effort of trying to hold fast.

When the third swipe stopped to change its direction Tolund's and Lindris' bodies did not. Losing their handholds completely, each of them rolled and tumbled beneath the surging water. When they broke the surface of the river to get some air, they saw that Bex had held on to the far side of the 'ride' with both of his feet sticking up in the air. Though the boy was a coughing, sputtering mess when that swipe was finished, he still clung stubbornly to the giant tail. "Well done, Bex!" Heather cheered. "You can do it! Just hold on for one more trip!"

"Oh, I think that coin's stayin' in my pocket, Little Missy!" joked Scrounger. While Bex caught his breath above the foaming waters, he wrapped his thick arms around the scaly tail with a look of tired determination. Old Scrounger now slapped Miss Respect's side three times.

This time the tail exploded through the water. Bex's muscled arms, pulled to a full stretch, held on desperately. With a wicked little flick, the tail angled up just a bit sending the now-dislodged boy hurtling straight up into the air. Bex let out a shout of alarm as his body flew up and then plummeted in a great crash into the swirling waters. When his dizzy head broke the surface of the river he joined with everyone else in a fit of hooting and laughing.

"A fair effort, Lad," shouted Scrounger, "but still a long way from winnin!"

After a brief rest the three swimmers begged to try another round of 'tail-whips.' Scrounger happily agreed. The second round was even less successful than the first as they were all sporting tired arms now. Still, no one cared about anything now except the joy of this experience. It was clear that they were having the time of their lives today. Though it was difficult to tell, Tolund felt like the great riverdragon was enjoying herself as well.

Once the rides were finally over and the weary swimmers clambered up the ladder of the platform, they all sprawled out on the warm deck to dry out and catch their breaths. Heather, though a bit sad at missing out on all of the action, was having fun explaining to the other three how silly they looked trying to hold on to Miss Respect's tail. Scrounger helped heal their pride a bit by explaining to them that greater warriors than they had failed this challenge and that he'd won quite a few wagers over the years with Miss Respect remaining undefeated at every attempt.

As Tolund rested on his stomach with the warm sun on his face and hearing the laughter of his friends, he thought to himself that this was about as perfect as an afternoon could get.

Another week upon the river passed. Getting back to their daily routine, Tolund was happy to notice that the extra attention from his trainingmaster was reaping rewards. At Breyligh's Hold fighters had to share their trainingmaster with dozens of others which made Mr. Pierce's time with them quite rare and precious. On this unique trip, Mr. Pierce only had to divide his counsel among four fighters which gave them a much more intense, but also a much more effective training regimen. Tolund, indeed, all of the young fighters, could feel themselves growing in skill and strength. Even Heather, the most inexperienced among them, was making impressive gains.

So it was that on the end of this last day, as everyone relaxed on the platform after the evening meal, Mr. Pierce surprised them with an announcement. "I think it's time we discussed our plans for tomorrow," said Mr. Pierce. "We've a little errand to perform for this flea-ridden weasel here." Their trainingmaster gave Scrounger a friendly kick as he said this.

"Errand? You never said anything about an errand," said Lindris.

"There are many things I don't say anything about, Miss Lindris," grumbled Mr. Pierce. "That should come as no shock to you after all of these years."

"Aye," interrupted Scrounger, who was picking at his teeth with a thin trout bone, "did ya think these fine traveling accommodations were free?" The young fighters shared puzzled glances.

"We've managed to cover an impressive distance today," said Mr. Pierce, "If the weather and river oblige us we should cover about the same distance tomorrow. That will put us near the corrupt village of Serist at around sunset, which is where our errand will be performed."

"Sir, what do you mean by 'the *corrupt* village of Serist?" asked Tolund.

"I suppose this is the time to prepare you," responded Mr. Pierce. "I've agreed to help Scrounger remove a particularly nasty thorn from his side on this trip."

"Aye, and it's a thorn in the side of anyone that's moved up n' down the river to the coast these past years," griped the old riverman.

"Here's the tale, Fighters," continued Mr. Pierce, "years ago the Ash was an easy, straight path to the Coastlands. This worked in the favor of everyone who traveled her to make a living by trading or moving folk up and down the river. All of that changed one winter. Under the cover of a fierce storm, an unusual shaking of the ground changed the course of the lazy river by splitting it right down the middle. The course of the Ash was suspiciously divided just past the riverfront town of Serist"

"How can you split a river?" asked Lindris.

"Twas a great spine o' stone runnin' up through its middle," answered Scrounger. "It sent one 'alf of the Ash to the left on a windin' long path that added days n' days to the journey to the Coastlands and then it sent the other 'alf down a long river wot moved in a line as straight as a spear! The first way was the long, long way to the coast and the second way was the fast, easy way."

"Then, almost as quickly as the landscape had been shifted, a massive iron gate barred the entrance to the straight waterway," explained Mr. Pierce. "It seems that a wealthy rotter by the name of Derger had the amazing 'foresight' to buy up all of the land where the new path magically appeared overnight. In only a day or so the great iron gate, that Derger just happened to have crafted beforehand, was secured before this waterway's entrance and now all passage through that swift path would cost travelers dearly in goods, silver, or gold. All of these events ensured that the Derger family would earn even greater wealth than they had known before. Of course, any fool could see that the Dergers had conspired with a stonelock to sculpt their new land in a way that would give them total control over the best path of the river."

Scrounger spit over the side in disgust, "Wot's that slime need with our poor earnings! We either pay the stinkin' toll for straight passage or we takes the long ways round costin' us more in time n' money!" Tolund looked over at Heather and lifted his eyebrows in a curious expression.

"I saw that, Boy," grunted Mr. Pierce. "You're wondering what all of this has to do with us. Well, Scrounger and I, along with some friends of mine in the Protectorate think that it's high time for a change in this river's course. It's been a foregone conclusion that the Dergers are in league with at least one stonelock order, possibly more. Unfortunately, there's been no actual proof of an alliance between the two so the Protectorate cannot be involved officially, so it's up to our little band of humble travelers to do something. As that wicked family gains wealth so too does their warlock partners. We're going to put an end to that.

Bex smiled broadly in anticipation of some excitement, "What do you want us to do?"

"Gather round and we'll discuss your roles in our little war," smiled Mr. Pierce.

Two mornings later and further down the Ash river an intense Mr. Pierce, followed closely by Tolund and Heather, strode along the footpath beside the river toward the gated entrance of the bustling town of Serist. Equipped as simple foot travelers, the three of them failed to draw a second glance from any of the townsfolk or river traders. Tolund noticed how Mr. Pierce's keen eyes took in every detail both on the waters and about the town gate.

The town itself and the wide docking platform beside the river were surrounded by a tall wooden fence, except for the entrance gates which were made of bars of spiked iron. Two protectorate soldiers manned Serist's front gate and another three walked the docking platform. "Don't let those trappings of authority fool you," cautioned Mr. Pierce, "those soldiers have been bought by Derger's gold and are not to be trusted."

The pace of the morning was increasing. Traders, barterers, carts, and shops were everywhere as people moved all about. Old Scrounger had told them how the great upheaval had turned Serist from one of many small stops along the river to the most important center of business anywhere on the banks of the Ash. As predicted, three unknown travelers would not be noticed in such a crowded, frantic market.

This was the first part of Mr. Pierce's plan. He told them that Tolund and Heather would join him to set things into motion by journeying into Serist just before midday. Scrounger had assured him that 'Lord' Derger always came to market at midday to select the best wares Serist had to offer and, more importantly for his own pride, to parade about before the largest crowd of the day. This was exactly what Mr. Pierce was counting on.

Tolund, who did not care much for crowds aside from those in the fireshows, was annoyed by all of the noise and mingling bodies. Heather liked these even less than Tolund. Following their training-master's burly form, they moved behind him as he led the way through the bulk of the crowd. To the boy's surprise, he actually found himself wanting to stop and look at some of the wares that could only have come from the Coastlands. Huge seashells, odd-looking trinkets and weapons, and small trained monkeys for sale all caught his eye. Mr. Pierce, who somehow knew what the boy was thinking without ever looking back, stifled his growing curiosity. "We've a job to do today, Lad," he said gruffly, "you can see all of those new things and more when we actually arrive in the Coastlands. Until then just keep your mind on the task before us."

Heather gave him a friendly elbow to his side. Without even seeing her face, Tolund knew she wore an amused smirk at his slight rebuke. He laughed softly and gently elbowed her back. After walking a little further, Mr. Pierce stopped and smiled, "Ah! There's our 'prize' at last!" Heather and Tolund could tell by the mocking tone of Mr. Pierce that he was less than impressed with his quarry.

Parting the crowd about twenty strides before them was a magnificent coach adorned with four silk flags pulled by four fine horses. The largest flag bore a proud eagle that flew over a solid background of gold— the remaining flags were half the size of the first and each bore a hawk over a background of forest green. Tolund saw that the same patterns were draped over the horses that drew the coach. Walking before the horses and barking at the people to get out of the way was a tall, strapping young man in fine clothing. Oddly, he was armed with an exquisite sword and wore a silver shield upon his back.

When a broad smile spread across Mr. Pierce's face, Tolund knew that something was about to take place. Moving directly to the middle of the road, Mr. Pierce stood firmly with both arms crossed in front of his broad chest. As the crowd parted before the young man he almost stumbled over the obstinate dwarf.

"Stupid Runt!" the young man scolded. "What do you think you're doing blocking our way? You're lucky I didn't step on you!"

"Now, now," scoffed Mr. Pierce in an amused tone, "don't wrinkle your fancy little tunic! The way I see it, all of these fine folk were here first and you and that gaudy eyesore behind you are the nuisance here."

Thrusting the reins out of his hands, the young man drew his fine sword from its expensive scabbard. "Loud-mouthed Dwarf! You need to learn how to respect your betters!"

"Well, hold on just a moment, Young 'Prince,' I'm not even armed," announced Mr. Pierce loud enough so that as many people as possible could hear him. The market street had cleared just before the horses so that only the young man and Mr. Pierce stood in the middle of the dusty street. Tolund and Heather now stood at the edge of the ring of bystanders who pressed in to see the excitement. Both of them could hear the whispers of contempt for the young man from the common folk. All of the whisperers were enjoying the insolence of this strange dwarf even as they hoped he wasn't seriously injured or killed.

The anxious crowd gave way to the left as Mr. Pierce playfully rummaged through a shopkeeper's display of cooking pots and utensils. "Aha! This ought to do nicely!" shouted the dwarf as he produced a long iron soup ladle and held it up high over his head. Tossing a coin to the shopkeeper, Mr. Pierce turned quickly toward the young man and held the ladle with both hands as he would hold a broadsword. The haughty youth glared at the soup ladle as bursts of laughter erupted from the crowd.

"It's bad enough I have to deal with this grunting pig," the rich lad smirked, "but this one's lost his mind as well!"

Mr. Pierce's comical expression now soured into one of intense concentration. "You're about to find out how wrong you are about this 'grunting pig,'" the trainingmaster scowled.

Sneering, the tall youth slashed forward with his sword. Like a striking viper, Mr. Pierce snapped the round end of the ladle directly onto the boy's knuckles that gripped his sword hilt. In a squeal of pain the young man dropped his blade and grabbed his sword hand with his other hand.

"*That* was for calling me 'pig!'" shouted Mr. Pierce. "And *this*," he said as he cracked the ladle down hard upon the boy's left shin bone, "is for drawing cold steel upon an unarmed visitor!" Now the 'prince' hopped up and down on his right foot while clutching his left shin with both hands. The crowd roared with laughter as Mr. Pierce stepped to the side of the young man and delivered a stout kick to his backside which sent the boy sprawling onto the dirt street. "*That*, I must admit, was just for the fun of it," laughed Mr. Pierce.

"Enough!" bellowed a voice from behind them. Emerging from the coach was a tall man with a large belly, also dressed in fine clothing, pointing a bejeweled finger at Mr. Pierce. "Stop this nonsense at once!" Tolund noted how the tall man spoke with a manner of someone who was accustomed to getting his way.

"Now, who is this?" questioned Mr. Pierce even though he knew full well who it was.

"I am Lord Derger and this is my town. You do not come into my town and disrespect my son."

"Oh, your son earned his disrespect without any help from me." Mr. Pierce responded sternly.

The tall fat man glared at the crowd all about him. Remarkably, everyone ceased to be amused and moved away from the scene, taking great care not to show their faces to Lord Derger as they scurried away. Instantly, the man took a deep sigh and his expression melted into a generous smile. "I'm afraid you've misjudged us, Good Dwarf," pleaded Lord Derger, "my son is a bit over-protective of me. Please don't mistake that for actual malice. In fact, as a gesture of Serist hospitality, please allow us to buy you a good meal as proper introductions are made. As my great grandfather always said, 'There is a reason that eagles fly with eagles.'"

"Why not?" replied Mr. Pierce pleasantly. "I've never been known to turn down a full table. And perhaps I've been a bit hasty in my judgements as well." Heather furrowed her brow at their training-master's uncharacteristic change of heart.

"Mr. Pierce is one step ahead of all of this," Tolund whispered to Heather, "you can be sure of that."

Moving to an extravagant inn, the small party sat down to a fine table which was now being arranged for unexpected guests. "We dine here often," smiled Lord Derger. "I'm hoping you'll enjoy the food here as much as we do. I highly recommend the roast chicken, it's surprisingly exquisite. Now then, I think some proper introductions are in order. I am Gerald Derger and this is my youngest boy, Braden." The older man motioned to his son who forced a nod and a slight scowl in their direction.

"Well, Sir, please call me 'Everett.'" Both Tolund's and Heather's eyebrows shot up in surprise for they had never heard him called anything else other than 'Mr. Pierce' or 'Trainingmaster Pierce.' Now the scheming dwarf gestured toward the two of them, "These are my young charges. Don't worry about their names, they're just traveling with me to learn more about the wide world outside their homes. Just call them 'boy' and 'girl' and that'll be good enough for the day."

A bit taken aback by this vague introduction, Lord Derger smiled, "Hmm, very good then. I can tell you that even living on the shores of a trade river we don't refer to new visitors in such a manner."

"Well, you don't want to get too attached to them as you never know when the little birds will learn to fly off on their own," replied Mr. Pierce. "Isn't that right, 'Little Birds?'" Tolund and Heather nodded and smiled.

Soon a lavish meal was set before them and everyone enjoyed the food except for Braden who was trying, unsuccessfully, to hide his damaged pride and distaste for Mr. Pierce. During the meal Lord Derger asked question after question about Mr. Pierce's background.

Tolund noticed how his trainingmaster deftly eluded giving the rich man any information of substance about himself or Heather or Tolund. The more Derger pressed him for information the more vague Mr. Pierce became, using witty remarks or distracting questions of his own to confuse his host. In the end, all Lord Derger could glean from the cagey old dwarf was that he was an accomplished bodyguard who had traveled all about Vedris and that he made a living by training others in the art of personal combat.

As the meal concluded and the small party made their way out toward Derger's opulent carriage, Lord Derger shook Mr. Pierce's hand vigorously and smiled warmly, "Well, Everett, I would very much like to hire you for an evening in hopes of training Braden and his older brothers to handle themselves better should the need ever arise. I'll pay you handsomely for your time. What say you?"

"Of course, of course," smiled Mr. Pierce. "I would be more than happy to, but I am only in Serist for one more day."

"How about tonight then? Shall we say eight o'clock?"

"Most certainly," said Mr. Pierce.

After providing him with directions to the Derger home and several more enthusiastic handshakes and pats on the back, Lord Derger and Braden made their way back down the main road with their garish coach forcing people aside as it plowed deliberately through the crowds. "That went even better than I'd hoped," grinned Mr. Pierce. "Old Scrounger was right on the mark about this one. Come on then, Fighters, it's time we headed back to Miss Respect."

Once out of Serist, as they walked the dirt path beside the river, Tolund spoke up, "Sir, I noticed that you never gave Lord Derger any real information about any of us. What was the purpose of lying to him?"

"Lying?" responded Mr. Pierce in a bemused tone, "I never spoke a single lie. I merely gave him a few leaves instead of the whole tree. You see, Fighters, handing knowledge over to wicked men is dangerously foolish. All I really gave him was the nick-name of 'Everett' that I picked up as a youth— it's not my actual birth name. So, as of this moment we've managed to annoy the Dergers, but if all goes well tonight we will become their most hated enemies."

"But why would we want enemies?" asked Heather.

"Ah! Because having the right enemies means you are the right kind of person," Mr. Pierce said with a grin. "Now, as I was saying, the Dergers know very little about us and that is how it should be. We now have a way into their little castle which will give us the means to ruin their false kingdom. We'll speak of this more with the others. By the way, do both of you have the gifts of the White Council with you?"

"Mine's right here," said Heather as she lifted her shiny grey pendant out of her cloak.

"I have my sword wrapped in my things back in Scrounger's shack," said Tolund.

"Good," smiled Mr. Pierce. "See to it that you have them with you tonight. Our success might well depend on how bravely you wield them." As Tolund shot a look of panic at Heather he saw the same fear in her eyes.

"Trainingmaster, are you sure they'll be necessary?" asked Tolund nervously.

"Sure? Of course I'm sure!" growled the tough old dwarf. "What do you think they're for? I want both of you to hear me and hear me well because I won't say this again—those gifts, like all true gifts, only exist to be given to others."

"Given to others? What do you mean?" asked Heather.

"What I mean is that gifts like natural talent or gifts of possession are not given to you to be hoarded. Those who are blessed by the High King are blessed for a reason. Tolund's sword isn't a decoration or trophy, it's a weapon of magic that should serve to defend and protect the defenseless. Your pendant's enchantments are worthless if they are not used to help others. The commonfolk of Serist and the Ash River have been badgered long enough by these petty tyrants— your gifts are going to help put an end to that. And I might as well tell you now that the two of you alone will be charged with restoring the Ash river to its rightful path. My task will be to deal with the Derger family. However, as I realize this is all a far cry from arena fighting, I won't expect you to take up this cause unless you wish to, no one will think less of you if you choose to pass on all of this."

Without another word Mr. Pierce quickened his pace up the path leaving a terrified Tolund and Heather to follow and to ponder his words.

CHAPTER 5

CLOUDLESS THUNDER

Just after sunset the five travelers finalized their strategies. Mr. Pierce would be meeting with the Dergers at eight o'clock as planned. Bex and Lindris were going to Serist to 'distract' Lord Derger's protectorate lackeys. Lastly, Scrounger was to deliver Tolund and Heather, who both agreed to take a hand in helping these poor people, to the great spine of stone by way of the rivergate path. At half past seven Mr. Pierce slapped each of them on the back and wished them all good hunting. He also warned Heather and Tolund to be cautious of their steps for Lord Derger's prize ridge of stone would not be left unguarded. "Look for a darkstone at the center of the spine. A spell so great must have required one. Sunder the darkstone and you will sunder the spell." He then left them with a wild laugh as he trotted down the dark path toward Serist with Lindris and Bex close behind.

"Oh, Tol!" sighed an anxious Heather, "I'm not so sure we should have agreed to help! We don't know what we're doing, we don't know how to find this darkstone, and who knows what kind of nightmares are guarding it!"

Tolund chimed in, "Worst of all is that everyone and everything depends upon our success. If we fail, everything fails."

"If'n you two are done bellyachin' I'd like to get underway," interrupted Scrounger. "Seems to me you two best save your strength for wot's waitin' for ya' anyway." Both Heather and Tolund shuffled to the very front of the platform as Scrounger ordered Miss Respect forward into the dark waters of the Ash.

Silently they weaved down the river with the immense form of the riverdragon holding to the shadows as best she could. "It's good fer us that there's no moon tonight," whispered Scrounger. Tolund was amazed at how Miss Respect could slip down the river so quietly. The boy noticed that the only hint of their passing was the sudden silence of the bullfrogs and crickets at their approach. Just before the docks at Serist, Scrounger ordered her to stop and wait.

They all watched the two protectorate guards at their posts on the main dock. After a very short time both of the guards crumpled to the wooden planks, each a victim of a stealthy attack from behind. Bex and Lindris slipped out of the shadows and stood over them. "Heh, they're good all right," smiled Scrounger. "Time to go." Gliding past the docks they gave their two companions a quick wave. Bex smiled and waved back while Lindris only gave them a slight nod as they began tying up their captives.

"The next part's even trickier," said Scrounger. "Now you two've got to get around the rivergate and its guards without raising any alarm. Miss Respect is as silent as the grave in the water, but she's just too heavy and big over land in order fer us to get around that stinkin' gate. This is where we'll let you off, but don't you worry because once that mountain o' rock crumbles the gate should fall and we'll be right there to pick ya up." He gripped them both on their shoulder with his weathered old hands and gave them both a good shake, "Blessings on you, Pups! I'll throw up some prayers fer ya while I wait back here."

"Scrounger," asked Heather in an earnest voice, "you seem to hate that rivergate so much, why is that?"

The old man stared deeply into the waters of the Ash as he answered, "Maybe it's hard fer ya to understand, Pups, but I only have two things in my whole world—Miss Respect and this here river and one's not much good without the other is it? Y'see when that blighter moved in and stole the river from us he stole a large part o' my world. When ya don't have much it don't take a whole lot to take it away." He looked back at Heather and Tolund with fire in his eyes, "I gots freedom on this here river. It's the only place that I'm somebody. When some dirty thief steals that freedom from ya he steals who ya are. When that cursed gate falls I gets my life back— I'll get to be somebody again… and that's why me and everyone else on the Ash has been hatin' that blasted gate since the day it was put up."

"Well then, I guess we'll just have to put an end to it tonight won't we?" smiled Tolund.

Scrounger smiled back and slapped them both on the shoulder again. "Step lively, Pups! Just follow that path to the left and it'll take ya to the spine. I know ya can do it!"

With his sword slung over his shoulder, Tolund led the way with Heather close behind carrying her spear. They each looked back and smiled nervous smiles at the old boatman. Now their task had truly begun.

"Very prompt," called out the voice of Gerald Derger. "I like that." He stood atop his magnificent castle and called down to Mr. Pierce who approached on foot. Even the worldly old dwarf was shocked by what he saw. Surrounded by a well-kept moat, the Derger castle looked exactly like a normal castle with its drawbridge, high walls, and parapets, but resting over the center was an extraordinary sight. It looked to Mr. Pierce that a giant eagle had landed on the castle and spread its wings protectively over its walls before being turned to stone. Its wings even spread over the front walls and dipped into the waters of the moat. The monolith's head lay directly above the drawbridge and the light from the watchfire inside of it lit up its eyes in an eerie, menacing manner. Lord Derger called to the approaching dwarf from the left eye of the intimidating statue. Mr. Pierce also noticed that the same smaller flags that adorned the Derger coach also waved over each castle parapet.

"Welcome to the Derger Castle, Everett!" invited Lord Derger as the drawbridge lowered in dramatic fashion.

"Very impressive," replied Mr. Pierce as he crossed over the thick wooden drawbridge, "I must tell you that I've never seen a castle like this one before."

By the time Mr. Pierce made it to the inner courtyard Lord Derger had moved eagerly down the winding staircase to the bottom and now greeted his guest with a strong handshake. "We're quite proud of it, I must say. It took some time for my craftsmen to complete it. You would have appreciated them as they were dwarves of exceptional talent."

"Indeed," replied Mr. Pierce with raised eyebrows, "In my many years I've never known any dwarves who could craft a statue like that one. One might say their talents must have been almost… unnatural."

Lord Derger's lips pressed in a tight line for a quick second and then he smiled politely, "Yes, well let me show you around the old place." As the tour of the courtyard, armory, stables, and main quarters began, Lord Derger and Mr. Pierce were soon flanked by Derger's three sons and five other guardsmen. The stout dwarf seemed to disappear in the midst of a forest of larger, taller men. Along the tour Mr. Pierce took note of how ostentatious the furnishings and trappings were. It was clear that the entire castle, like the Derger's traveling coach, only existed to flaunt the wealth and position of this smug family. The trainingmaster also noticed how the two archers that shadowed him along the upper walkway of the castle walls each held their bow at the ready.

The tour ended back in the main courtyard. "Now then," stated Lord Derger, "why don't we get your lesson underway?" As soon as he said this the men all about Mr. Pierce stepped back to form a large circle about him. The dwarf narrowed his eyes and gave his host an inquisitive tilt of his head. "I'm afraid the lesson that I speak of, Good Everett, is for you." Gerald Derger's eyes suddenly burned as he scowled, "No one disrespects my son in my town. That was the last mistake of your pitiful life. Guards!" Lord Derger motioned with his hand toward Mr. Pierce and two arrows were loosed from the high walls on either side of him.

Heather and Tolund walked along the riverbank stealthily until they were around the heavy bars of the rivergate and the four men guarding it. There were two guards on each side of the river, one holding a bow and the other a spear. Clinging to the shadows, with their own weapons at the ready, they were able to sneak past the guards without incident. Once they had moved far enough up to the path to talk, Heather whispered, "I'm glad we didn't have to use these."

"So am I," smiled Tolund. "I've never actually used this sword in real combat. The only time I've drawn it for battle, aside from tonight, was when we encountered that reaper in the alley."

"I've never used this spear either, except to practice," added Heather, "let's hope the same luck holds for tonight." Tolund nodded in agreement and they moved on quietly.

They were pleased to see that even without a moon in the night sky the starlight made it fairly easy to see once their eyes got used to it. Once past the rivergate, the waters of the Ash split to the left and to the right almost immediately. At first the ground lifted in the middle with some scattered rocks and boulders lying about, but as they walked up the middle path they saw the dirt and grass give way to nothing but stone which formed a high ridge in the center and sloped down on each side. There was an unnatural stillness all about the rocks. Nothing green grew anywhere on the white stone and no birds, beasts, or insects could be seen or heard. It was at this point that Tolund paused.

"What's the matter?" asked Heather.

"Heather, do you think we can trust Mr. Pierce?"

"What? Are you serious?"

"I have to be," Tolund answered grimly, "you weren't there in the Boglands. You weren't there when Jareg and Mr. Kessing revealed their true colors."

"So you think Mr. Pierce is also an agent of the warlocks? That he's sent us into a trap tonight?"

"Before that night in the Boglands I would not have thought like this, but trusting too much almost cost me my life. I have to question things now. I have to assume people are not what they seem. Until now Mr. Pierce has led us along easy paths, but now he's sent the two of us out alone into a dangerous place in the dark of night where no one can help us and no one would ever find us if something did happen. You don't think that's suspicious, or at least unusual?"

"I don't know," Heather looked genuinely confused, "...Mr. Pierce has always seemed so honest and trustworthy, but it is odd that he would send us out alone when Bex or Lindris could have come along."

"My point exactly," said Tolund firmly. "Maybe it's all of the strange dreams I've been having that's making me nervous, but maybe I'm right to be nervous about all of this." An uneasy hush settled upon the moment as the two anxious friends looked up at the eerie stone ridge ahead of them.

"So, what do we do?" asked Heather.

"I'm not sure—if we go on and it is a trap then I guess we deserve what we get for allowing ourselves to be fooled again. On the other hand, if we don't go on we'll ruin the plans and waste the efforts of the others tonight. Badgers! I wish I knew what to do here!" Another moment of heavy silence crawled by.

Finally, Heather broke the silence, "My father always used to say, 'doing nothing is wasting something.' We need to just pray about it, make a decision, and step to it." Without another word, Heather took Tolund's right hand and dropped to one knee. Following her lead, he did the same. In an earnest prayer to the High King they prayed for wisdom they didn't have and courage they desperately needed. As they finished and stood up, a firm breeze rose up behind them gently pushing them in the direction of the ridge.

Heather smiled in relief and took a deep breath, "I think that's our answer. Let's go!" Without hesitation she stepped forward with Tolund's hand still clasped in hers from the prayer.

"I hope we're right about this," he grumbled softly.

"Well, we'll know one way or the other before the sun comes up won't we?" smiled Heather. As they moved up the ridge she was more than a little surprised at how good Tolund's hand felt in hers. Not only did it calm her nerves a little, but for some reason it felt different tonight than it had in all the years that they had been friends.

"What?!?" screamed an outraged Lord Derger. The instant after the bowstrings snapped forward Braden Derger and one of his personal guards cried out in pain. Braden clutched his right thigh, which was skewered by one of the arrows. The guard was sprawled, unmoving, upon the dirt of the courtyard with the other arrow lodged in his chest.

"It looks like you've still some lessons to learn tonight, Derger!" scoffed Mr. Pierce. "Well met, Fighters!" From the shadows of the upper walkways Lindris and Bex stepped forward.

"Guards, protect your masters!" ordered Lord Derger as he fell back behind his men. "Boys, make your father proud and bring me the head of that loud-mouthed dwarf!" Braden's two older brothers unsheathed their swords and moved toward Mr. Pierce.

"Take care of the rabble," Mr. Pierce called out to Bex and Lindris who had clambered down the ladders to the courtyard. Each bore the real versions of their wooden arena weapons, Bex with his black iron axe and iron shield and Lindris with her two curved steel swords. "I'll handle these lumps."

"Handle us?" mocked the oldest Derger 'prince,' "you don't even have a weapon. We'll have you in a pine box straight away!" The tall young men closed in on the dwarf.

"You forget," growled Mr. Pierce as he dashed to the wall and pulled two torches from their iron sconces. Whirling about like a panther he held them up like two swords, "...I came here to give you pretenders some lessons and I'm not leaving until I do!" With a hop to his left Mr. Pierce set the thatched roof of the stable afire with one torch while he blocked the slashing blade of the eldest Derger son with the haft of the other. In a casual move he then set fire to his attacker's fancy tunic. Dropping his sword, the Derger boy screamed and rolled upon the dirt to extinguish the flames. Mr. Pierce readied himself for the lad's brother.

With a shout of anger the second Derger boy charged in swinging his blade wildly.

"Bah!" called out Mr. Pierce, "you lumps don't merit real weapons." In one fluid motion the dwarf again blocked the sword with one torch, but this time burned his opponent's sword hand with the other. In a squeal of pain the tall boy dropped his sword and backed up against the stable wall as Mr. Pierce thrust a torch straight toward his chest.

"I submit, I submit!" the boy cried out in a panic.

"Aye, that you will, Lump," growled Mr. Pierce. "Now, take your fool of a brother out of the castle and see to his burns. Also, here is the lesson I promised— battles are not won by words or weapons, but by the warriors themselves. If you dare to ever cross blades with me or mine again, the pine box will be yours!" Nervously, the boy scurried toward his brother and began to drag him to the front gate.

Behind the dwarf the fire had spread from the castle and over the roof of the main house. Huge flames lifted up in the night sky and smoke and cinders filled the air in the courtyard. Mr. Pierce was pleased to see that Lindris had finished dispatching her adversaries who were strewn about her, disarmed and wounded, while Bex was buckling the shield of his last overmatched opponent. Quickly the vanquished guardsmen were all herded or carried out the front gate to the lowered drawbridge where Lord Derger and his humbled sons saw to their wounds; Mr. Pierce was also relieved to see that the servants and stable beasts had managed to safely escape the fire he'd started.

"You think you've won a great victory for yourself here tonight, Dwarf?" barked Lord Derger. "We'll see now who rules in Serist!" Pointing in the direction of his fields, Derger announced the approach of hundreds of angry villagers bearing weapons of their own.

"Something's happening with my pendant again," whispered Heather urgently. "It's tingling like it did in the alley with the reaper, only this time it's stronger."

"That can't be a good sign," said Tolund, "we'd better be ready for anything." By this time the two of them had made their way to the summit of the rocky spine without incident. Nothing seemed out of place and there was no sign of a darkstone. They continued to follow the ridge as it angled down gradually.

"Wait," warned Heather, "there's some kind of opening or hole up ahead." Both of them squinted hard and did indeed see where the ground opened up into a hole scarcely large enough for a grown man to crawl down into.

"That has to be it," Tolund said. Moving faster, they closed in upon the hole at a slight jog. Suddenly the rock beneath their feet softened, yanking them down violently. Tolund felt like he was drowning in thick mud. Impossibly, the rock had become liquid and sucked them down like a whirlpool. All was black and Tolund could not find Heather. He knew they only had a few moments before they would drown. He was trying to swim, but he didn't seem to be moving no matter how hard he kicked his feet or paddled his arms. Matters grew more deadly when he felt the liquid rock thicken about him. If he didn't get out soon he would be entombed here forever.

Why he thought of his sword at this moment of near-panic he did not know. His right hand shot toward the shoulder scabbard and drew the enchanted blade. Magically, the hardening rock about his body softened back to liquid again. With a life of its own the sword pointed above the boy and began to lift him out of the swirling rock. Gasping once he hit the surface, Tolund felt the black blade dragging him toward the 'shore' where solid rock was still solid. Coughing and hacking, the boy spat out the watery rock in his mouth only to see it turn to hard stone once it hit the ground.

"Heather?!?" he screamed as he jumped to his feet. She was still inside the trap and he had no idea where. Cautiously, he touched the spot where the rock was swirling a moment ago— it was solid now, just as natural rock should be. Tolund knew that Heather was not only trapped, but almost out of air by now. This vile pool of stone had hardened around her and was about to become her grave.

"I don't know what to do! What do I do?!?" he shouted with tears filling his eyes. A slight shimmer caught the corner of his eye. His sword seemed to be reflecting the starlight in a strange way. Tolund gave one hard look to his blade and then, backing up to get a running start, dove headfirst, with his sword leading the way, into the center of the living rock. The instant the sword tip pierced the surface, the stone softened to liquid once more. As if it read his mind, the blade pulled its master to the still body of Heather Bonwell. Tolund grasped her arm with his free hand and pointed his sword tip up to the surface of the trap. Again the blade drew them up like a bucket pulled up from a well.

Once on solid rock, Tolund shook Heather's still form and turned her on her side while shouting her name. His eyes filled with tears of relief when he heard her begin to cough. Soon she was spitting out the wet rock from her throat and gasping for air. "I'd thought it was over," he stammered, "I…I thought we were dead."

"Are you all right?" Tolund asked as she slumped onto the hard ground, exhausted.

"I am now," she smiled.

"I guess we didn't see that one coming did we?" Heather joked weakly.

Tolund laughed out loud at her silly question, "Oh, I don't know, we get pulled into rock whirlpools, almost smothered, and pulled out by magic swords all of the time! Why should tonight be anything special?" They both laughed at this absurd peril more out of shock and relief than anything else.

Looking over at the area of shifting rock they were surprised to see a macabre warning of what had almost become their fate. Thrust out from the now hardened pool of stone were the bones of a previous victim. The skeleton hand and rib cage and the very top of a skull now stuck out from the surface of the rock. "It looks like we weren't the first ones looking for the darkstone," said Heather.

"We must have disturbed this poor soul's bones when we escaped the pool," Tolund surmised. "I wonder how many victims have been claimed by that trap. It's treacherous enough. Someone might look out for a bog or quicksand to try and drown you, but who would ever suspect a shelf of rock?"

"Another sure sign that a warlock's behind Lord Derger's success." The scorn in Heather's voice was obvious, ever since her time with her adopted brother, Eli, she'd learned to hate these ruthless beings. "What do you think we should do now, Tolund?"

"We have to look into that hole, but I think we'd better examine it carefully. If your pendant acts up again we need to pay better attention to its warnings, we rushed right into that whirlpool trap like a pair of mindless flies into a web."

Stepping carefully, with his sword out in front, Tolund approached the hole in the rock. Heather followed behind clutching only her pendant as her spear had been lost in the stone whirlpool. Just a step away from the hole, Heather called out urgently, "Tolund wait! The pendant's tingling again, even more than before." Both of them froze, waiting for something to leap out of the hole at them. Tense moments passed without a threat or attack.

"I guess the smoothstone's warning us about something down in the hole," said Tolund. "Wait here for a moment, I have an idea." Walking to his left, he made his way to some long tree limbs that were hanging over the stone ridge. Tolund quickly hacked off a long branch and scurried back up the ridge to where Heather was waiting.

"What are you going to do with that?" she asked.

"This," he answered as he shoved the tip of the branch into the hole. Instantly crude, razor-sharp spikes of stone thrust out from all sides and shredded the tree limb. Tolund pulled what was left of the branch out of the hole. Only a splintered stump with a few leaves remained.

"I'm glad we didn't jump in with both feet," Heather said anxiously.

"I think I can make out a rounded tunnel, but those spikes just grew out of the tunnel walls the instant I put the branch in," said Tolund. "Even if I could hack off a few of them with my sword I'm sure to be gored to death by the other ones. The darkstone has to be on the other end of this tunnel, but I don't know how to get through. What do you think Heather?" There was no answer from behind him.

"Heather?" Tolund turned around to a shocking sight. Heather stood rigid with both hands gripping her pendant with white knuckles and her eyes were glowing with the same fiery green light that was emanating from her pendant. "Heather!" he shouted, fearing this was another deadly trap.

With a loud gasp the young girl's eyes returned to their normal state and the pendant shone fiercely and then stopped. Panting heavily, Heather smiled, "I know what to do, the pendant told me what to do!" Perplexed, Tolund grimaced and tilted his head to one side.

"It's going to seem impossible, but I know it will work. Follow me."

Stepping quickly down the right side of the ridge, Heather led them to a shallow pond not far from the river. "Why are we way down here?" Tolund asked.

"You're going to have to trust me on this, Tolund. Just hold onto my hand and jump in with me. Whatever you do, don't let go of my hand." The lad was thoroughly confused and gave his best friend another dumbfounded look. Heather whispered a prayer and her pendant burned a bright green again. Tolund's mouth hung open when he saw that, once more, the same ghostly hue shone from her eyes. Without hesitation she jumped into the center of the small pond, dragging Tolund in with her.

In a quick rush of water and bright light, they fell into the shallow pond only, incredibly, their feet didn't touch the muddy bottom as they should have. Instead, they plunged down and bobbed up right away into someplace else. It was dark wherever they were except for a round opening far above them. "Where are we?" asked Tolund.

"Look around you, look up." Heather said in a pleased voice. "It actually worked!"

Tolund looked down in the dim light and saw that they were standing in a shallow pool of water which was to one side of a crevice scarcely the size of a small room. "I still don't…" he looked up at the tunnel above them that led up to starlight. "Wait! Is that the tunnel in the rock?!?"

"It is," answered Heather. "The pendant brought us from the pond above to this spring below. We are down inside the hole and past the tunnel with the spikes. Isn't that amazing?"

"But…but how did you know how to do that?" asked Tolund.

"The pendant just seemed to come alive and talk to my mind, almost like I was dreaming. It showed me a picture of what we needed to do, where the pond was and everything. I can't believe that…"

"Look, over there!" interrupted Tolund. As he was listening to Heather a slight reflection in the very back of the crevice caught his attention. There, imbedded in the sloping back wall, was a gleaming black darkstone. "Heather, we found it!"

"Quick, use your sword to shatter it. You said it was supposed to be the 'bane of all things evil.' It should work."

"I'll give it a try," said Tolund. Drawing the sword again from the sheath along his back, he held it up with both hands and prepared to strike.

"Wait," warned Heather. "How do we know it's safe to shatter it? Couldn't it kill us?"

"I don't know," he answered. "I've never split a darkstone with a magic sword before; what are you asking me for?"

"I guess we don't have much choice, do we?" An awkward moment of silence hung over them as they hesitated. Heather wrapped her arms around her old friend and hugged him as hard as she could. "If we don't survive this at least we'll both arrive in the High Kingdom together."

Tolund gave her a bemused grin, "Are you ready?" Heather clutched her pendant with both hands again and gave him a worried nod. Fighting the queasiness in his stomach, Tolund ignored his fear and brought the black edge down as hard as he could upon the darkstone.

Grey sparks exploded as the evil stone splintered into tiny shards. Both Tolund and Heather were slammed to the rocky floor by the booming sound of thunder. In a quick breath the stone all about them shuddered and turned to dust, smothering both of them. Now a huge rush of cold water hit them from both sides. Their young limbs thrashed and kicked as the surging currents engulfed them. This was the second time tonight that they were helpless and drowning.

It was a tense moment before the Derger castle. With the fire behind them and the mob of armed villagers before them, Mr. Pierce, Lindris, and Bex stood trapped on the drawbridge. They stood there, weapons at the ready, while Lord Derger and his family and servants moved to the open ground in front of the moat. Armed with their own weapons or tools such as fishing pikes, pitchforks, or shovels, the mob moved in around the Derger party and blocked the front of the drawbridge. "How many of them are there?" asked Bex grimly.

"More than a hundred," answered Mr. Pierce, "it looks like most of Serist has been roused."

"How can only three of us fight off a mob of that size with a fire at our ba—" Bex's anxious question was interrupted by the clap of nearby thunder. A collective gasp went out; the heads of all assembled looked up to find a cloudless night sky. Now the rushing of great waters echoed out over Serist.

"Do you hear that, People of Serist?" bellowed Mr. Pierce. "That is the end of this fool's reign. The stone ridge has been leveled and the Ash is one river once more. Derger's iron gate is now as useless as he is!"

Angry murmurs erupted from the crowd as they looked back and forth at each other and Lord Derger. Bex and Lindris steeled themselves for the coming battle. An angry call went up from within the mob and they turned and converged upon Derger's party. The self-proclaimed 'lord's' history of smug cruelty had just decided his fate. The two young arena fighters were genuinely surprised by this quick turn of events, but their wise trainingmaster showed no surprise at all.

Mr. Pierce rushed forward waving his torches madly, "Stop!" he cried out. "These fools are not worth the blood that would stain your hands!" The vengeful crowd halted.

"You don't know what it's like to live under his heel!" a man's voice protested from the center of the mob. "Derger walked on gold while we groveled in the dirt! Always demanding, always mocking us and treating us like we were dogs."

"They stole from us! They ordered us about like we were slaves!" cried a woman's voice. "And his boys were just as bad as he was; they all deserve what they get!" Howls of agreement filled the air.

Again waving his torches to gain their attention, Mr. Pierce addressed them, "That is why we were asked to come here. We have broken his hold over this river and this town tonight, but we need more from him. Gerald Derger is merely the lapdog of his warlock masters, those whose power split the river and sculpted this castle. We need to bring Derger and his servants back to Ansalion so we can determine the measure and means of his alliance with these warlocks.

It is within your power to spill his blood, nothing I can do can prevent that, but I would ask that you forego your vengeance for the sake of the greater good. The warlocks are a threat that will return to plague you if we waste this opportunity to uncover their inner workings."

The mob hesitated and grumbled amongst themselves for a few moments. Finally, a respected elder spoke up, "We'll honor your wishes, Good Dwarf. We all want the warlocks out of our lives, but that doesn't mean we can't make Derger and his followers more 'presentable' for their journey back to Ansalion!" With that, the mob pressed in on Derger, his sons, and his guardsmen. A roar went up as they vented their long-stifled frustrations upon them with fists and boots. Bound and beaten, the captives were now carried back to Serist over the heads of the cheering throng.

Bex and Lindris looked on as a handful of village elders spoke with Mr. Pierce. Soon, their trainingmaster walked back to them, "Everything's arranged," he said. "Derger and his fellow traitors, including the guards stationed in Serist and at the rivergate, will be held in the town until the protectorate officials can arrive and take custody of them; although I'm pleased to report that all of the prisoners will be adorned with pitch and goose feathers for the trip." A satisfied chuckle accompanied the last part.

"So, we're not going back to Ansalion after all of this?" asked Lindris.

"Of course not," answered Mr. Pierce. "I told all of you that we were heading to the Coastlands for some arena matches and that is still the plan."

"What about the others?" asked Bex in a concerned voice. "Do you think they're all right?"

"I hope so, Lad. We'd best get over to the river and see for ourselves." Once rushed 'farewells' were shared with the village elders, the three companions hurried off in the direction of the thunderclap.

Rolling end over end, Tolund fought to reach the surface. The angry currents from the two smaller rivers that were now smashing together into one larger river hammered the boy mercilessly. Tolund began to panic as he realized that swimming was futile in this ruthless deluge. With the rush of the water in his ears and everything going black, Tolund did not notice that something was tugging on his cloak. In a violent pull the lad's body broke the surface of the raging tide and landed firmly on wooden planks.

"Are ya still breathing, Pup?!?" called Scrounger's raspy voice.

"Tolund, can you hear me?!?" cried Heather. Coughing for air and shaking the water from his head, Tolund's vision came back. The first thing he saw was Heather's worried eyes. "Are you all right?" she pleaded.

"I…I think so," he stammered. "Are you?"

"Only just," she smiled weakly. "Miss Respect snatched me up just before she found you."

"I don't know how she does it, but my old girl here can find a tadpole in a whirlpool if ya ask her to!" laughed Scrounger. "Now then, let's get you two to dry land." No sooner than he'd spoken the words,

Miss Respect thrashed her tail and angled them all to the shore. After the initial surge, the waters now began to calm down.

"Thanks for coming to our rescue, Scrounger," said Tolund.

"Believe me, t'was my pleasure," grinned the old riverman. "To see the Ash back to the way she should be is all the thanks I need. Besides, 'tween the thunder and the rivers crashin' back together, t'was the best show I'd seen in a long, long time!"

CHAPTER 6

SUMMONED

It was late afternoon when Cleric Michaels stepped out of the coach and stretched his arms up in the air with a groan. He smiled at the sight of the Gold Quarter before him; it had been far too long since he'd seen its familiar beauty. Collecting his bag, sword, and cloak, the cleric walked toward the White Sanctuary with an eager stride. Thoughtfully, he stopped and placed his hand upon the smooth white marble of the entrance wall and smiled again. Preparing to enter, he removed his boots and stockings and washed his bare feet with the towel and basin provided at the doors. "Well, well, look at who has returned!" a voice called cheerfully.

"Ah! Cleric Marston," grinned Cleric Michaels, "how are you?"

"Quite well, thank you. And you?"

"I still dislike long coach rides, but it's worth the stiff back and smell of dust and horse to be back in the Gold Quarter again. It's hard to believe that I've been away for so many years."

The two friends walked past the entrance and down the long hallways toward the high-reaching staircase. As they walked, Warren Michaels breathed in the smell of the candles and enjoyed the feel of his bare feet on the white stone floors. "How is your lovely wife and the now-famous town of Glendien?" asked Cleric Marston.

"Everything's pleasant enough. Rachel's fine, the church is fine, everyone's getting along all right. Although, the recent excitement has brought new visitors to Glendien. They're mostly from neighboring provinces and harmless enough, but a bit of an annoyance to the locals who, for the most part, are tired of telling and re-telling the story of the 'Bogland War.' Rachel takes great joy in boasting about our two young heroes, but I think Tolund and Heather are fairly lucky to be here in Ansalion otherwise they might die of embarrassment at how often their names are being bandied about." Cleric Michaels let out an amused chuckle at this last statement.

"Do you know much about why you've been summoned so suddenly?" In spite of himself, Cleric Marston could not resist changing the subject so abruptly.

"My, my," scoffed Cleric Michaels playfully, "things must be pretty dull around here for my small plans to become such an interest for my brothers in the White Sanctuary!"

"Heh! True enough, true enough," laughed his old friend. "Still, with your post in Glendien becoming such an eventful one recently you have to admit that an unexpected summons to the Council is a tantalizing curiosity. And you should know that you were not the only one summoned." Cleric Michael's eyebrows raised in a silent query.

"At this point I'm only concerned about getting washed up and having a bite to eat before the meeting," he responded flatly. "Is that all right with you?"

"Well, judging by your bored tone, I guess it will have to be," joked Cleric Marston. "You know, you were a lot more fun when you were younger, Warren."

"So were you, you old codger. So were you," chuckled Cleric Michaels. Arriving at the proper floor, the two old friends exited the staircase and found the guest quarters reserved for Cleric Michaels. Bidding his fellow cleric farewell, Cleric Marston informed him that his time with the Council was set at an hour past the evening meal.

Later that night, at an hour past the evening meal in the highest floor of the White Sanctuary, Cleric Warren Michaels took his seat in the hallway a few strides away from a young protectorate captain whom he had not met before. Glancing quickly at one another, each one wondered what this meeting was all about and why only the two of them had been invited. Suddenly, one of the large wooden doors opened up. "A blessed evening to you Captain Shaw, Cleric Michaels," smiled the friendly face of Cleric Green, "The Council is ready for you now."

The deep of night crept up upon the Coastland village of Berbago. There was nothing unusual about the winds that came in from the sea and moved gently over the old fishing village. The sights this night were the same for the handsome, dark-hued people who had lived all of their simple lives close to the shore—starlight over open sea was an enchanting vision that they were all too familiar with. Tonight, however, the sounds had changed.

Along with the music of coastal breezes moving the palm leaves about and the rhythm of the waves crashing upon the shore came a ghostly melody. Like the moaning cry of a widow in mourning, it began to weave its way to the ears of the sleeping villagers amidst the sounds of the wind and the waves. Lovely and haunting, it carried with it a spell of overpowering need. Someone was singing a horrific song that the villagers could not resist. The lure of the urgent call had an immediate and shocking effect upon its helpless victims.

Every man, woman, and child that heard the beckoning song rose from their sleep and stumbled like creatures half-dead toward the seashore. Old and young, all that could stand and walk made their way toward the song upon the waters. Once the village had emptied out onto the edge of the shoreline, oddly, everyone summoned by the spell of the music stretched themselves out on the white sand and fell into a deep, relentless sleep. From the small island a half-league offshore the author of the song ceased its chilling cry.

For some time the mesmerized villagers slept in their oblivion, unmoving and unknowing. Suddenly, the foam of the surf began to move unnaturally as hundreds of shiny forms emerged from the sea. From all along the waterline they skittered greedily, their black shells glistening under the night sky. Without a single conscious witness to their incursion, the army of gargantuan ebony crabs swarmed upon the entranced villagers. Impossibly, each crab was the size of a large wolf and bore powerful pincers and quick skittering legs. Without sound, the frenzied swarm went to work.

There was no hesitation or confusion in their assault. Moving furiously to find their own victim, each crab claimed a villager. Scampering up to their throats and chins, the crabs placed their own mouths over the lips and nose of their victim and began to spew a large, clear bubble. The bubble, thick like glass or crystal, moved and bobbled, but did not pop. Once its quarry had their strange bubble in place, the crab scurried to the sand by their victim's feet and grasped their ankles with both claws. Now, in a show of effortless strength, each crab began to drag its victim into the surf and under the waves. Through all of this no eye fluttered, no voice cried out, and no hand stirred. In a matter of moments the only things left upon the shore before the village were the drag marks in the sand of all those lost in this vile culling. The village of Berbago had been harvested.

CHAPTER 7

THE SACRED VAULT

Night had fallen by the time the Lockslayer had reached the vault of the Frostland dwarves. It was high up in the northern passes between two towering mountains, hidden deep in the snow-swept ravine between them. For all his supernatural speed, the lead of the warlocks had proven to be too great for Eli to overcome. He had failed to intercept them before they had reached the vault. Now, the warlock presence here was all too obvious.

Before the huge stone door of the sacred vault were the fallen bodies of dozens of dwarves who gave their lives in its defense. A slight grim smile lifted in the corner of Eli's mouth as he noted the fallen bodies of four casters and two dragons in the snow. "At least a heavy toll was paid before they entered here," the Lockslayer thought to himself.

Moving nimbly, Eli landed and examined the carcass of the icedragon. The beast had not been dead for long. Now voices could be heard from within the vault itself. Dismissing his wings, the great warrior summoned his shield and longsword. His senses told him that the dragons had already departed this place, but he knew that he had to investigate the vault. Though he had missed the battle itself, voices from within meant there were survivors and survivors would mean information.

After the ruined entrance, the vault opened up quickly into a larger chamber. Carved out of the stone of the mountain itself, it was a solid, well-crafted stronghold. Eli saw that on either side of the only pathway that led deeper into the vault were several fortified posts from which archers or spearmen could rain death upon any who dared enter. He also noted that the corpses of those brave defenders were charred or frozen from the combined assault of the icelocks and stormlocks. A furious battle was lost here by the dwarves, but, again, Eli had to respect the bravery of these warriors in the face of such overwhelming odds.

Several strides into the vault the warlock snare was tripped. Suddenly, the very air froze sharply into four thick walls of ice that successfully trapped the Lockslayer. "We marked your footsteps in the snow," a voice called out from further down the vault. Eli moved close to the wall before him, trying to make out the approaching figures through the icy barrier. With the wall at least four feet thick, all he could spy were the forms of two taller figures holding what might be spears or staves. "Our masters told us you would be coming. They even honored us with the task of delaying you."

Instantly, the air about Eli's chest and shoulders froze about him, wrapping him in a sheath of mystic ice. Instinctively, the great warrior summoned his firewings, but found that the ice blocked their appearance. Shifting to his other wings, he found that they too would not appear. "Impressive," Eli called defiantly, "but it won't save you."

"Unfortunately, we would have to agree with you," called a voice different from the first one. "You are the legendary Lockslayer and we are but a pair of humble casters. Still, that does not mean that we cannot give you pause." Instantly, lightning exploded within the four walls of ice.

Eli gritted his teeth in pain, but refused to cry out as the vicious bolts scorched and shocked his armor from all sides. Dismissing his sword and shield, he clenched his fists and flexed his iron muscles against the ice that held him. With a grunt he shattered his restraints, but before he could summon his wings an impossible gust of wind slammed him against the back wall of his sorcerous prison. This tactic continued with brutal efficiency. Again and again, faster and faster, the storm winds smashed him against the four ice walls, which instantly healed any crack or damage the impact might have caused, granting them continuous invincibility. Now the lightning joined with the winds adding searing pain to the attack.

The Lockslayer knew this trap was wrought carefully and was proving to be deadly, even to him. The constant shock of the lightning coupled with the spinning and pounding collisions against the walls made it impossible for Eli to concentrate enough to summon his weapons or wings. Fortunately for him, his rage grew as his agony increased. Finally, his savage instincts were unleashed.

In the chamber just beyond, the icecaster and stormcaster concentrated on their tasks. Suddenly, the stormcaster ceased his violent spell and lowered his staff. "Something's changed!" he said fearfully. "His form is gone; I don't sense him inside my storm anymor—" Above them the roof of the stony vault exploded.

"Your tortures are undone and now you are mine!" called the Lockslayer from above them. With open sky behind him, he was held aloft by his white wings and held his bow in his outstretched hand. Before the two casters could redirect their attacks to his new position, Eli loosed two swiftly summoned arrows from his bow. The first arrow of red struck the icecaster in his shoulder; his death screams filled the air as he burst into flames so blistering that even his freezing spells could not expel them. The second arrow of blue stuck into the ground just before the stormcaster, creating a whirlwind that swept him up into the ceiling of the vault. Broken in numerous places, the shattered corpse of the caster slumped to the ground without a word.

Gliding lightly to the ground, Eli discovered three dwarves, bound and gagged, lying on the floor by the back wall of a small side chamber. Cutting their bonds and reassuring them that he was not here to harm them, he began to question them about the attack. Grateful for their rescue, they were all too happy to oblige him.

They quickly explained how the dragons first ambushed the outer guard from the sky. As the dwarves engaged the dragons, the warlocks and their casters flanked them on foot. After a bloody battle, they fell back to the vault, but their defenses proved to be completely ineffectual against the merciless spells of the icelock and stormlock that led the attack. "Once defeated, the warlocks left two of their casters behind to ambush you," said the eldest guard. "We were the only survivors of their attack and the casters were planning to use us as hostages if their trap failed."

"If you don't mind my asking, Great Lockslayer, how did you escape that death box they trapped you in?" asked another of the guards.

Staring over at the staff of the fallen stormcaster while he answered, Eli explained his escape to the anxious guards, "I must admit that it was a masterful strike, one that was far stronger than it had a right to be. However, their 'box' was imperfect. The ceiling of the vault was only natural stone and not living, healing ice. I was able to grasp the rock with my hands when I was smashed up against it. Tearing through the rock to the open sky above, it was a simple matter to fly above their position and use my weapons to breach their ceiling and finish them off."

"Yes," answered a dumbfounded dwarf, "...a 'simple' matter."

"Hmph," grunted the Lockslayer as he knelt down to inspect the stormcaster's staff, "this would explain their unexpected power. There are four darkstones bonded to this staff!"

"That was the treasure of this sacred vault, Milord," added the eldest guard. "Unbound smoothstones collected from many places have been guarded here. All that remain here now were the eight used by these casters to stop you, the rest were carried off by their masters."

"Tracking them will be simple enough," Eli thought aloud. "How many smoothstones did they carry off?"

"Oh, several hundred at least, Milord."

Looking hard at the large vault that was now empty of every last smoothstone, the Lockslayer took a deep, drawn-out breath. "May the High King have mercy on us all."

CHAPTER 8

CINDERS AND SOOT

In the hours of early morning Tolund and Heather were reunited with all of their companions. Over a cold breakfast of bread and cheese the party shared the details of their parts in the liberation of Serist. As they ate and reveled in their victories, Miss Respect carried them further down the now-restored Ash River.

Everything seemed bright and everyone pleased, except for Tolund. Even as he explained his part in ruining the schemes of Derger and his warlock allies, the boy's eyes narrowed whenever they settled on Mr. Pierce. When Mr. Pierce spoke Tolund refused to look at him and stared out at the river's surface instead. Heather held her breath a little every time she noticed this; she hoped that Mr. Pierce would not notice Tolund's distant mood toward him.

After a while, once their small celebration was over, the tired party took their usual places on the platform and fell fast asleep. Scrounger and Miss Respect, herself, were enjoying moving down the Ash River that was again as it should be. Like a queen touring her beloved homeland, the great riverdragon paraded herself through the waters while Scrounger allowed joyful tears to stream down his wrinkled cheeks. Their home, at long last, was restored and all was well in their little part of the world.

That next evening, once everyone had slept almost the entire day, Scrounger ordered Miss Respect to the shore where they would camp for the night. Just as Bex volunteered to gather firewood for the cooking fire, Mr. Pierce interrupted him and told him that he and Tolund would take care of that chore instead. Mildly surprised at this, Tolund followed behind his trainingmaster without complaint. He did, however, glance over at Heather with a bewildered look. Heather's only reply was to shrug her shoulders and give him a befuddled look of her own.

The two of them walked briskly until they were just out of earshot from the others. Mr. Pierce stopped abruptly and pointed a stubby finger at a small boulder, "Have a seat, Lad."

"What's the matter?" asked the surprised boy. "Aren't we gathering firewood?"

"All in good time, Tolund. It seems you and I have something to discuss first." He gave his charge a good long stare as he waited for Tolund's reply.

"Um, I'm not sure I know what you're talking ab…"

"Don't waste my time, Boy," the tough old dwarf said flatly. "I'm a trainingmaster, remember? I read faces and expressions like scholars read scrolls. Something's bothering you all right, something that concerns me. I'm the only one getting the 'snake eyes' from you today. So, quit wasting my time and tell me what's under your skin."

Cornered and nervous, Tolund looked down and took a long breath to gather his thoughts and courage. "All right, Sir," he said firmly,

"I'm frustrated about the other night. I don't understand why you sent Heather and I out on such a dangerous mission by ourselves." As he spoke these words his voice grew more intense. "We almost died in those traps. We were the youngest ones on this trip and you sent us out alone! You should have sent Lindris or Bex with us or gone with us yourself!"

Even in his frustration Tolund couldn't look the intimidating dwarf in the eye. Now the boy just looked down and waited for the trainingmaster's response to his outburst.

Mr. Pierce took a thoughtful breath of his own and stroked his thick beard for a moment. "I think I understand what this is all about now," he said calmly. Moving over to Tolund, he leaned in close and stared the boy right in the eye, "Tolund, am I someone you should trust?"

Taken aback by the abrupt question, Tolund mumbled the first thing that he could think of, "Um, of course you are, Sir."

"Why?" the dwarf asked sharply.

"Well, um, because you're a respected trainingmaster."

"Wrong!" Mr. Pierce gave Tolund's forehead a slight knock with his burly knuckles like he was knocking on someone's door. "Position and reputation mean nothing. You trusted the well-respected Mr. Kessing last year and look where that got you! Now, let's try it again… am I someone you should trust?"

The boy rubbed his forehead and studied Mr. Pierce's face for some clue of how he should answer. Seeing no help there, he tried to come up with a better answer, "Well, I guess you should be trusted because you've never lied to me or to Heather. In fact, if anything, I think you're too blunt and honest with everyone. That's why people trust you."

"Wrong!" The wide, hairy knuckles gave Tolund's forehead another quick rap. "How do you know I never lie? If I'm good enough at it you wouldn't know I was lying until it was too late. You of all people should know that!" Tolund's pride was stinging now and his face began to turn red. Mr. Pierce's scolding continued, "Your young friend Jareg was a loud-mouth, just like me. Just like me, he didn't seem like he could keep his mouth shut about anything. You didn't think he was lying until he turned on you, isn't that right??"

Bringing up Jareg was the last straw for Tolund. Forgetting who he was talking to, his temper flared as he stood up and took a step back from Mr. Pierce. "Fine! Then you tell me why I should trust you! I'm just a novice fighter too stupid to figure it out for myself! The way I see it, maybe I shouldn't trust you at all after the way you sent us out on our own last night!"

"Good!" snapped Mr. Pierce. "That's the first speck of sense I've heard from you tonight!" Tolund's brow furrowed and his head tilted in confusion. Mr. Pierce continued his lecture, "The truth is, Boy, that you really don't have a lot of reason to trust me. Like most fools, you toss your trust around like you're tossing leaves in the air. The only difference is that after all you've been through you should know better, especially when you've made the kind of enemies you've made." Now the dwarf took a step back and again stroked his beard casually. "I like the fire in you, Lad, the fire I see in your eyes right now. That's the kind of fire that will keep you from stumbling blindly into the traps of people you never should have followed."

"But, where does that leave me?" asked Tolund earnestly. "Are you telling me that I shouldn't trust anyone?"

Mr. Pierce walked over and placed a strong hand on Tolund's shoulder, "Not quite, Tolund, not quite. I'm glad all of this came up because it's revealed the difficult nature of 'trust.' Blind trust, even blind trust in your trainingmaster, is a fool's gambit—one that may get you killed. Real trust, however, is worth more than a chest full of gold, gems, and smoothstones. You are my charge and you should obey me in most things, but how do you really know that I am not in league with your enemies? Even now, how do you know that this conversation might all be a ruse to lure you into foolishly trusting me?" He could see that the poor lad was more confused than ever. "The way I see it, Tolund, is that the only one on this trip you can really, truly trust is young Heather."

"What about you?" asked Tolund. "After all of this you're telling me that I shouldn't trust you?"

"That's exactly what I'm saying," the dwarf said with a satisfied smile. "I don't want you placing too much trust in anyone, even me, unless they've earned it." A happy Mr. Pierce gave his fighter a good slap on the shoulder and began to walk the other way.

"But… but how will I know when someone's earned it?" asked an unsettled Tolund.

"Ah!" Mr. Pierce answered cheerfully, "that's for you to figure out!" Without another word, the dwarf began to collect wood for the fire. Tolund knew this was his trainingmaster's way of ending their conversation. With a sigh of resignation the confused boy joined in the search for firewood. Not another word was spoken between them that night.

The following days were pleasant for the entire party. Scrounger continued his appreciative mood and took great joy in pointing out more landmarks and particulars of the Ash River. Mr. Pierce, after allowing a full three days of complete rest for his fighters, began to rigorously drill and train them again. The four fighters, themselves, were eager to get back to the demands of the arena and the thrill of seeing their prowess and skills increase. The travelers carried on like this for days until Scrounger pointed out to them the change in the air itself.

"Do ya feel it, Pups?" he asked as they awoke one morning. "It's gettin' warmer. That's how it starts. The Ash'll take us down a few waterfalls and then the air will get a little more damp and thick. And then we're almost there."

"Almost where?" asked Bex.

"To the place wot's doin' two things at once," he said thoughtfully. Tolund could tell that the old riverman was again enjoying his chance to be the voice of experience. "First, it's the place that shows us why the river had its name changed to wot it is now. Second, it's the place wot marks the beginnings of the Coastlands." A proud smile spread over his sunbeaten face, "Believe me when I tells ya, Pups, that it's a sight ya don't never forget even though you'll want to!"

Just before sunset of that day, just as Scrounger predicted, they came upon the first waterfall. In practiced fashion, Miss Respect slipped up to the shore just before the waterfall itself. Moving in her twisting steps, she made her way down the path that ran alongside the river without upsetting a single crate or cup upon the platform that rested on her great back. That night, over the cooking fire, Scrounger and Mr. Pierce regaled the young ones with descriptions and tales of the fabled Coastlands.

Boasting a variety of remarkable darker-skinned people, the villages that dotted the shorelines and islands of the Coastlands were guaranteed to show the fighters a new way of life. Scrounger talked at length about the magnificent food and drink unique to these lands and of the call of the sea that almost claimed his own wanderer's heart. Mr. Pierce spoke of the relaxed way of the Coastland dwellers and how they had a way of blending in with the rhythm of life near the ocean. He also shared tales and warnings of the dangers of these lands, of pirates and deadly tribes and the monsters of the deep. The audience of four sat entranced by the stories and memories of this enchanting place. Even after allowing for the exaggerations of old storytellers, they all knew they were in for an adventure to remember.

Two days after they traversed the first waterfall, Miss Respect slowed as they approached the roaring mist of the second, greater waterfall. "Now, yer all about ta see the grandfather of all waterfalls!" Scrounger called out above the roar of the falls.

Heather giggled as the cool tingling of the mist touched her skin. Turning away from the others, she drew back her cloak and let the mist touch her scars. Closing her eyes, she could almost imagine herself back in her blessed valley again. It seemed like several lifetimes had passed since she'd left there. A prayer of thanks moved over her lips in a whisper that only the High King could hear. It was moments like these that made her grateful for her time in that valley, that made her feel like she was being allowed a glimpse of the High Kingdom's splendor. Once the mist had soaked her long hair, she shook her head from side to side with a playful laugh and drew her hood back over her face.

Once more Miss Respect lifted her hulking form out of the water and upon the river's bank. This time, however, Scrounger informed everyone that they would have to walk behind her as she moved down the winding path that followed the course of the Ash. Now they could hear the thunder of the impending waterfall and see where the Ash rolled over and down at the top of the falls. Moving in awe of the natural spectacle beside them, the travelers made their way down the muddy trail. Both Mr. Pierce and Scrounger smiled as they read the wonder on the faces of the fighters; it pleased them both to see even young ones as bold as these show a humble reverence for the grandeur of creation.

At the top of the falls the path angled down sharply. The little party stopped and gaped at the scene that now unfolded before them. "Allow me to introduce ya to 'Penance Falls!" Old Scrounger shouted above the roar of the surging waters. To their right was the top of the gigantic waterfall where the waters rolled over and down in a wide furious sheet. The river had widened toward the top of the falls to the point where Tolund guessed that if you shot an arrow as far as you could it still wouldn't make it to the opposite side of the waterfall. Now the boy looked down at a sight most folk would never see in their lifetimes.

Higher than the tallest trees, higher than the waterfalls in the accursed giant's valley, the storm of Penance Falls cascaded down to the valley below. The wind whipped their hair and cloaks about and the crashing of the water was almost too much for their ears. Everyone was soaked to the skin by the misty air, but no one seemed to notice it. Tolund, Bex, and Heather shuffled carefully to the edge and looked down. A shudder went up their spines at the dizzying height and relentless fury of the crashing water. Unable to resist this time, Tolund tossed a small stone over the side to see how long it would take to strike the bottom. After a long, long drop the stone was engulfed by the whitewater storms that exploded at the base of the waterfall. Carefully stepping back from the edge, they now surveyed the valley around the base of Penance Falls. The valley itself was as shocking to behold as the waterfall.

For many leagues in all directions, the land was blackened and charred. Smoke and cinders drifted up, urged forward by the winds from Penance's wrath. No trees remained from whatever fire caused all of this; only an occasional hill or boulder interrupted the flatness of the land. Nothing green lived, even along waters of the Ash River that snaked through the center of this scorched valley. Moreover, the touch of foul magic was in the hazy air. This wide shelf of land was a lifeless ruin. Lost in the eerie spectacle before him, Tolund was roused by a tap on his shoulder. Mr. Pierce was directing the party to move down the steep path, following Miss Respect's hulking form.

Once at the bottom, the great lizard slipped happily into the waters and waited for the travelers to board the platform again. Stepping down from the muddy path to the dead ground of the valley, Tolund could feel the gritty soot under his boots. His hands waved away the ash and cinders that swirled in the air in order to keep his vision clear. Soon they were back on the platform and gliding down the river.

Now, past the noise of the falls, Scrounger addressed their silent questions, "Here now, keep yer hoods over yer noses and mouths and lissen up. Ya can feel it, can't ya? Like these lands're tryin to swallow ya up inta their ruin. This here's why the river wuz renamed the 'Ash' and why the falls is now called 'Penance.' Long, long ago they were places full of beauty and life. This valley wuz green and thick with trees; folk would camp here as they moved down the river ta trade in the Coastlands. But those folk, and the folk all along the river proved to be fools. Ya see, the lands all along the river, though they wuz beautiful, were not fit to live in because of the presence of the warlocks. T'was widely known that the forests about the river and this here valley were places where those fiends would hide out.

At first, those monsters used the river and the lands around it to escape whatever soldiers or paladins that were chasin' em, but in time they became bolder. When they were still few in number, maybe only a few scattered bands here and there, the folk along the river ignored em,' hoping they'd just go away. But evil never just goes away." As the ragged old voice of the riverman told the tale, the young fighters stared nervously at the burnt valley that still smoked and fumed around them. Scrounger continued his tale while Mr. Pierce began to prepare the cooking fire for the evening meal.

"Word must've gone out to more n' more of those vile things because all too quickly their numbers swelled up. By keepin' quiet out of fear, the folk of the river made a sanctuary for these butchers. It turned out that two warlock orders took hold in these parts; the firelocks laid claim to the land above the falls while the beastlocks made this here valley their home. It wasn't long before war broke out between em."

"But I thought they were hiding out in these lands," interrupted Bex, "why would they start to attack each other and draw attention to themselves?"

"You haven't seen how these creatures hate one another," answered Tolund with obvious contempt in his voice. "I've seen them up close. Even when they're working together you can feel their hatred— like they can't wait to put a knife in the other's back at the first opportunity. I don't think they can help themselves, they're like mad dogs who will attack anything that comes near them."

"Aye, that sounds about right," echoed Scrounger. "Anyway, go ta war they did. It started with raids and skirmishes here and there, nothing so big that the protectorate wuz called in, but then something riled the firelocks. No one living knows wot set them off, but one night all of their locks, casters, and reapers poured down the same trail we just came down and into the valley. Though surprised by their boldness, the beastlocks were ready for war too. For two nights and two days their final battle raged and scorched this land. When the protectorate fliers arrived on their dragons the fires were still burnin' high. At this time a lone firelock named Dreytis still clung to life as he spat out a curse over the smoking corpse of his vanquished rival, the beastlock leader called Azlial. Seems Dreytis, with his dying breaths, managed to burn Azlial after he'd been mauled and torn up by the beastlock. Fore he died, with the magic of his own soul, he laid down a curse upon the beastlock's bones so that every night, when the last rays of sunlight have disappeared from the sky, Azlial's bones rise up and wander this blackened valley. Dreytis doomed his enemy to an eternity of unrest, forcing Azlial's spirit to suffer a thirst for vengeance that could never be slaked because the object of his wrath was already dead and gone."

"Wait," Heather spoke up with a tremor of fear in her voice, "you mean Azlial's bones are still out there, walking around even now?"

"No, not now," smiled Scrounger, "the sun hasn't set all of the way yet." All the young fighters now looked out over the smoking lands with wide-eyes. The old riverman laughed at their response, "Don't worry bout that skeleton. 'Ol' Azzy' doesn't swim anymore and we're not goin ashore tonight."

"Have you or Mr. Pierce ever seen this thing walking around?" asked Lindris.

"Oh, many times, Lass, many times," answered Mr. Pierce. "All the travelers of the river have seen his old bones stalking about the banks in the dark. Everyone knows that you keep to the river in this valley."

"Does he howl or scream or anything like that?" asked Heather.

"No, leastways not that I ever heard," answered Scrounger. "But I have seen his bones shift and twist into different forms, like animals all mixed together. I guess even cursed bones don't forget all of their tricks."

Bex shot a quick glance at Lindris, giving her a skeptical grin and a roll of his eyes. She nodded back in agreement. Tolund could see how the tale of 'Ol' Azzy' might be Scrounger's way of having fun with them and deep down he hoped that that was exactly the case.

After eating, everyone settled down into an uneasy slumber. At first Tolund dreamed of his usual dreams of skillful victories in the fireshows and then those dreams shifted into those of utter fantasy.

He dreamt of himself as a giant, large enough to cover the entire city of Ansalion in only a few steps, dragons were the size of sparrows to him and he was so high above the people that he could not hear them call out to him. Tolund liked this dream and smiled in his sleep for some time. Finally, a new dream blurred into his mind.

Now the boy was back to his normal self and was joined by his mother and sister. He warmed to the sight of Gwendolyn and Emilyse laughing with him as they picnicked along the green shores of the Barrier river back in Glendien. After finishing their perfect meal Tolund had fun tickling his sister's feet until she kicked her feet and laughed so hard that she snorted. Gathering their things, Gwendolyn led them to a small boat and they all enjoyed a relaxed sunlit ride upon the river. Suddenly, Tolund spied something moving along the far shore in the shadows beneath the trees. The tone of the boy's dream had now changed. Instantly, the sky was black and without a moon or stars. Tolund was all alone in his boat and now the thing that moved in darkness shot forward. Glaring at him from empty eye-sockets, a giant skeleton followed his movement down the river. In his dream, the cursed bones of Azlial were stalking him with fangs snapping and claws raking the night air as if they were yearning to reach the boy and rip him to shreds.

Shaken from his sleep, Tolund awoke in a cold sweat. He fought to slow down his breathing and the frantic beating of his heart. As he started to settle himself, relieved to find that it was all a dream, a scuffling sound caught his ear. Over the waters and on the shoreline, Tolund stopped breathing altogether at the sight of the cursed bones of Azlial stalking him with fangs snapping and claws raking the night air as if they were yearning to reach the boy and rip him to shreds.

Without shout or roar, the haunting skeleton made its malice toward the boy apparent.

"What is it with you, Dellender?" whispered Bex in a baffled tone. "I've been up for a long time trying to get that thing's attention, but all it seems to notice is you, even when you were still sleeping. It's almost like it's following us just to get close to you— like it has a grudge against you or something."

Surprised that he wasn't the only one awakened by Azlial's bones, Tolund shrugged his shoulders, "I don't know, Bex. Maybe beastlocks can still smell their enemies even after they're dead."

"That's a scary thought," answered Bex. The two anxious boys watched the undead Azlial following them in silence for several moments. Unnerved, Bex ventured another question, "Is this what it's like?"

"What?"

"You know, to get mixed up with warlocks and monsters?"

"I suppose," whispered Tolund. "You're never really ready for it; it always makes your skin crawl and your stomach knot. This thing's different than the others, but they're all sickening. This one was able to crawl inside my dreams and hunt for me in there. It's like it could stalk me even in my own mind and soul. I wish it would just leave me alone."

All of this was almost too much for Bex to deal with. The disturbed lad took turns staring at the twisting, flailing skeleton along the shore and then at Tolund. Tolund could feel Bex's eyes upon him just as he could feel the burly lad's confidence wilt. "How can you stand against horrors like that?" Bex asked with a slight tremor in his voice.

"With a lot of faith in the High King…and with this." As he replied the boy brought forth his enchanted blade. Tolund took to one knee and then held its black edge aloft in the direction of the cursed Azlial. Instantly, the skeleton rolled and twisted in a silent fit of rage. Azlial's long-dead bones kicked up soot as it writhed and thrashed into various monstrous shapes. The bones steamed, cracked, and then melted again and again as they contorted into the bones of panthers, wolves, serpents, and more. The creature seemed to be trying to frighten Tolund off with its threatening display. Before long Tolund swiped the air with his dark sword in Azlial's direction. Twisting now into a spidery form, the bones skittered back into the darkness away from the shoreline.

"I can't believe it," whispered a frightened Bex. "Your sword scared that thing off. It ran away from you like you were the Lockslayer himself!"

"I wasn't sure how it would react to it," responded Tolund, "but I'm glad it did the trick. I think we can get some real sleep now." Tolund wrapped himself back up in his cloak and stretched himself out on the deck again, only this time he held his unsheathed blade alongside his body. "Good night, Bex. See you in the morning."

Even after closing his eyes, Tolund could feel the older boy's eyes upon him. After a few tense moments he heard Bex whisper, "I could sleep soundly too if I had a blade like that." Eventually Tolund could hear Bex settle down and hear his breathing slow and deepen, telling him that the boy had finally drifted off to sleep. Even so, with Mr. Pierce's words about misplaced trust echoing in his mind, Tolund kept his magic sword close to his side through the rest of the night.

CHAPTER 9

THE DEAD MOUNTAIN

"Nagon, how many warlocks are on this block of ice?" Lord Gresk's question could hardly be heard by his cleric over the screams and clamor of the battle. All about them dwarves clashed savagely with the reapers and casters of the invading army.

"I can mark only two, Milord!" cried Cleric Nagon. "One is definitely an icelock, but the other is a warlock that I've never sensed before."

"What does that mean?" bellowed the dwarf lord as he speared a stormcaster with a mighty throw.

"I'm not sure what it means. All I can sense is that it must be a warlock, but of no kind that I've ever come across. It's at the center of this fortress and I would urge caution as we approach it."

"You're getting ahead of yourself, Cleric!" laughed Lord Gresk as he smashed down another icereaper with his hammer. "We've a long way to go before we've breached their stronghold!" Continuing their battle, Gresk's mind sought to find a strategy that would gain the upper hand in this grisly conflict.

Following the Lockslayer's command, the northern dwarves had quickly marshaled their forces and launched their ships in pursuit of the warlock army. Using their own powerful clerics, the trail of the enemy was marked and followed. Eventually, they sailed along their own coastline to a collection of frozen islands that the dwarves had dubbed, 'dead mountains' for they looked like mountains of ice upon the water, but their drifting, lifeless paths reminded them of gravestones on the sea. It was on the last and largest of these that Gresk's forces spied the warlock's stronghold. Following wave after wave of dwarven arrows, the footsoldiers were able to land upon the snowy shores and begin their attack. Again and again the ferocity and skill of the dwarves pushed the warlock defenders back, but the tunnels the enemy had burrowed into the dead mountain were too well wrought and no ground could be gained without losing too many dwarves so they were forced to retreat and recover. Back and forth, the attackers and defenders played this deadly game with neither side gaining any true advantage in the conflict. "They're wasting our time," Lord Gresk barked to Clanleader Delek, "I can feel it in my bones!"

"We've cornered them in their own lair," answered Delek, "all they're trying to do is survive."

"No!" snapped the wary dwarf lord. "I've fought warlocks for over a hundred years. Their army wouldn't stay cornered in their fortress like this if they've got two warlocks waiting within. Trust me, old friend, they're holding out for a reason and we won't survive this little war if we wait upon them to make the final move."

"But how can we breach those tunnels?" asked Delek as he loosed another arrow toward the enemy. "Everytime we've tried we've failed and lost too many of our soldiers."

"You're right, the tunnels are not the answer. We have to come at them from a point they won't expect." Gresk withdrew several paces and stroked his long beard as he surveyed the frozen island from the highest summit to the surface of the water. Suddenly his bushy eyebrows lifted in revelation. "Nagon, Valos, Rund!" Quickly, the three dwarf clerics within earshot circled around Lord Gresk. Delek looked on as they debated and made urgent plans. Finally, all four heads nodded in agreement signaling the end of their brief counsel. Gresk waved Delek over.

"You will lead our forces while I try a new avenue of attack," ordered the clanlord. Delek returned his new orders with a bewildered look.

"Milord?"

"I've no time to explain! Just continue to press them at every turn without losing too many good dwarves. If our new course is successful the day will be ours."

"And if it isn't successful?" asked a puzzled Delek.

"Then this dead mountain will live up to its name and our old bones will lay frozen out here forever." With that, Lord Gresk let out a savage laugh and struck his old friend across the face with his burly fist.

"Hah!" laughed Delek. "I always knew I'd end up rotting beside your mangy carcass someday! Our wives always said we'd be the death of each other!" Delek spit the blood from his mouth once and then smashed his own fist across Gresk's bearded chin. After a quick laugh the two friends nodded farewell to each other and set about their tasks.

Lord Gresk strode purposefully away from the battle and in the direction of the icy shore. Following closely, the three dwarven clerics cleared their minds and took deep, long breaths. On the water's edge Gresk gave a nod to Cleric Rund. Dropping to one knee, the cleric whispered a prayer to the High King with one hand raised to the sky. A slight breeze moved across the curtain of grey clouds overhead to allow a single thread of sunlight to pour through directly upon the cleric's upraised hand. Cleric Rund smiled and touched the surface of the water with his other hand. A golden light danced upon the rippling circles that moved outward in wide rings. "The summons is given," he shared. "It will only take a few moments."

"Well done," said Lord Gresk. "Now, let's see to the rest." Positioning herself next to Gresk, Cleric Valos steeled herself for the next part of their plan. Standing before their commander and their colleagues, Clerics Nagon and Rund stretched out their arms toward them and began a new prayer. After a moment of silence the new spell sparked to life. Gresk and Valos felt their skin tingle and grow warm. Now Lord Gresk's weathered old hide began to itch as a coat of thick white fur grew out of his body— even his hair and beard turned to white fur. His fingernails hardened into stout black claws and his teeth stretched into sharp white fangs. In only a dozen anxious heartbeats Lord Gresk had shifted into a were-creature that had the basic form of a dwarf, but was mostly a white bear of the north. Cleric Valos' transformation was even more drastic. With her boots removed and her legs held together beneath her robes, her skin began to melt together and twist into a new shape as if she were made of candle wax. Also her skin became smooth and slick and shaded in color to a deep blue. When her spell was complete she had slumped to the snow with the tail and hide of one of the small whales that inhabited these waters. Even her eyes had become wholly round and black and a large fin had formed in between her shoulder blades. Using her arms, she crawled into the frigid water.

Breaking the surface she smiled, "I can hear our new ally approaching."

"Good, we've no time to waste," answered Lord Gresk. In a massive swell of water the black and white form of a Monarch Whale swam alongside Cleric Valos.

"He'll bear you to your destination," said Cleric Rund, "but take care with your new claws and hammer, you should hold on with the strength of your legs."

"Aye," Gresk snarled playfully, "this is one mount I don't want to anger!" In a rush of icy water the strange party was on its way.

Diving swiftly, the whale followed the graceful new form of Cleric Valos. As he held his breath, Lord Gresk was pleased to find that his new form felt quite comfortable in the freezing waters. His new eyes widened at both the beauty of the blue waters from down below and at how much larger the frozen island was beneath the surface than above.

Valos was carving an urgent path through the currents as she spied the ridges and hollows of the floating ice mountain furiously. Soon she came upon a spot that seemed to please her. Turning to the whale, she voiced an eerie song. Immediately, the powerful beast shot up toward the surface. Once they surfaced, Lord Gresk, recognizing her intent, took two long deep breaths and then held his third breath while nudging his magnificent mount with his heels. The Monarch dove down again to meet Cleric Valos.

A glowing green light burned in one spot upon the side of the ice mountain. Valos nodded to her commander. Pushing off from the whale, Lord Gresk held his enchanted stonehammer in both hands. His first strike broke huge chunks of ice off, sending them floating in all directions. His second blow actually broke through the hollow of the ice mountain; bubbles poured out of the thin cracks he'd made. His last strike shattered a large hole in the ice. Valos let out a whale-song of triumph as Gresk swam up and into the new entrance he'd created. With another song Valos asked their new ally to return to the surface and bring down the other two clerics. After the whale had done this, she asked him to gather his brethren and patrol the waters about the frozen island to prevent any warlock surprises or reinforcements. The great lord of the deep eagerly swam off to fulfill his new duties. Valos sang him a song of blessing and smiled. She knew that nothing short of a sea dragon could challenge a gathering of these powerful whales. The waters about their battleground were now secure.

Before long, Lord Gresk and his three clerics all crouched in the ice tunnel they had broken into. Cleric Nagon worked to restore Gresk and Valos to their normal forms while Cleric Rund wove a warming spell to dry them all off and prevent them from freezing to death. "Well done," whispered Lord Gresk, "our ocean path into their stronghold seems to have gone unnoticed. Now we must press our advantage. If we can catch them off guard, we can take out their warlocks and the day will be ours." Though tired from all they'd already done this day, Gresk's faithful clerics smiled at his bold words. Drawing their own axes, they moved silently with their clanlord into the winding tunnels of ice.

Their hastily formed plan bore a rich harvest. With brutal efficiency the four dwarves stalked and dispatched ten reapers and three casters before the hour was out. With the attention of the enemy on the siege that raged above ground it was a simple matter to ambush the unsuspecting villains as they moved within their lair. Encouraged by their easy success, the small party made its way to the center of the dead mountain where echoing voices and sounds told them that a large cave or chamber lay up ahead. "Hold, Milord," urged Cleric Nagon, "something's amiss. There is more to this assault than a warlock raid upon our lands."

"I'm forced to agree," added Cleric Rund. "The warlocks must have shrouded its presence with a masking spell, but now that we are so close it is unmistakable."

"What? What is unmistakable?" whispered Gresk.

"They're not alone in that chamber," said Cleric Valos. The baffled dwarf lord's eyebrows narrowed.

"What do you mean 'they're not alone,' what's in there with them?" he asked.

The three clerics shared worried looks with another before Cleric Nagon answered, "Something more powerful than we've ever come across, something wholly evil." The old cleric stared intently in the direction of the shadowed cave up ahead and dropped his head and let out a quivering breath, "We are all going to die."

CHAPTER 10

THE MEETING

"It's good to see you Warren," smiled Cleric Green, "it's been a long time."

"Most definitely, Brother," Cleric Michaels smiled back. "Now, before we hear what all of this is about, tell me more about this young soldier here." Cleric Michaels gestured toward Captain Shaw who stood silently in the doorway in a formal stance.

"Yes, yes," responded Cleric Green, "please allow me to properly introduce you to Captain Nathanial Shaw of the Protectorate Guard. His particular duty as a member of that Guard is to maintain the immediate lands that surround Ansalion."

The strapping warrior stepped up confidently, "My responsibility, Good Clerics, is to ensure that the great city is secure from without just as the paladins keep it secure from within." His squared jaw and stern brown eyes, as well as his impressive physical form, made clear his warrior's bearing.

"As I'm sure you've noted, he has earned the rank of 'Captain' at an unusually young age," shared Cleric Jin, a Coastlands cleric who moved to greet them. "His prowess in battle and his exceptional leadership skills have served him well in his short time with the protectorate. He has already earned many…"

"Begging your pardon, Sir," Captain Shaw interrupted, "but your invitation seemed quite urgent and I've duties to attend to. May we dispense with the personal histories and get down to the matters at hand?"

"Ha!" Cleric Michaels laughed. "All business this one! I can see why he's made such quick strides in the protectorate. That, and he may be the tallest soldier I've ever stood beside."

"Yes," replied Cleric Kellesh, "I suppose he's right. We can all exchange pleasantries later, you're both probably dying to know why we summoned you here so ominously." The cleric gestured for everyone to take their seats at the long table of polished oak and then took her own place at the table. "The simplest way for us to begin, I believe, would be for each of you to describe for us your dreams of late."

"Milady?" Captain Shaw's head angled slightly, reflecting his surprise at this request.

"Your dreams, Captain," reiterated Cleric Kellesh, "tell us of any that have stood out in your memory lately."

The young man stared about the room curiously to see if this was a serious request. Finding only expectant faces awaiting his response he surmised that this was either a test of some sort or a legitimate request. "Umm, well I suppose there has been one in particular," said Shaw. "I don't usually remember my dreams, but I can't seem to get this one out of my head and it's been recurring every night for the last week. Odd isn't it?" Cleric Michael's head turned sharply in his direction; his interest suddenly piqued.

"Each night the dream begins the same. I'm walking alone in the countryside just beyond Ansalion's walls, in front of the Bronze Quarter, I think, and I'm in full armor with shield and sword in hand. All at once a foul wind rushes in from the east and my armor and weapons dissolve into sand and are blown away in the wind." Now Cleric Michaels' eyes narrowed. "I'm standing there defenseless in my normal clothing when it begins to rain."

"Only the rain is like a black oil instead of water," interrupted Cleric Michaels.

"Umm…exactly," answered a startled Shaw. "How did you…"

"Allow me to finish the scene for you," Cleric Green added. "It begins to rain a black oily rain until you are soaked. The downpour intensifies until you are up to your knees in the foul-smelling oil. Now a loud roaring assaults your ears and, from the same direction of the wind, you see it. . ."

"A towering wave of filth and pestilence," Cleric Michaels nervously interjected, "flooded over the land and crashing directly toward you."

"Yes…yes," said an anxious Captain Shaw, "the last thing I remember each night is the wave crushing me, engulfing me, and, I suppose, the city behind me. But how did all of you kn—-"

"We've been dreaming the same dream for as many nights as you two, we and all of the High Clerics here in our sanctuary," said Cleric Jin. "Only in all of our dreams you two are standing side-by-side before this great wave."

"That is why you were both summoned," said Cleric Kellesh. "These dreams are warning us, giving us a chance to prepare for this calamity. The High King is speaking and it is imperative that we listen and listen carefully."

"But…but how can you be so sure?" questioned the young captain.

"Experience, Good Captain," smiled Cleric Green. "Faith only grows in strength when it is exercised rigorously. Our faith speaks to us more clearly on this matter than the sound of your voice in this room. This horror is coming and we must be ready to meet it."

"So what must we do to prepare?" asked a determined Cleric Michaels.

CHAPTER 11

THE COASTLANDS

"It's like we've landed in another world altogether," exclaimed Heather.

"I know," smiled Tolund. "We only moved down two more valleys and past a few more waterfalls, but it feels as different as high summer from deep winter."

The best friends sat awestruck upon the wooden deck as Miss Respect cruised along the southernmost waters of the Ash river. This was their first morning in the lush, thick jungles of the Coastlands. They had actually descended the last waterfall path the night before, but the shadow of the canopy overhead gave them little light to appreciate the wonder of their new surroundings. Now, as the sun rose, all of the color, sound, and splendor of these unique lands had the newcomers mesmerized.

Mr. Pierce and Scrounger smiled to each other as they prepared breakfast. They'd been hoping for this kind of joyful reaction from the young ones and they were happy to see that they weren't disappointed. Even the usually stoic Lindris was smiling widely as she pointed out the small monkeys that flitted and leaped about the upper canopy of trees. Tolund thought he had seen greenery before, but nothing could compare to the impenetrable fortress of bushes and trees that pressed in upon the river on all sides. He wondered aloud what it would be like to explore this tropical wilderness to which Bex only laughed and wagered how long it would take Tolund to get himself hopelessly lost. Heather found herself falling in love with the myriad colors that flourished all around her— so many magnificent jungle flowers and plants in shapes and hues she'd never seen before. Lastly, Bex joined Lindris in marveling at the strange new animals and insects they were discovering for the first time. They all spent the better part of their morning asking Mr. Pierce and Scrounger question after question about the new world they were caught up in.

So entranced by the verdant majesty of the jungle were they that they failed to notice the thick air and growing heat until high morning. The sweltering weather of the deep jungle reminded Tolund of the Boglands, but this heat pressed down upon him as if it were a living thing itself. A quick change of clothing was in order for everyone as boots, cloaks, and thick shirts were now more of a cruelty than a comfort. As they took turns changing in the small shack upon the platform, Tolund noted how Heather waited until the last and then emerged still hooded in her cloak. When Scrounger encouraged everyone to take a quick dip in the river to relieve the midday heat, the poor girl declined and stayed in the shade of the trees and the cover of her hood. Tolund found that her recurring anxiety over her appearance only made him love his good friend all the more. He decided to sit with Heather instead of plunging into the inviting waters. She gave him a smile and shoved a playful elbow into his arm; it was her way of thanking him for his little sacrifice.

Soon they were moving down the river and deeper into the jungle. Scrounger informed them that they would be visiting some old friends that night. He said this with a wry grin as if he were saving a surprise for them all. True to his mischievous smile, they found themselves halting at dusk to a shocking sight.

Where they came from none of the young fighters could fathom, but rising from the water before and around Miss Respect and slipping out of the dense brush on both sides of the river was the unnerving sight of small, dark-skinned savages brandishing spears, clubs, and stone knives. They wore only animal skin loincloths and were painted in bright colors of orange and indigo over most of their lean, strong bodies. Heather felt her thumping heart skip another beat when she looked up to find that even more tribesmen were also perched on the branches of the giant sloping trees that lorded over the wide river. Old Scrounger showed no sign of anxiety as he ordered his riverdragon to stop.

"It's all right, Pups," he reassured the young fighters. "These here are the 'Jyn-laka.' I call em' the 'Frog Bleeders,' because that's wot Jyn-laka means in their language. I've been a friend o' theirs for years and years. We've been traveling in their territory for the last couple of hours; I was waitin' for them to show themselves. Hope ya weren't too spooked by em." Tolund looked around to see that the others were just as unsettled as he was, except for Mr. Pierce who still sat comfortably in his chair with his feet up and his arms folded behind his head. "It's 'Frog Bleeders' because they use the poison of the jungle frogs on their weapons. That's also why they paint themselves up like that. Like the frogs they copy, they're letting everything around them know that they're deadly."

"Are you sure they're friendly?" questioned Lindris. "They look like they're about to cut us to pieces."

"Aw, don't worry. They always look like that outside of their village. Believe it or not, they're happy to see us." The scowling faces and glaring eyes did little to communicate happiness, but soon they had gathered alongside the riverbank and were talking excitedly with Old Scrounger in a tongue that only they, and he, could understand. After a few moments of this, they quickly moved in a single file line directly into the jungle to the left of the river. Mr. Pierce ordered everyone to follow while Scrounger informed them that they were all going to spend the night in the village of the Jyn-laka as their guests of honor.

As he followed behind, Tolund could feel his sense of distrust rising. In only a half dozen strides from the riverbank the heavy foliage of the jungle smothered the view of the Ash River completely. The boy could hear the current moving and even hear Miss Respect shuffling herself into the mud for a long slumber, but all he could see when he looked back was a wall of green. Ignorant of his apprehension, the long line of little tribesmen plunged deeper into the forest. No words were spoken, even by Scrounger, and Tolund noticed how the eyes of the small savages were constantly darting about as if they expected some threat to ambush them at any moment. This unnerved the boy even more when he thought that this, according to Old Scrounger, was the heart of their territory. "They don't seem to feel safe in their own homelands," the lad thought to himself. "Why are we even here?" Moving further into the maze of thickets and giant trees, Tolund was glad to feel his broadsword sheathed across his back.

As it turned out, it was not a long march to the Jyn-laka village. In a little over an hour they had reached the high wall, which was literally covered with poisoned wooden spikes that protected the center of their savage world. Two large gates creaked open as women and children met the returning warriors with wide smiles. Tolund was relieved and more than a little surprised to find that the fierce demeanor of their hosts disappeared instantly as they showed themselves to be loving fathers and husbands. The otherworldly feel of the small tribesman faded once they were safe inside of their primitive fortress. "Didn't I tell ya?" smiled Scrounger. "Though they could kill ya before ya knew they wuz even next to you out in the jungle, if you're their friend, they're as friendly as yer own kin inside of their village."

Soon, as the darkness of night closed in upon it, the village fires were built up and the cooking spits were filled with the meat of some large lizards Tolund had never seen before. After a surprisingly tasty meal of grilled lizard and sweet jungle fruits everyone relaxed before the central bonfire and watched Scrounger and the Jyn-laka chief exchange customary gifts. First, the chief presented both Scrounger and Mr. Pierce with long thick reeds that served as dart-throwers for the tribe as well as a pouch of darts coated with frog poison. The old riverman then produced a fine iron dagger for the chief along with a leather belt and sheath. It was only a regular dagger by a weaponsmith's standards, but on the chief's diminutive form it looked like a longsword on a tall warrior from the north. The delighted people clapped and howled in approval as their chief strutted about the fire with his new sword at his side. Despite himself, Tolund found himself reveling in the strong sense of fellowship displayed by these little warriors.

As the night wore on, the high spirits and loud talk died down. Most of their new friends had retired to their thatched huts for the night leaving only the sentries along the walls and the chief himself still awake. As he lay stretched out on the sandy ground, Tolund could hear the urgent tone of the chief as he spoke in his strange language to Old Scrounger. The boy also noticed how the chief lowered his voice so that his own people could not hear what he was saying to the riverman.

Soon the chief finished his hushed conversation with Scrounger and retired for the night to his own hut. With an uneasy scowl, Scrounger joined their party about their campfire. "What's under your skin?" asked Mr. Pierce.

"Old Basiri is pretty spooked and he gave me an earful about wot's got him scared." Everyone edged a little closer to hear Scrounger's words. "Seems that their tribe is runnin' scared these days from what they calls 'spirit monsters.' Basiri says that about three months back strange tracks were being made throughout the jungle. When they followed the trail o' these footprints the tracks would suddenly change form into those of a different creature— sometimes a familiar animal and sometimes some frightening tracks that they'd never seen before."

"A beastlock," interrupted Mr. Pierce ominously.

"That's sure what it sounds like," said Scrounger. The young fighters sat transfixed by this news. Bex and Lindris shared the concern of their trainingmaster, but had never encountered an actual warlock before. Tolund and Heather looked deep into one another's eyes for a moment for they had hoped never to cross paths with these terrors again.

Old Scrounger continued, "He also said that these tracks led them to an even more disturbing sight. Three times the tracks led to the carcass of what these tribesmen call the 'Moving Mountains.' That's what these natives call the local landdragons. Each time they found the jungle flattened down and bloody due to a great fight and the bones of the giant landdragons picked clean." Heather shuddered in fear while Tolund drew his arms about his sheathed blade more closely. "And there's one more thing," said Scrounger, "the chief also said that all the snakes in the forest have run off. He says that they haven't seen a single one since they first sighted one o' the strange trails three months back. At first they wuz happy to be rid o' them, but then it began to worry them, like the jungle wuzn't whole anymore. They started lookin' for em' on purpose, but couldn't find a single one under any rock or on any tree.

"What does all of that mean?" asked Tolund. Scrounger shrugged his shoulders and gave an inquisitive look to Mr. Pierce.

"I'm not sure what it means," Mr. Pierce offered in a clear, sober tone. "It sure looks like there's a beastlock involved in all of this, but to what end we have no way of knowing. So far, in over three months, it hasn't moved directly upon these people so I think it's safe to assume that they are not part of its plans. Maybe it's just staking out new territory or maybe it's just passing through these lands. For our part, I think we should just continue on to the coast and keep our eyes and ears sharp as we go."

"It seems like everywhere we go we can't get away from these fiends!" scowled Tolund.

"Well, what did you expect?" remarked Mr. Pierce. "Evil goes where it will; only a fool hopes for a charmed life. You must assume the worst on all paths and prepare yourself accordingly. Whether we encounter this evil or not, we will be ready to meet it. Is that understood, Tolund?" Tolund nodded with a heavy sigh. "How about the rest of you?" The other three fighters also nodded in agreement. "Good!"

growled Mr. Pierce. "Now, let's stop wringing our hands like frightened children and get some sleep. We still have a long way to go before we reach the sea and we still have some arena battles to train for."

After a gruff 'good night' Mr. Pierce stretched himself out before the dwindling fire and went to sleep. The rest of the party did the same. As he said his silent prayers before going to sleep, Tolund felt Heather's hand grasp his own. Amid the savage jungle, under a strange sky, the two friends fell asleep hand-in-hand, finding strength in one another's company.

The village of the Jyn-laka woke before the first rays of sunlight touched the canopy overhead. Fires were stoked and morning meals were prepared as the night sentries stepped down from their posts along the top of the high wall to make way for the morning guard. Scrounger was pleased to report that nothing unusual had been spotted by the watchmen during the night.

During another meal of jungle fruit, Mr. Pierce informed the party that they would be leaving for the fishing village of Ibago immediately after breakfast. As hospitable as the small tribe had been to its guests, the dwarf was not surprised to see the relief in the faces of the young ones when they heard this news. This was especially true for Tolund who seemed to be of great interest to Chief Basiri this morning. Even as they ate in a large circle around the morning fire, the old savage would stare intently at the boy as if he were trying to uncover a secret of some kind about him. Tolund found this to be quite unnerving and Heather found it to be rude. "What is so fascinating about Tolund this morning?" she asked Scrounger as she nodded at the chief's staring.

"I'm not sure," he answered. Now the riverman questioned the chief about this in the savage's own tongue. "He says he had what he calls 'dangerous dreams' about our boy here. He dreamt of shadows and screams stalking Tolund in these jungles. He says that the sooner this boy leaves his village, and his jungle, the better it will be for his people." Watching intently as his words were translated to his guests, Chief Basiri spoke again. Once more, Scrounger relayed his words, "He also says that he believes that, though evil is drawn to the boy, his heart is strong and his spirit is bright. Out of respect for Tolund's spirit, the chief himself wishes to escort us to the river's end."

All of his companions, as well as the elders of the tribe who sat at their fire, all looked at Tolund to study his reaction to Basiri's words. Tolund was trying not to look anxious about this dark announcement, but his concern was still obvious to all. The boy noted how Mr. Pierce was the only one who seemed indifferent to these words. He also noted that Bex was staring again at the sword sheathed along his own back.

It wasn't long before the small party was moving back toward the river with a stout contingent of the small warriors leading them. Heather loved the early morning cool and the dampness of the jungle. Far above her, the canopy dripped the morning dew down upon them like a light rain. She also noticed that their escorts were more on edge this morning; their painted heads darted this way and that at the slightest movement or sound. "I think the chief's dreams really got to them," she whispered to Tolund.

"Can you blame them?" he whispered back. "Would you want me in your jungle if I was drawing evil things to your home?"

"Of course I would, Stupid," Heather teased, "because once those 'evil things' got close enough to smell you, the smell would kill them all off! It would be the perfect trap!" Tolund's only response was a friendly shove that pushed her out of the single file line they were traveling in. A slight giggle behind him caused him to look back. Lindris was amused by their banter and had let out the giggle. The instant the boy caught sight of her lovely green eyes he blushed quickly and snapped his head forward again. Now he grimaced at his clumsy response and silently chided himself for looking like a fool to the older girl. Heather caught all of this and grew strangely quiet for the rest of their trek to the river.

When they arrived at the river they found a slumbering Miss Respect burrowed happily into the thick mud. In no time she was awakened and was now bearing their party down the river while the tribesmen trotted along the right bank. It was almost late afternoon when the young fighters first heard low thunder. "What is that crashing sound?" asked Bex.

"We're almost to the sea," answered Old Scrounger. Tolund could smell salt in the air. Apparently, Lindris could as well as she had closed her eyes and tilted her head up into the inbound ocean breezes to catch this new scent. Heather was still busy marveling at the incredible stamina of the little tribesmen.

"They've been running alongside us for the better part of the day," she exclaimed.

"Like dwarves, they're much more formidable than their lessened height might suggest," Mr. Pierce added proudly. "Pull to the side here, Scrounger. This is as a good a place as any to say our 'goodbyes.'" The old riverman did as instructed and soon they were all gathered by the shore with the Jyn-laka.

Chief Basiri, glistening with sweat and recovering his breath, stood with his men behind him and spoke proud words to Mr. Pierce. "He says t'was an honor to host the young warriors from the highlands," shared Scrounger. "They are glad that you are all safe at the edge of their kingdom. Also, he says that you are always welcome at their fires." Now the chief moved deliberately over to Tolund and peered into the boy's eyes.

"What is he doing that for?" Heather asked sharply. She could see how nervous this made her friend and she didn't like it. Now, the chief spoke again.

"He's telling Tolund that he can see the doubt in his heart, that the world is still too big for his young eyes."

"Well, what does he think I should do about that?" Tolund asked.

Scrounger shared his question and the chief answered quickly and with a tone that suggested great meaning. "He wants ya to remember these words, Tolund; he wants ya to carry them close to you when you feel the darkness pressing in around you. He said, 'passing rain changes nothing, but a strong river can carve stone.'" Basiri carefully studied the boy's eyes as he heard these words. Lastly, he smiled, said something else, and then turned back up the river with his men. In just a moment all of the savages had gone.

"What was that last thing that he said?" asked Lindris.

"He said that keeping his sword close was not a bad idea either," chuckled Scrounger.

CHAPTER 12

TROUBLED SEAS

Once more, worlds seem to change in a matter of moments for the young fighters. As Miss Respect swam closer and closer to the new breezes that rushed into the jungle, the crashing sounds grew louder and louder. Following the river's last turn, the towering green of the forest now gave way to the wide open view of the great Southern Ocean. The four young ones stood up straight and stared, open-mouthed, at the long stretch of glimmering sand that bordered the endless blue water.

Foam from the pounding waves sprayed high into the air and caught the bright afternoon sun in a brilliant display. White gulls cried out as they soared and drifted with the ocean winds. Those same warm winds moved over them like the greeting of an old friend. Heather wondered if even the High Kingdom was as beautiful as this. It was all so dazzling and clean.

Tolund could see where the river before them met the blue of the sea. Now he was aware that the riverdragon that carried them was slowing. "This oughta do," said Scrounger. Reading his command, Miss Respect curved to the side of the river. "She's never cared much for the sea; I'm thinking it's the salt water that puts her off," the riverman commented. "I guess I'll camp with you tonight and then the old girl and I will be sayin' our goodbyes in the morning and move back up the river."

In spite of the joy of their first swim in the warm ocean waves and their first night by the seashore, the young ones were all sad at the thought of losing the company of Scrounger and Miss Respect. Though gruff and unnerving, the odd pair had become a part of their journey. Tolund didn't think that things would feel right anymore without them along for the adventure.

Mr. Pierce, sensing their somber moods, took it upon himself to raise everyone's spirits. After picking a good spot on one of the higher sand dunes, the dwarf set about building a stout fire pit. Next, using Scrounger's magic net, he secured an impressive number of large fish from the ocean and began roasting them over the fire. While the fish cooked, he instructed them all to flatten an area of sand and to stretch out their bedrolls upon it. "Tonight the sky itself will take your breath away!" he promised.

The meal was magnificent; Tolund could not recall ever tasting better fish. True to their host's word, the sky blazed as the sun dove into the line of the sea upon the horizon. It looked like the entire sky was painted with molten gold. Soon after the sun was completely swallowed up by the ocean, the stars began to fire amidst an indigo sky. Now the heavens blinked to life with the dancing white light of countless stars. Scrounger regaled them with ancient tales of men and elves who explored the waters and islands of this mysterious realm. The last thing Tolund could remember as his eyes grew too heavy to keep open was the warm caress of the ocean winds and the crashing surf that was singing him to sleep.

That night Tolund's dreams were both disturbing and fantastic. At first, he found himself walking barefoot along the seashore at night in perfect comfort and contentment. Soon, however, the jungle to his left began to hiss and rustle unnaturally. To the lad's horror, he saw thousands of snakes suddenly twist out upon the sand dunes and slither madly toward him. Their eyes burned a menacing green, as did their venomous fangs. Realizing that flight was impossible as he was hemmed in on all sides, all he could do was stumble back into the wild surf and hope that the waves would somehow deter them. Almost instantly he found himself swimming in the breakers, struggling to keep himself from being tossed about by the powerful waves. Tolund's heart sank as he saw that the snakes were not slowed by the water at all and, in fact, swam faster than they had slithered. Panicking, the boy started to swim furiously out into the deep water where the waves were cresting; his only hope was that the waves themselves would push the serpents back. But now, as it often happens in dreams, another surprise occurred.

Above Tolund, in the night sky, a pure light sparked and then roared. Even above the din of the pounding surf his young ears were deafened by these new sounds. Looking up, he gasped as he saw a number of the white stars in the sky burning and plummeting toward the shoreline. They grew brighter and larger as they hurtled down toward the advancing horde of snakes. Now the dunes exploded in fragments of shimmering silver as the stars rained down upon the snakes. The celestial hailstorm seemed to go on forever. When the barrage finally ceased and the silver light dimmed, the sand upon the shore was now a sparkling white as if every grain of sand had been transformed into specks of diamond. The only thing that marred the beauty of it all was the sight of thousands of scorched serpents. This moment in the dream startled Tolund and he awoke with a gasp.

It was deep in the night and all of his companions were fast asleep on the sand dunes. The only fire in sight was the sullen orange glow of their waning campfire. The moon was only a newborn sliver in the sky and the stars were small and high up in the heavens just as they should be. Tolund was relieved to see there were no snakes, scorched or living, anywhere upon the beach. The boy marveled at how real his strange dream had seemed as he took long deep breaths to steady his nerves. Oddly enough, now he fell asleep with the thought that the army of stars shimmering high above him were actually watching over him and guarding him as he slept. This comforting thought was the last thing he remembered before morning.

The following day began with an odd mix of strong emotions. The young fighters and their trainingmaster saw to their 'farewells' with Old Scrounger after an early breakfast. Though the gruff riverman tried to hide his feelings even the young ones could tell that he'd grown quite fond of their company. "I must admit that I'll be lookin' forward to the return trip back up the river with all o' you," he said. "Til then, we'll be exploring the smaller rivers that run through the jungles here. Miss Respect'll like that I suspect."

"I expect our tour of the villages will take the entire month," said Mr. Pierce, "You should look for our return, at this spot, in about four weeks."

"Very good then," smiled Scrounger. "I hope you bring us back something that glitters for our efforts."

"How you didn't end up a pirate I'll never know," laughed Mr. Pierce. "Take care of yourself, you muddy old rat!" The dwarf added a firm handshake to this last remark. Once these old friends were done with their goodbyes the moment became awkward. The four fighters, all of whom were initially wary of the riverman and his giant pet, had become accustomed to their presence. All of them were a bit sad to see them go, but also a little relieved as they still did not quite know how to take their strange way of life and rough manner. Politely, they all fumbled through their goodbyes. No one could bring themselves to embrace the weathered old man, but they did manage grateful handshakes and good wishes. The riverdragon, herself, never so much as glanced their way and seemed eager to return to her beloved river. In short order they all found themselves waving to them as the odd pair moved back up the river and into the thick green of the jungle.

"Well, that's that," barked Mr. Pierce. "Time to move on. Look to your things and have them bundled up and ready to move; we've a good stretch of the legs ahead of us if we want to make 'Ibago' by nightfall."

"Is that one of the villages we'll be fighting in or are we just visiting there?" asked Lindris.

"Oh, we might find a taker or two, but there are no real arena-fighters in Ibago, just a lot of old friends who know their way around a cooking pot. You young pups are going to love filling your bellies on this trip. You're about to eat dishes unlike anything you've eaten before!"

True to his word, Mr. Pierce urged them along at a taxing pace. Tolund suspected that part of this was to make the village by sunset, but the other part had to do with building his fighters' stamina after so many long weeks of being limited to the small space on Miss

Respect's platform. In either case, breaks that day were scarce and it was with great relief that the tired, leg sore party spied the outline of a small village silhouetted against the setting sun. Mr. Pierce paused with a puzzled look upon his face, "That's odd. There are no torches or cooking fires lit. That's not right."

The seemingly tireless dwarf jogged ahead at a brisk pace. The young ones, following his lead, did the same. Quickly, they were in earshot of the dark village and Mr. Pierce began calling out names unfamiliar to the four of them. His only reply was the lapping of the waves and the sound of the palm leaves shifting in the wind. "What do you think has happened?" Bex inquired of their trainingmaster.

"I'm not sure yet," replied Mr. Pierce as he stopped abruptly. "Let's prepare for the worst; leave your packs here and arm yourselves. I'll take the lead and you four follow behind within the sound of my voice. If I order you to run that is precisely what you will do. You will run just as hard and as fast as you can and you will not stop for anything. Understood?"

"Yes, Sir," they all replied nervously.

Mr. Pierce stalked forward and melted into the shadows of the nearest row of thatched huts. None of the young fighters could see or hear anything up ahead. The tense moments stretched on. "I hate how loud silence can get when you're scared," whispered Heather.

"Just be ready to run…or to fight," Lindris whispered back with conviction.

"All right, Scrappers!!" called the big voice of Mr. Pierce, "come on in, and bring the packs with you." Quickly, everything was gathered and carried into the village. In its center they found their trainingmaster stroking his beard with a baffled look upon his face. "None of this makes any sense," he growled.

"Where is everyone?" asked Bex.

"Gone," answered Mr. Pierce, who was obviously concerned. "Every living soul, young or old, is gone. And, judging by the cold fire pits and empty cooking pots, they've been gone for some time. On top of that, the only markings that I can make out move from the huts to the tideline of the beach."

"Tideline?" questioned Lindris.

"That's the highest edge of the water at high tide," answered Mr. Pierce. "These marks look like things have been dragged through the sand. I suppose they moved further down to the water, but there's no way to tell if they veered to the left, to the right, or if they boarded a ship of some kind."

"Well," Bex interjected, "it doesn't look like any of their fishing boats are missing." The boy nodded in the direction of the boats which were all tied off in their usual places on trees above the tideline.

"Aye, that looks to be all of them," Mr. Pierce confirmed. "And it doesn't look like they've been set to water in a while. Also, the village itself is unspoiled. No food stores, weapons, or valuables seemed to have been taken. Hmmph! This is a tough stone to crack!"

"Well, what do you think we should do now, Sir?" asked Heather.

"Not much we can do tonight, Heather," the dwarf answered. "We'll set ourselves up here tonight and try to get some rest; if there are answers to be found we won't find them stumbling around in the dark of night. Boys, once our camp is in hand, you two will have the first watch. At about midnight wake me and I'll keep watch until sunrise."

That night, at Mr. Pierce's urging, no fire or torch was lit and the small party clung to the shadows of the huts they slept in just in case unfriendly eyes were watching Ibago. To the relief of all, a restless night passed quietly and daylight came without incident. With the benefit of the morning light Mr. Pierce made another discovery. "Aha! Tracks!" he called out. "There are some strange tracks that lead away from here."

"This is a mess of tracks!" offered Bex, who knew a little about tracking from his father's protectorate training. "It looks like one set of footsteps of one small man, or possibly a woman, and the tracks of probably more than one dog, but I'm not sure what these straight lines are— maybe a cart being pushed?"

"Not the way they follow the person's footsteps," corrected Mr. Pierce, "that's a litter being dragged in the sand or I'm a fool."

Tolund couldn't make sense of any of this. "So, what does that mean?"

"I haven't the foggiest idea, Lad," answered the dwarf. "But since these tracks are the only clue we have to go on, then that's what we are going to follow. That village was full of old friends. Ibago was a peaceful fishing village whose folk never troubled anyone or anything. You can be sure that I won't rest until I've uncovered the truth of what went on here and set things right. I only hope my own fears prove to be wrong." With that, their trainingmaster did something that his young charges had never seen him do.

Reaching into his large pack, he brought out a wicked double-bladed axe head with strange runes carved into its middle. Kissing it with reverent lips, the dwarf whispered something they could not hear. Next, Mr. Pierce brought out two metal shafts that slipped into a groove together to form one long handle. When he finally snapped the top of the handle to the axe head it was crafted for, the dwarf let out a fearsome growl as he swung the axe in a vicious arc. "Prayers are in order, Scrappers!" he barked. "Prayers for my friends to be found safe and, if they are not, prayers for whoever's responsible because if I find them this axe will be the last sight they will ever see!"

Tolund shuddered at the frightening sight of his trainingmaster in this moment. Even in Serist he did not seem so deadly. This was also the first time the boy had ever seen Mr. Pierce with an actual weapon of his own. Such was the dwarf's prowess that he never had to rely on any one weapon so seeing him actually bearing an axe that was crafted for his own hands made it all the more threatening.

Before long, the small band was following the trail of the tracks. A resolute Mr. Pierce led the way with his fearsome axe gripped firmly in both hands. No one dared to even speak to him as he stalked forward shooting wary glances in all directions. Tolund thought he looked like one of the great cats on the trail of its next kill. In spite of the ominous mood, the day was uneventful. That night they camped hidden away in a thick grove of palm trees off of the main path.

"We've the good fortune that our trail is still easily marked," Mr. Pierce said over their evening meal. "If we keep moving along the shoreline like this we're bound to reach the next village some time tomorrow."

"Which village would that be?" asked Bex.

"Just another fishing village," replied the determined dwarf. "This one's called Berbago."

Gwendolyn Dellender awoke with a start long before daybreak. It was no dream or even nightmare that woke her from a sound sleep this night. Unable to put her finger on what disturbed her, all she could identify was a feeling of great dread and a sense of fear for her son.

Slipping on her robe, she strode to Emilyse's room. With a sigh of relief, she saw that her lovely daughter was slumbering peacefully. Gwendolyn brushed her baby's soft hair to one side and smiled at how healthy and beautiful Emilyse was now. Gazing at her now, it seemed hard to imagine that the lass had ever known a moment of sickness in her young life. Now, reassured that Emilyse was safe, she made her way to Tolund's room. Everything was neat and arranged perfectly, just as it was the day he left for the new training season at Breyligh's Hold. Sitting down on the edge of his bed, Gwendolyn placed a trembling hand over her own heart; the frantic beating seemed to grow stronger now that she was in his room among his things.

Somehow, her mother's heart moved beyond all reason and urged her to pray, "High King," she sighed heavily, "please look after my boy. Forgive me if these strange fears are meaningless, but if they are not please watch over him. Please go where I can't go and provide what I can't provide. Also, look after dear Heather and the others. Help me to remember that they never leave your sight and that your strong hands are always holding them close. By Your will, Amen."

As expected, her prayers calmed her anxious heart. Though still unnerved by these feelings, her prayers helped to remind her of the proper order of things. After their great ordeal of the previous year, she had learned to trust the High King's will more than ever. Looking out of her son's window she whispered a gentle reminder to him as if he could somehow hear her over the great distance between them, "You stay close to Him too, Tolund. You stay close to Him too."

The Lockslayer was furious. He was not used to being thwarted in the hunt. Though the path his quarry had taken was childishly simple to mark, he could not close the gap between them. Savage, ruthless winds pressed against him as he flew. So powerful was this constant assault that Eli was forced to dismiss his white wings of speed in order to rely upon his brown wings of strength. Though he hated to slow his pace, the great winds were actually forcing him back; only his brown wings could overcome their fearsome power.

He was also aware that this defense not only prevented his gaining upon the thieving warlocks, but also allowed them to widen the gap between them. Though he could not guess their destination and purpose at this point, he knew that their possession of so many unbound smoothstones could only bring death and calamity upon Vedris.

Cursing his foul circumstances, he pressed on as best he could.

CHAPTER 13

ORPHANS

"Look!" called out Mr. Pierce, "in the distance, that's Ibago's 'sister' village of Berbago." The four young ones were both relieved and nervous at this announcement. All of them had been pushed to their limits by the pace their trainingmaster had set for them this day. Rest had been brief and infrequent, but none of them dared complain in light of Mr. Pierce's vengeful mood. Either way, they knew that reaching Berbago would give them a chance to rest their burning legs and lungs. However, their anxiety piqued at the thought of what they might find in this new village.

The tracks they'd been following continued past the village itself. Mr. Pierce did not wander from the trail to inspect the village huts, but he did carefully spy Berbago's condition. "It's exactly like the other village," he said quietly. "We can only surmise that whatever happened in Ibago also took place here in its neighboring village."

"Should we take a closer look?" asked Lindris.

"No," answered the grim dwarf. "My instincts tell me that this trail will lead us to more answers. If I'm wrong we can always double-back and see if there's anything different here than in Ibago."

Without any further discussion the five of them strode past Berbago. All of them could feel the sense of dread that hung over the empty village. Tolund, following the example of Mr. Pierce, looked about sharply in all directions and listened carefully for any sound above that of the lapping waves and their footsteps in the sand. On they marched for almost another hour.

"Hold," ordered Mr. Pierce in an urgent whisper. "The tracks have changed." The small party halted and knelt down to inspect the trail.

"It looks like all of the dog tracks have split off to the left and the right," shared Bex.

"Aye, and the ruts from the litter continue to move forward," said Mr. Pierce.

"What do you think that means?" asked Heather.

"Hard to say," answered the dwarf. "Something could have scared the dogs off or maybe they went after something. My guess is that these beasts must be trained by the bearer of this litter as it looks like they all traveled together in one group."

"So, do we follow the dog tracks or the other ones?" Tolund wondered.

"We follow the litter," said Mr. Pierce firmly. "If it bears someone from Ibago then that's where my duty lies."

With that, they pressed on for a short while longer. Suddenly, Mr. Pierce halted them as the sound of quick movement within the jungle to their right caught his ear. "Form a circle and keep your weapons ready!" he ordered.

"What do you think it…" Heather's worried question was interrupted by the forms of seven large dogs that burst out of the thick bushes baring their fangs and growling fiercely. Instantly, from the high sand dunes to their left, three more large dogs leaped forward flanked by six smaller ones. The smaller dogs barked their high-pitched yelping barks. The menacing pack formed a wary ring about the five intruders.

"Stand your ground, but make no sudden moves," barked Mr. Pierce. The dogs kept them hemmed in, but did not advance on them. The tense posturing continued for long moments.

"Shouldn't we attack?" asked Bex "There are a lot of them, but they're no match for our blades!"

"Don't be too quick to feel those teeth, Boy," grunted Mr. Pierce. "You might be right about our advantage, but there's no way we could engage them without taking some serious wounds…or worse."

"So, we're just going to stand here until they become bored with us and decide to leave us alone?" asked Heather

"Oh, you can be sure that that's not going to happen, Heather. As I'd suspected, these mongrels have been trained by someone. Their job is to keep us from going any further along this path. My guess now is that their masters will be along shortly in response to the yapping of those little ones." Now Mr. Pierce dropped to one knee and nodded to his charges to do the same. "Try to look calm, but be ready in case I've read these beasts wrong."

In a few moments the largest of the pack, a dark grey wolf-like dog, ceased his growling and sat on his haunches while staring intently at their party's every move. Immediately, the rest of the pack did exactly the same thing. After a short time where no one moved, Bex shifted from one knee to another. Instantly, all of the dogs snapped to their feet, bared their teeth again, and snarled in his direction. Reading their warning, Bex froze. Soon, again following the lead of the grey dog, the beasts settled down and just stared at them.

Within the hour, the dogs' ears lifted high and they all began to circle about their captives frantically. "Young Ones," said Mr. Pierce, "I think we're about to find some answers." The whining and short barks of the pack seemed to reaffirm Mr. Pierce's statement. From the direction of the sand dunes more barking dogs could be heard.

"If you stand still they won't hurt you!" a young voice called out from the cover of the dunes. Tolund exchanged questioning glances with his companions.

"If they keep their distance we won't kill them!" snapped Mr. Pierce. The dwarf's scowling face quickly shifted to a look of surprise when the owner of the voice stepped into view.

Shuffling carefully toward them was a tall young man of no more than twenty years in age. All of the travelers were surprised to see him relying upon his wooden staff to mark the path before him. "He's blind!" Heather whispered to Tolund.

"Not completely," the young man added with a smile. "Now then, who are you and what are you doing on my land?" His worn clothing, wild hair, and faint beard did not carry a sense of menace to the travelers.

"Oh no," growled Mr. Pierce, "you will answer our questions this day or you will be sorry you ever stole from the village of Ibago!" With this the dwarf resumed his scowl and stood up, holding his axe at the ready.

"Stole?" wondered the young man. "You believe I had something to do with…?" Now the stranger squinted hard at Mr. Pierce for a moment and then whistled twice to his dogs. Instantly, the pack sprinted happily to their master's side. Now he smiled as he stroked the grey dog's ears with his free hand. "Are you defenders of Ibago then, here to set things right?"

"I said I want answers!" snapped Mr. Pierce. "Those folk were old friends of mine and all the curs in the world will not save you from me if you've brought harm to those good people."

"Well then, you can lower your weapon, Sir," the stranger answered calmly, "for I had nothing to do with Ibago's or Bergago's fall, but I do have news for you, both good and ill. My name is Alden. We should not stay out in the open too long. May I offer you my hospitality as we discuss these dark events?"

Mr. Pierce gave the young man a long look of his own. "'Alden' is not the name of a Coastlander, nor do you have the darker hair and dusky skin of these folk."

"My family traveled here from the north before I was born," Alden said firmly in response to the dwarf's doubting tone. "This village is where I was raised. Though I am a descendent of the higher lands I've never even set foot on them. I am a Coastlander in everything but heritage. Now, do you want to follow me to shelter or not?"

"Very well," answered the dwarf, "but know that any treachery on your part will cost you dearly in blood."

"As will yours, Good Dwarf, as will yours." Turning about, surrounded by his loyal pack, the young man moved back the way he'd come with his staff swinging in front of him to help guide his path. Mr.

Pierce nodded to his young fighters and they all followed the strange procession of a blind lad and his beasts into the maze of sand dunes.

Surprisingly, it didn't take them long to find the opening between two huge slabs of rock that served as the entrance to what Alden referred to as 'his castle.' After the opening, a winding dirt path eventually led them to an enormous underground cavern that had been carved by an ancient river that used to find its way to the sea. "We're beneath the sand dunes now, just a little inland from the ocean," explained Alden.

"Does the sea water make it this far back?" asked Lindris.

"Only during a great storm," answered their new host. "And even then only a small current gets this far back. I think you'll find that this is as safe a place to live as just about anywhere in the Coastlands." Heather smiled an amused smile at Tolund; she was beginning to like this wild boy's manner.

Alden continued to boast about his hidden home, "It has only one entrance which, as you saw, is almost impossible to find. It's easy enough to have some of my dogs guard it." Now, as they moved in, lighted torches marked the footpath that led deeper into the cavern.

"How weak are your eyes, Boy," asked Mr. Pierce

"I can see well enough to get around in bright daylight," Alden answered without a hint of embarrassment. "Light is easy enough to follow, but in the dark of night, when the moon is faint or there is no torchlight, my eyes are all but useless. But it's a simple matter to stay in my home at night and trust in my dogs to look after me."

"Speaking of which," interrupted a curious Lindris, "where did all of these dogs come from?"

"Most of them are orphans, like me," replied Alden. "Either they're unwanted by the villagers who have too many or they're strays I've come across. So I give them a home and we all look after each other." Now the winding footpath opened up into a larger area where the bleating of goats could be heard.

Tolund was surprised to see how ingenious this boy had been in settling this cavern. Torches on the walls and a great firepit in the middle brought warmth and light to the whole chamber. The bleating was coming from a natural cave that had been sealed with a crude wooden gate so it could serve as a pen for livestock. He saw several goats and one milk cow within. Another very small cave was also penned in and served as a chicken coop. On the far side of this large opening was a flat area with old blankets spread about for the dogs. The last small cave on that side also had its own gate, but a different sound was echoing out from within.

"Babies?" blurted a shocked Heather, "You've got children in here?!?" Heather's instincts overcame her as she bolted toward the sound of the infants. Before she could reach the wooden gate she was stopped by four of Alden's snarling dogs.

"They won't let you near that room unless I order them away," Alden explained. "They will do the same to protect the animal pens as well."

"But where did these children come from?" demanded Mr. Pierce. "And how many of them have you stolen?"

"I didn't steal anything!" At the sound of their master's raised voice the posture of the dogs became agitated and the fur on their backs stood on end. Alden snapped a quick command at them and every single dog sat down attentively. "Here, let me show you,"

Leading them all to the room with the children, the travelers were relieved to see that the seven infants Alden was caring for were all bundled up in warm blankets and looked strong and healthy. "I found these three in Berbago on the morning after the strange night; the other four I found that afternoon in Ibago when I went there to find help."

"What do you mean 'after the strange night?'" asked Mr. Pierce.

"Not long ago my dogs woke me up in the middle of the night. Their ears were up and they were whimpering as if something they could hear was hurting them. Whatever it was was beyond my ability to hear, but the dogs all huddled close to me like something was threatening them. I couldn't get them to settle down so I just stoked the fire and stayed up with them the rest of the night trying to keep them calm. The next morning, after failing to find anything unusual around my castle, I decided to go down to Berbago and see if any of the villagers had seen or heard anything unusual the night before."

"And what did you find?" asked Mr. Pierce.

"It was empty, abandoned— like everyone had just walked away in the middle of the night." Alden's voice quivered a bit as he spoke. "My dogs kept sniffing the sand up to the tideline and whining in the direction of the sea…and that's when I heard the first baby crying. I searched the huts and found that all of the infants had been left behind. What could make good people abandon their own babies?"

"So you gathered them up and took them back to the safety of your hidden cavern," Tolund surmised.

"Eventually," confirmed Alden. "First I set out to the nearest village, Ibago, to seek out their help, but instead of help I found that that village was also abandoned except for the four newborns that were left behind. The only thing I could think of was to bring them home and keep them safe with me."

"And that's all you know?" questioned Mr. Pierce.

"I'm afraid so. Nothing else has happened until you made your way to my doorstep." After Alden's last words Mr. Pierce gave him another long look and then looked over the infants once more.

"Well, what about you?" challenged Mr. Pierce. "What brings you to live in this hidden place when you claim the local villagers are your good friends?"

"You are the suspicious one, aren't you?" smiled the blind boy. "Fair enough, I've nothing to hide. The truth is that I was raised in Berbago. I lived all of my life in that little village; it wasn't until a few years ago that I made this series of caves my home."

"So you say," scoffed Mr. Pierce. "Though it's been almost thirty years since I've visited both of these villages. I've never heard of lighter skinned folk being born here."

"I never said I was born in Berbago, only that I was raised there. You see, my parents were merchants who fell in love with these lands and sought to make a new life for themselves in Berbago. I was only a few years old when they moved here." Young Alden paused sadly before his next words, "Unfortunately, my mother died from a fever and my father was bitten by a venomous snake only a year after that."

Tolund thought of his father's sickbed and his last days as he listened to Alden's tale. "So, who looked after you after you lost them?" he asked.

"There was an old widow who was never able to bear children of her own. Her name was Ayana, I called her 'Old Mum'; she was the only family I'd ever known." Alden looked down somberly at the grey dog by his side and scratched his ears and smiled, "Except for these cave rats."

"Where is she now?" asked Lindris respectfully.

"Old Mum passed away in her sleep the year before I left the village. Everyone in the village had been very kind over the years, but without Old Mum there it just didn't feel the same. Besides, I was ready to prove that I could make it on my own and too many of the villagers wanted to pity me. So, I bartered away our hut and the things I no longer needed, gathered up all of Old Mum's livestock and my dogs, and set myself up in here. I like it better in here. In my castle it's peaceful and quiet and I get to be in charge."

"Where did all of this stand with the villagers?" asked Mr. Pierce, whose tone still carried a hint of mistrust.

"It took some getting used to, for all of us, but in time even the elder fishermen understood why I needed to be on my own. They never ceased to be my informal family and I often dropped in to visit and barter with them. They've come to count on me as a watchmen for the western path to the village; nothing escapes the notice of my dogs."

Alden smiled with pride as he spoke these words.

Mr. Pierce gave him a hard stare for a moment and then relaxed his grim demeanor. "Hmph…may lightning strike me if I don't believe you, Young Alden. I remember Ayana and I remember how soft-hearted she was. So I guess you've truth enough in your story." The dwarf's words carried a hint of relief with them. "Now, the question is, what is our next move?"

"The sun will be down before we can make it back to Berbago to look about so we may as well settle in for the night. I'll be happy to get started on some supper for all of us," offered Alden.

"Then we will accept your gracious invitation," smiled Mr. Pierce.

Before long, the wild boy produced a tasty meal of grilled fish with wild onions and goat cheese. He even brewed up some hot tea procured from some native leaves near his home. It was all surprisingly delicious and quite enjoyable to his new guests. With the calming sound of the ocean waves they all reclined in the sand before Alden's firepit and enjoyed a second round of tea as they discussed what to do about the mysterious event that claimed both of the hapless villages of Ibago and Berbago. They determined to inspect Berbago in the morning, hoping that the sharp eyes of the travelers might uncover clues that Alden missed. In light of his strange dreams of late, Tolund felt uneasy about the whole matter. He could not imagine any outcome other than a tragic one, but the more he spent time with Alden the more he found himself respecting this courageous blind boy.

Eventually, Alden's dogs settled down in their usual sleeping spots and fell fast asleep. Tolund was relieved to see that a number of them stretched out before the only entrance to the cavern ensuring that nothing and no one could gain entry without alarming the wary beasts. Soon, the children and adults also drifted off to sleep in the warmth and comfort of a castle ruled by orphans.

CHAPTER 14

THE CROSSING

They came upon the emptiness of Berbago an hour after first light. Cautiously and quietly, Alden and his pack led the way. Mr. Pierce and his fighters, save for Heather who volunteered to stay behind and look after the infants, followed behind with drawn weapons and wary eyes. To the relief of all they only found seagulls, the morning breezes, and the endless waves. Berbago remained undisturbed and silent.

"This is exactly as I found it before, except for the children," Alden shared.

"Aye," echoed Mr. Pierce, "Ibago was like this as well. Their food was untouched, their weapons were left in their huts, and anything worth taking or stealing was ignored."

"Their boats are still here, just like the first village," Lindris added as she looked at the small fleet of fishing boats tethered to palm trees far above the lapping waves. Suddenly, she fixed her eyes on deep marks upon the sand, "Trainingmaster, there are more of those drag marks here in the sand." Everyone moved closer to the place where the village ended and the sandy shore began to dip toward the tideline.

"Exactly like those in Ibago," said Tolund.

"Yes," Mr. Pierce agreed. "All moving from the village to the water, but without any footprints or bootprints anywhere about them. Judging by the way the sand was pressed down, it looks like something heavy has been dragged to the sea."

"Could that have been the fate of these people?" asked Bex.

"But that doesn't make any sense," Alden protested. "How could two entire villages of stout men and women be overcome and hauled into the sea without any sign of a struggle or even a single footstep? And why would their conquerors leave the infants and everything in the villages untouched?"

"I don't know," answered Mr. Pierce. "I've never come across anything like this in my travels."

"So what do we do?" asked Lindris.

"My grandfather loved to share his own proverbs with our clan as often as he could fit them in," grinned Mr. Pierce, "one of his favorites was, 'Instead of wasting time fretting over what is unknown, follow the path of what is known.' I do believe that is the counsel we need right now."

"But we don't know anything," Bex said flatly.

"Not so," answered Mr. Pierce as he rummaged through his own pack, "we know that the only signs in both villages lead to the sea." Now the dwarf produced a mariner's looking glass from his pack. "If we are to assume that the people didn't drown themselves then it stands to reason that they either boarded ships or were forced to board ships; either way, their path was the open water off of these shores without the use of their own boats." Putting the looking glass to his right eye and closing his left, Mr. Pierce surveyed the open waters. "Master Alden, what am I to make of that small spit of land straight from us as the crow flies?"

"Small...? Oh, that would have to be what we call 'The Nest,'" answered Alden. "It's just a speck of an island infested with vermin and snakes. No one ever steps foot on that rock if they can possibly help it. The elders even ordered all the fishermen to stay far away from it for fear of a curse bound to its shores."

"Well, cursed or not, I mean to explore that island," asserted Mr. Pierce. "As I see no ships anywhere in sight the only place for us to look would be that 'Nest,' as you call it."

"But there's another reason we give that island such a wide berth," Alden protested. "Living in the deep coves all about that island are what we call 'Firewhips.'"

"Firewhips?" wondered Tolund.

"Others have called them 'Ghosts of the Sea,' but we've always called them Firewhips. They're giant creatures of living slime that float under the surface with dozens of long whips, like tentacles, that will hook into you and burn you like fire with their venom. When I was little, one of our fishing boats made it back home after a Firewhip attack. Two of our bold young men dared to get too close to that island. Without warning, their boat was attacked from below. One of them was wrapped up in the poison whips and was pulled down to his end, screaming in agony. The survivor slapped away the whips with his oar and managed to paddle out of their reach while the monsters bore down upon his comrade. I still remember the way those whips had shredded and blackened the wood of that boat. Only a fool would venture into those waters or on that cursed island."

"Hmm," grunted Mr. Pierce. The dwarf began to stroke his beard while he stared in the direction of the island. Tolund sighed anxiously and shot a look of concern toward Lindris; the young fighters knew their trainingmaster well enough to know that his mind was already set upon exploring that island. "Well, Master Alden," the dwarf said with a sharp edge in his tone, "it seems we have some planning to do. I will set out for this island one way or the other, but, as I am fond of my own skin and the skin of my fighters, I would appreciate your help in finding a way to survive these slime-beasts."

"It looks like the stubbornness of dwarves wasn't just a myth from old stories," smiled the blind boy. "Still, if you're set upon this course, I think I have an idea or two that the elders used to talk about over evening fires."

Following Alden's instructions, the young fighters spent most of the day scavenging along the nearby coastline for large clumps of seaweed. They were to gather as much as they could and pile it upon the sand in front of Berbago. Alden, with Bex's help, searched among the huts and boats to find the best line of thick rope that he could. Mysteriously, Mr. Pierce had excused himself to Chief Kelaka's hut and left strict orders that he was not to be disturbed as he had his own errand to attend to. By late afternoon Alden, who seemed satisfied with the amount of seaweed gathered, called everyone to the center of the village for an early supper.

"This should be enough," said the boy as he gestured to the large pile of seaweed. "Bex helped me pick out the sturdiest boat and the finest rope in the village. The idea is to use the rope to weave the seaweed all about the boat; the elders believed that this would not only form a barrier against the firewhip's tendrils, but it might also fool the beasts into thinking that it was only a floating clump of seaweed and not living prey."

"Might?" wondered Lindris.

"Well," grimaced Alden, "no one's ever been foolhardy enough to give it a try. Besides, we've never had a reason to visit that dark place. The only reason we know that it's infested with foul creatures is because of tales passed down over the ages. Now, I suggest we prepare and provision your boat right away. It will take you the better part of the night to reach the island and the cover of darkness should conceal you from any unfriendly eyes."

"So you believe that those responsible for taking the villagers are still nearby?" asked Bex.

"I do," answered Alden, "either along the coastline or upon open water. I know it sounds mad, but there's been an evil wind upon these shores lately; I can feel it in my soul. Nothing feels safe right now."

"I concur," said Mr. Pierce. "For that reason our task is best done in shadow. We will leave as soon as it's dark enough."

While Alden, Bex, and Lindris lashed the seaweed to the boat in the shallow water, Mr. Pierce sent Tolund to retrieve Heather. Before long, he and Heather returned pulling the litter full of children. Alden happily cared for the infants while Heather and Tolund helped to finalize the 'disguised' boat. Tolund asked about Mr. Pierce's whereabouts and Bex informed them that their trainingmaster had slipped into the jungle just after Tolund began his errand. The dwarf ordered them not to follow him until he called for them.

As the very bottom of the setting sun began to drop under the horizon, the last of the seaweed clumps were tied securely to the hull of the boat and all seemed as ready as it could be for this strange voyage. With nothing else to do but wait, Heather and Tolund walked a short distance from everyone else, sat down upon the still warm sand, and watched the daylight wane.

"Isn't it strange, Tol?" asked Heather.

"Isn't what strange?"

"The ocean," she mused. "It can be so lovely and crystal blue in the day and then so black and haunting at night. It's all the same ocean, but its moods are as different as can be. It's like a dream in one hour and a nightmare in another."

"Are you scared about tonight?" Tolund asked.

"Of course I am," she chuckled. "Aren't you?"

"I was pretty nervous about it, what with never traveling on the ocean before and these firewhip creatures, but now all your talk of 'haunted waters' has me really spooked. Thanks for that," he teased sarcastically.

"Glad I could make myself useful," she teased back.

"But, honestly," Tolund continued, "so much of these dangerous things look different to me now, at least, from far away."

"What do you mean, 'from far away?'"

"I mean, when something terrifying is right in front of you it still feels the same, but from far away I'm not so scared anymore. Think about Azlial's bones. When I saw them creeping around it was strange and frightening and it made my heart beat faster, but from a distance I know that I'm not looking at them alone. I'm never really alone.

After our trials with Celnumus, I've learned that the High King really is watching out for us. When I have time to think, I realize that we are caught up in a larger current that is carrying us along to where He wants to take us. So that makes the journey a lot easier."

"What you just said wouldn't have made sense to me a few years ago," Heather smiled, "but now I know exactly what you mean." Still smiling, Heather drew back her hood, closed her eyes, and allowed the coastal breezes to whip through her hair and over her face. Tolund knew that she did this because no one else was close enough to see her scars and he also smiled because he liked the idea that she felt safe enough around him to be completely herself. The boy whispered a prayer of thanks to the High King for this peaceful moment as the two friends soaked up the final rays of daylight.

Not long after full darkness had pressed upon the village, Mr. Pierce called out from the thick of the jungle. "Everyone walk to the sound of my voice," he insisted. "Young Alden, I'll need you to bring every one of your dogs with you." Alden's head leaned back a bit with a confounded expression on his face. The four fighters smiled at one another as they were all familiar with their trainingmaster's love of secrets and surprises. Leaving the litter full of children to Heather, Alden carefully worked his way toward the jungle.

Tolund watched as Alden struggled to see anything in the dark, relying mostly on his staff and the leading of his faithful dogs. It dawned on Tolund that every day of living was an act of bravery for Alden. Yet, never once did he hear the boy complain of his lot in life or his failing eyesight. There was a deeper form of courage walking before him on this night, deeper and more profound than any warrior's conquest or king's triumph. Tolund whispered a prayer of thanks to the High King for the gift of crossing paths with this valiant young man.

After about twenty strides or so, the party found Mr. Pierce in a tiny clearing that was walled in by the jungle foliage. The dwarf was hunched over a meager fire that had burned down to only its coals. They were all intrigued by the grey-blue glowing of the coals. "Good Alden," Mr. Pierce began, "you've proven yourself to be both a generous host to strangers and a strong defender of your adopted people. As we take our leave of you tonight, I believe it's only fitting that you are left with a gift that suits your unsung valor. I've taken the liberty of collecting the village smoothstones from both Ibago and your village. Both your Chief Kelaka and my old friend, Chief Nikoa, held two smoothstones in hiding to safeguard their people in the face of great threats. With a total of four stones between both villages, I believe that one can be spared for a special blessing tonight." Removing his glove, Mr. Pierce reached for the center of the smoldering coals with his bare hand.

"Mr. Pierce!!" Lindris shouted in alarm.

"Relax, Lass," he smiled, "it's an unusual fire stoked for an unusual coal." Plunging his hand deep into the bed of eerie coals, the dwarf, showing no signs of pain or burning, lifted out the steaming smoothstone, which shimmered a magnificent blue. "Step forward, Alden, and bring your dogs one at a time."

Everyone looked on in awe as Mr. Pierce touched the smoothstone to the foreheads of each of the dogs in turn as he whispered a prayer beneath his breath. Though the beasts showed no signs of pain or discomfort from this, poor Heather still chewed at her fingernails anxiously. When all of the dogs in Alden's pack had been blessed, Mr. Pierce turned to the boy, himself. "Master Alden," he said as he touched the magic stone to the boy's forehead, "you have proven yourself, in spite of circumstance and limitations, to be as fine a protector as any chief or king could hope for. Therefore, it is my honor to bequeath to you this unique gift of power. May you use it to bless the innocent and terrify the wicked."

Though no outward sign or change could be seen, Alden smiled widely. "This feels fantastic! I feel so strong and light! What did you do to me?"

"It's a unique dwarven spell only used two other times in our world," nodded Mr. Pierce. "It took me the better part of the day to get the words from the ancient scroll clear and true, but you'll see it was worth it. For what you and your dogs now possess is the 'Blessing of Armor.'"

"Blessing of Armor?" Alden wondered.

"Aye," smiled the dwarf with a proud wink. "The mage of our clan had an ancestor that invented this spell. That ancestor made only four scrolls which could, with the use of a smoothstone and a good fire, create this blessing. The scroll I used and burned to stoke this fire was the second-to-last scroll in existence. It was a gift to me for saving our mage's life once."

"What does it do?" asked a fascinated Bex.

"Well, if I prepared it correctly, which I did, only one weapon in all of Vedris should ever be able to harm you. You and your pack can now withstand any assault, magic or otherwise, without suffering injury or pain of any kind. Allow me to demonstrate…" Drawing his dagger, the burly dwarf stabbed down hard upon the grey dog's back. So great was the strike that the large dog was dropped to the ground, but, impossibly, it showed no sign of pain. "You see?" Mr. Pierce continued. "The only thing worse for wear here is the point of my knife." Alden touched the tip of the dagger to find that his dog's hide had blunted the point of it as if Mr. Pierce had stabbed a blacksmith's anvil with it.

"That's unbelievable!" exclaimed the blind boy.

"It's the same for you too," added Mr. Pierce as he ran the side of the blade over the top of Alden's knuckles.

"Ahh!" the boy recoiled instinctively. "Wait…you're right. I didn't feel a thing! And no blood was drawn!" Alden stretched out his hand for everyone to see.

"Mr. Pierce," interrupted Bex, "what did you mean about 'only one weapon' being able to harm them? What weapon would that be?"

The dwarf nodded at the blade strapped over Tolund's shoulder. "The only blade created to undo magic, right, Tolund? Here, let me put my reasoning to the test." Motioning for Tolund's sword, Mr. Pierce waited as Tolund drew it from its sheath and handed it to him. "Master Alden," he said lightly, "if you would, please hold one finger up for a moment." Following his request, Alden held up the first finger of his left hand. Mr. Pierce ran his dagger's edge across it in a brutal swipe. The lad's finger showed no blood, cut, or mark. Next, using Tolund's black blade, Mr. Pierce carefully brought the tip to Alden's finger. Now, the boy winced slightly as a tiny drop of blood issued from a pinpoint wound. "Sorry about that, Boy," Mr. Pierce apologized. "Rest assured that that will be the last bit of pain you'll ever feel…that is, unless you and Tolund run afoul of one another." He said this last remark with a sarcastic grin and a slap on the back for Alden. "You and your dogs are now a match for any dragon, warlock, or army! Any tribe or village in the Coastlands or beyond would count themselves lucky to have the lot of you protecting them. One other thing you should know is that this spell is also contingent upon your adherence to purity." Alden's confusion at this statement was easily read upon his face. Mr. Pierce continued, "What that means is that if you ever abuse this blessing by engaging in acts of evil, the gift will fade instantly, never to return. This was a safeguard woven into it long ago by my ancestors, and a good one it was. I believe you'll use this wisely and your good deeds will be many. Speaking of which, we'd best be underway on our quest for these stolen villagers or else you'll have no one to protect."

"I don't know how to thank you for this, Master Pierce."

"No thanks will be necessary, Lad," replied the dwarf warmly. "You've already earned this gift by saving the lives of these little ones. The remaining three smoothstones I leave in your care. If we are successful in our quest then you may give them back to the two chiefs yourself; if we are not, then I know they will be safe with you. My only regret is that one of them was not a healing stone so that I might cure your eyes.

"Wait," interrupted Bex, "I have to ask, if this spell really makes people and animals invincible then why wouldn't your mage use it on your entire clan or even all dwarves? Why didn't you use it on yourself? You could withstand any challenge or win any battle with a blessing like that on you or your army."

"Come now, Boy, don't you know the minds of dwarves by now? No self-respecting dwarf from any of the clans would want such an uneven advantage in battle. They would rather die in honest combat then cheat for a false victory.

"So, if dwarves have no use for it then why did that mage give it to you?" asked Lindris.

"Oh, I suspect she knew my character well enough to know that I'd find a noble use for it in my travels." replied Mr. Pierce. "And, I daresay that I have."

"Does that mean that Alden and his dogs are immortal now?" asked Tolund.

"No, they'll live normal lifespans and then fall asleep peacefully when it's their time. After all, it's a 'Blessing of Armor' not a 'Blessing of Godhood.' That would be a blasphemy toward the High King and no good dwarf would have a hand in something like that."

"All right," added their trainingmaster, "I think we've asked enough questions. We've a lot of work to do and a long night ahead of us so we'd best get to it."

In short order everyone was wishing Alden well and saying their 'good-byes' while Heather made sure to hold and kiss all of the babies several times. Mr. Pierce was busy looking over the provisions that had been lashed down on the boat. Tolund was the first to notice Lindris' unusual posturing. The normally calm and confident fighter stood off to one side of the group wringing her hands in a nervous stance. "Lindris?" Tolund asked kindly, "Are you all right?"

"I don't know why we're doing this," she snapped in a low voice. "This is a fool's errand that's likely to be the end of us!" She had said these last words louder than she'd intended which captured the attention of the entire gathering.

"Lindris?" asked Mr. Pierce. "What's going on? This isn't like you."

"So what if it isn't?" she barked at her trainingmaster. "You want us to throw our lives away on a quest for some poor souls who aren't even out there!" The three fighters who knew Lindris stood speechless— none of them had ever seen her panic like this let alone lash out at Mr. Pierce so rudely.

Now the grim dwarf responded to her uncharacteristically with a gentle demeanor and a gentle tone, "What's troubling you, Lass? You know that you don't have to join us if you don't want to."

"It's not that I don't want to help," she protested, "it's just that… that I can't see us ever returning from those waters! And even if we make it to that accursed island alive all we're going to find is an empty rock! I mean, how can you ask us to risk our lives, to risk drowning or being dragged to the depths by monsters, for people who have already been lost? What if those villagers are not even out there??"

Mr. Pierce, showing no sign of anger or emotion, placed his strong hands on the frantic girl's shoulders. "That's the wrong question, Lindris. The real question is 'What if they are?' What if they are on that island and we abandon them to their fate for fear of our own?" The tall girl's only reply was to drop her head as she shut her eyes tightly to keep from crying. Her trainingmaster continued, "I have to know, Girl. For the sake of my lifelong friends, I have to be certain that I did all that could be done and searched even this distant, dangerous place before I gave up hope for them. You can stay here, you and any others, I will never think less of you for waiting here with Alden, but I am going. I am going because I have to know for sure."

Looking up with eyes damp with tears, Lindris stared out over the open ocean. By the scant light of the crescent moon the dark outline of the island waited ominously. "That ocean is so dark tonight. How could we ever hope to cross it with our lives?"

"I don't understand," interrupted Bex, "you braved the Ash River without a moment's hesitation."

"But that was just a river," answered Lindris. "If we ran afoul of something the solid ground of the shore was just a short swim away. Once we're out on these endless waters we'll be at the mercy of Alden's floating ghosts or some other monster of the sea. If something in those waters wants to pull us down or snap us up in its jaws then there's nothing we can do to prevent it!"

"Perhaps not, Lass," Mr. Pierce said with a firm, clear voice, "but that is the path I am taking. I understand your fears, and there is no shame in them, but we are losing time and the island still waits. Stay if you will, that goes for all of you, and I will return to you if I can. However, if you wish to come with me, fears notwithstanding, I would be glad for the company, but either way I am leaving and I am leaving right now." Turning about, the grim dwarf waded into the surf and clambered onto the boat without another word.

Bex squared his broad shoulders, gathered up his own pack and weapons, and walked toward the waiting boat. Again, Heather surprised herself with her uncharacteristic feelings. While gathering her own things, she felt both the urge to reassure the older girl and the urge to leave her alone. For some unknown reason she chose the latter and, without offering comfort or compassion of any kind to Lindris, she boarded the boat herself. Tolund's feelings at the moment were quite different.

As lovely as he'd found the tall girl before, her sudden vulnerability made her all the more beautiful to him. He felt his heart beating at a faster pace and his mouth was dry and sticky. Nervously, the boy walked over to the girl and put his hand on her shoulder, "You can do this, Lindris," he smiled. "You were born to be brave; it's a part of who you are."

Lindris pulled back her long straight hair on the side of her face closest to Tolund revealing her teary eyes of deep green. "How do you know who I am, Tolund Dellender?" She asked the question to herself as much as to him.

"Anyone can see it," he said with a wry grin, "you're the girl who never runs from a challenge, in or out of the arena. Everyone knows that you're on your way to becoming one of the best fighters Breyligh's Hold has ever seen. One reasonable fear can't change that. It can't change the fact that you're as valiant as any paladin or soldier or cleric in all of Vedris."

Lindris looked at him sternly for a moment. "You really believe that?" she asked.

"Of course I do," he answered firmly. "And so do you. Now, what do you say we get this whole mess over with? The sooner we get started, the sooner we'll be back here and you can say that even this haunted island couldn't get the best of you. It'll make a great story back at Breyligh's for years to come!"

She looked at him curiously for another moment. "You know, Tolund, I think I'm starting to see what's so special about you after all. All those tall tales are starting to make a lot more sense now." Leaning to one side to gather her swords and pack, Lindris wiped her eyes, let out a long, deep breath and strode for the boat. Tolund followed right behind and soon the five travelers were paddling their seaweed-laden boat over the waves and out to deep water.

At Mr. Pierce's direction, the small party remained silent as they paddled. For some time their strong, arena-trained muscles worked together to take them far out on the waters despite the drag of the wreath of thick seaweed that surrounded their boat. Fortunately, once they had passed the line of breaking waves, the current, oddly, seemed to move in the direction they were going which made this daunting task much easier.

After a long stretch of paddling Mr. Pierce ordered them to rest their arms for a bit. It was at this time that Tolund looked behind them and was amazed to see how far from Berbago's shoreline they'd come. Concerned for Lindris' fears he saw that she too had noticed how far out on the ocean they were. The urgent rising and falling of her shoulders revealed her panicked breathing. "Lindris," Tolund whispered, "why don't you ever talk about your family?"

In the scant moonlight he could see her head turn in his direction. "I don't know," she whispered back in mild surprise. "I suppose it just never came up. What do you want to know about them?"

"Well, who are they, where do they live? You know, all of the usual things," he answered.

"As I told everyone before, they are all just common people," Lindris added pleasantly. "My father is Lindin Alastrad, a simple cobbler, and my mother, Erris, helps to keep their little shop and manage their accounts. I have a younger brother and two younger sisters, I am the oldest child…" Lindris went on to talk of her family and home as they all resumed their paddling. She gladly talked of her home village, Longburrow, and the simple life that she'd left behind there. Before long, all of the young fighters chimed in with their own tales of home and loved ones. All of them shared their own stories over the long night of paddling. Soon, the dark crossing didn't seem quite so ominous.

Mr. Pierce allowed himself a wide smile of appreciation for what Tolund had done. By getting Lindris, and then the others, to talk of familiar joys and memories the threatening unknown of the sea seemed a little less threatening. Eventually, even Lindris herself realized what he'd done. "That was a very shrewd trick, Tolund," she shared with a smile, "distracting me from my fears by getting me to talk about my home and family."

"Well, my mother always said that the best way to forget about your bad dreams is to remember your favorite ones," he replied. "I guess she was right." Once again, Lindris found herself pleasantly impressed with the younger fighter.

"Aye," interrupted their trainingmaster, "that's all well and good, but we'd best be silent and on our guard from here on out. The island is a lot closer now and Alden wasn't able to tell us exactly how far out those 'firewhip' creatures were known to nest. Let's assume the worst and hope that we're quiet enough to slip by them without them knowing we were even here."

Tolund joined the others in pushing ahead as silently as they could manage. His muscles were burning from the continued strain. Even the 'helpful' sea current and the numerous rests that Mr. Pierce allowed couldn't prevent his shoulders and arms from aching. Still, they all followed the burly dwarf's lead as he urgently paddled forward. Eventually, outlined by the crescent moon, the shadow of the eerie island loomed before them. The thunder of waves breaking upon shore and rock boomed and echoed in the distance.

Bex was the first to notice the change in the air, "Do you feel that?" he whispered nervously.

"Feel what?" asked Heather.

"That tremor in the air," he answered. "It feels like lightning's about to strike, like just before a great storm."

"I feel it too," whispered Mr. Pierce, "the hairs on my neck and arms are on edge. Everyone draw in your oars; we'll allow the current to pull us in for a while. But stay sharp and don't make any sudden noises. Remember, we want these sea-ghosts to think we're just another lump of seaweed drifting about in the tide. If young Alden was right, they'll only attack us if they think we're invaders in their territory. Our best and only weapon is to blend in."

On they drifted upon the black current. The edge in the air grew stronger even as the sound of waves pounding against the rocks grew louder. Bex was the first to spot the strange lights shimmering from the depths. "There!" he whispered in a panic. "Over to the left of us!" More than a hundred boat lengths to their position, far beneath the surface, a pale blue-green light shifted and moved.

"Be still now, Fighters," urged Mr. Pierce in a voice so low they could barely hear it. "Hold fast and have your oars ready, just in case." Heather gave Tolund a skeptical look. Both of them knew there would be no chance of escape if these beasts chose to attack.

All eyes were set upon the eerie lights. At first the shimmering form seemed to drift away from their boat, but all of the sudden, with a shudder and a quick turn, the light began to move rapidly toward them. Tolund could feel his heart beat faster. It was unnerving to see the effortless speed with which this thing moved. Even more disturbing was the way it seemed to double in size with each passing moment. Tolund felt Heather's hand grasp his own as she squeezed his hand tightly to ward off her fear.

Even as he broke into a cold sweat, Tolund had to marvel at the beauty of this horror. As it drew closer, the lights of white, green, and blue danced and raced all about its ghost-like form like falling stars in the night sky. It was moving directly under their boat, its size now dwarfing the craft, even with its seaweed wreath. Now the air burned with power and Tolund felt the hair on his head lift up in all directions. For an eternity the firewhip floated slowly beneath them. Heather fought back tears and struggled not to cry out in fear. Bravely, the terrified group managed to stay quiet and still.

To make matters worse, now the first bulbous giant was flanked by two more of its kind. The firewhip to the right of it was much smaller, only twice the size of their boat, while the one to the far left was even larger than the one beneath them. They had made no sound as they haunted the waters, but now Tolund looked all around as the sound of something breaking the surface could be heard. In every direction smooth vine-like tendrils slithered up from below. Writhing and searching, dozens of glowing whips sought out the edges of the seaweed clump about their boat. Heather stopped breathing for a moment when she saw that the touch of these coils was causing even the wet seaweed to bubble and smoke. A shiver went up her spine as she thought of what these things would do if they brushed up against bare skin.

For a long stretch of time the firewhip examined the seaweed tangle as if it could somehow see through the ruse. A few times the tendrils snaked dangerously close to the wooden boat. The scent of burning seaweed filled the night air. Tolund silently shifted his grip from his boat oar to the hilt of his longsword. The boy noticed that Lindris had also taken up her blades in anticipation of the behemoth's attack.

Fortunately, defense would not be necessary. Eventually, the macabre creature ceased its investigation and drew its lethal tendrils back down to the depths. Like living clouds beneath the water, the three spectral forms drifted slowly down and far away. Everyone in the tiny fishing boat let out an exhausted sigh of relief.

"It looks like we fooled them," smiled Mr. Pierce, still whispering cautiously.

"I've never felt so small and helpless," Lindris exclaimed. In the faint moonlight Tolund could see tears of relief streaming down her face.

"That thing could have dragged us down as if we were nothing," added Bex.

"That'll be enough of that talk," Mr. Pierce whispered sharply. "It's still a long way to shore and we'll need to paddle quietly the whole way. The last thing we want to do is invite those nightmares back for a second look!" Nodding in agreement the rattled party took up their oars again and made their way toward the dark island that now loomed closer than ever.

He was failing. He was failing in his pursuit and he knew this would mean death for many if the warlocks were able to escape with their horde of stolen smoothstones. Defiantly, the Lockslayer pressed on against the merciless rush of wind that hindered him. Eli also cursed the direction their path had taken for they were now on a straight course for Ansalion itself. So focused was he on what this might mean that he did not sense their approach in time.

With this unnatural wind at their backs, the dragons that bore the two stormcasters moved faster than the swiftest arrow. They were upon him like lightning. Two slashing cuts from their glowing, ethereal longswords sent Eli into a tumbling spin. Whatever these blades were, they knifed through his vaunted armor as if it didn't exist.

Righting himself and clutching his left leg and right side where the emerald ghost-blades cut deep, he summoned his own shield and sword. Eli spied the two dragons curving about for another pass. "This time they will be against this evil wind while I can use it to my advantage!" he thought to himself.

Suddenly, the winds shifted and swirled about him as the laughter of the stormcaster echoed and danced in their midst. "These winds are ours to command, Lockslayer," called a mocking voice. "Did you think our masters so foolish that they did not plan your ambush with care?" Before Eli could respond the winds now pushed at him from both the left and the right. In the blink of an eye their two attacks flashed by him so quickly that he could barely make out the forms of their dragons and glowing blades. Again, he struggled to stay aloft as two new 'cuts' seared into his soul from both sides.

"This burns just like Celnumus' mist-wraith!" he thought to himself. Before he could catch his breath the winds twisted again. One stream moved from above and another from his lower right. Instinctively, Eli slashed his sword directly above himself, in the direction of the new winds.

"Ahh!" cried out the stormlock in surprise as the Lockslayer's blade forced him to veer his dragon to the left to avoid the strike. Pain burned again from Eli's lower right as the second caster's sword found its mark. "It seems your legendary cunning is no idle boast, Lockslayer, but on this field you are a snail trying to outstrike a viper!"

Beneath his faceplate, Eli winced at the truth of this jackal's words. The wounds of his soul were draining his life with every heartbeat. He could not defend their attacks even if his shield were to meet their ghost-blades, which would simply pass through it unhindered. Worse still, their murderous winds and flashing speed made it impossible to land a single blow upon them. "Enough!" he growled to himself. "This game must change."

Diving straight down with his mighty wings beating fiercely, Eli landed upon the ground with a crash. He heard the stormcasters' shouts of triumph move across the windstorm about him. Quickly dismissing his shield and sword, he summoned his ruby arrow. The winds curved again to his left and right, heralding the casters' next attacks. Without hesitation Eli stabbed the ruby arrowhead into the ground directly below his own body. With heat and fury a massive fireball exploded from the arrowhead scorching the Lockslayer and everything about him. The last thing Eli remembered hearing was the roars of burning dragons and the high-pitched screams of the dying stormcasters.

With great effort the exhausted party brought their boat over the breaking waves and onto the sand dunes that prefaced the looming jungle. "We can catch a breather under the cover of this high dune," Mr. Pierce said cautiously. Tolund had to lean toward him to hear his lowered voice over the crashing surf.

"Why do we have to be so quiet?" the boy griped. "We're all alone and the sound of the waves will drown out everything else."

"Don't be so foolish," the old dwarf chided. "We are in a strange place steeped in curse and shadow. Every instinct I have demands caution. Mind this lesson well, Tolund Dellender: caution can be more important than a dozen swords and shields. When we delve into that jungle I want us to move so silently and so carefully that the trees themselves won't know we've passed by. Every footstep, every breath must be guarded. If you're right and we are alone here then our caution will have cost us nothing but a bit of time, but if you're wrong then silence may very well save our lives. Think of how the 'Frog Bleeders' moved through their forest home; they were like living ghosts that became a part of their surroundings. That is what we must become. Does everyone understand?" The young ones nodded to their trainingmaster as they sat and rested upon the sand.

After as much of a respite that he could risk, which was at least long enough for a short nap, Mr. Pierce ordered them to get up and advance into the jungle. He informed them that first light would not be long in coming so they would have to use the remaining darkness to their advantage. Lindris was ordered to take point with both swords at the ready. Bex followed her, then Tolund, then Heather, and, finally, Mr. Pierce himself. As their trainingmaster directed, they moved without words or sound.

Tolund surprised himself at how quietly he worked his way through the thick greenery. As his eyes adjusted to the blackness, he began to make out the tangle of trees, bushes, and high grasses all of which were interwoven with the endless jungle vines that creeped down from the higher treetops. The vines seemed to rule over everything— like thick webs that were determined to strangle and smother everything in sight. The lad longed to chop through them with his sword in order to make a clearer path, but he knew the noise from this would ruin their stealthy approach.

On they crept until the thunder of the surf had given way to the sound of the forest at night. Had Tolund been able to say so he would have praised his friends for their careful silence. "Even the Frog Bleeders would be impressed by this," he thought to himself. Suddenly, Lindris halted and held up one blade which signaled that the rest of them should halt as well. The slender girl leaned forward, craning her neck to one side in order to listen for something in the shadows ahead. Tension and fear gripped the young fighters. Tolund looked behind to see if Mr. Pierce shared their apprehension. The boy's heart stopped as he realized that their trainingmaster had disappeared! Before he had the chance to alert the others, Lindris' cry of alarm broke the silence as the jungle clearing before her suddenly burst forth with the charging forms of dozens of giant black crabs.

CHAPTER 15

THE DARK CIRCLE

Even for the great Lockslayer the pain of his fire storm was agonizing. His suffering was immediately eased by the sight of the charred remains of the two stormcasters and their dragons. Taking as little time as he could, Eli managed to soothe his burns with the magical salve provided for him by the High Clerics. He applied the medicine to wherever the flames scorched him past the protection of his armor. With his great physical strength he knew he would heal quickly as he continued his hunt. In only a matter of moments his burns were numbed and he was taking flight again in the direction of the fleeing warlock party.

The sorcerous winds that fought against him had not relented. Still, with his powerful brown wings, he took up the chase once more. It would be dawn before long. Eli silently cursed the drawn out pursuit for he knew that his enemies' presence anywhere near the great city could mean nothing good for those who lived within. After an hour of flight he was surprised once more when the winds that had held him at bay for so long suddenly ceased. The dread warrior slowed his flight for a moment trying to sense if another attack or trap was imminent. He sensed nothing. Wasting no time, Eli shifted his wings to his wings of speed and flashed through the sky in a furious rush.

Eventually, his trail moved up to the left, turning toward the foothills above the grassy plains. The Lockslayer now slowed his flight and called forth his battle-axe and shield. Directly ahead of him, at a solitary unassuming farm, the trail of the warlock party ended. His mystic senses alerted him to two things—a fading presence of an intense, restless evil and the pungent aroma of dead things.

Warily, Eli circled the small farm twice; first in a wide cautious arc and then in a tighter one. The blackened carcasses of the livestock littered the yard around the humble barn and cottage. Though black as if they'd been burned by fire, the bodies of the chickens, goats, cows, and horses were not consumed in any way. The Lockslayer settled to the ground for a closer look. His eyes had not betrayed him; the poor creatures had not been burned even though their remains were as dark as pitch. What slew them he could not determine, but he could tell that whatever killed them did so in the blink of an eye, before they had a chance to take even a single step. A greater stench of death was pouring out of the little stone and thatch barn.

With a stout kick he sent the wooden door splintering into the opposite wall. All was silent within. Leaping in, he held his weapons at the ready. Eli's gaze narrowed as he beheld the sight of what looked to be all of the stolen smoothstones set upon the dirt floor of the barn. He noticed that they were not dropped or scattered randomly, but set down in a deliberate circle, row upon row. Each of the smoothstones were now bleached and crumbling as if every last vestige of power had been leeched from them. Surrounding the circles of ruined smoothstones were the skeletons of the six warlocks who looked to have been the creators of this spell. All of them were still frozen in their kneeling position with heads bowed low. Their bones were oil-black and shiny as pitch. He also noticed that in the very center of the circle, where an opening was designed, there was a great charred spot, like a fire had burned there even though there was no evidence of ash or soot. A shudder ran up his spine as he realized where he'd seen this blasphemous mark upon bare ground before. "It is the same mark the Fallen Ones left upon the Boglands," he thought to himself. "It is the same sign they left when they dragged Celnumus to his death."

CHAPTER 16

THE JUNGLE

Tolund, caught completely by surprise, was stumbling backwards, trying to fend off the attacking crabs with his sword as best he could. Each crab was the size of a large dog or wolf. The loud clicking noises and snapping pincers of these monsters had him terrified and unnerved. It was even worse for his companions.

As if the size and ferocity of these giants weren't enough, Bex, Lindris, and Heather soon found that their thick shells were impervious to their weapons. Strike after strike all they were able to do was back the advancing crabs off for a second or two. Nothing they could do could hurt them. They also discovered, painfully, that the massive claws of these beasts were both strong and sharp. Each of the fighters soon had gashes and cuts where the claws or spiked shells of the black crabs had raked across their skin or snipped through their clothing. "Watch those claws," Lindris cried, "they can take off an arm or leg in one strike!"

"Quick, get up in the trees," ordered Bex. "It's our only chance!"

Following his advice, everyone began to make their way to the base of the nearest tree. Bex had been closest to one of the forest giants and had been the first to scramble up to the safety of its stout branches. He was relieved to see that Lindris and Heather had also found trees of their own and that Tolund had almost fought his way to the base of one. Suddenly, Bex's eyebrows lifted in surprise as he saw that a swipe from Tolund's sword had easily sliced into the crab that he was retreating from. "These beasts must be magical so Tolund's sword can affect them," he thought to himself. "The greatest blade there is in the hands of someone who doesn't know how to use it!"

Leaping down instantly, the burly lad sprinted in Tolund's direction. "Bex, what are you doing?" shouted Lindris.

Ignoring her, Bex rushed to Tolund's side with a kick that sent the other boy flying. As he slammed to the damp ground, Tolund's hand released his ebony sword. In one smooth motion, Bex took hold of the hilt and slashed a wicked cut right down the middle of the crab that was lunging at Tolund. With a sickening sound, the creature's thick body was cut in two. "You see, Dellender," Bex cried, "that's how you use an enchanted sword!"

"It's my sword, Bex," snapped Tolund, "give it back!" Before Bex could reply, a strange call rang out from ahead and the jungle all around them came alive with dozens more of the monstrous black crabs. As Tolund and Bex both scampered up into different trees to avoid this new wave of crabs, mocking laughter could be heard in the foliage straight ahead.

"Not a good time to be squabblin' now is it?" Emerging from the thick undergrowth, riding atop a huge crab that was three times the size of its brothers, was a cloaked savage. He wore armor crafted from the black shells of the crab swarm he commanded. He also carried a staff that bore one of the spiked crab claws at the top; eerie red embers floated out of this claw which faintly glowed red. "You come to our island lookin' for somethin? Hmm?" called his deep voice. "I'm thinkin' that all you be findin' is death!"

Heather was close enough to spy the darkened blood veins on his arms. Staring harder at his strange shell-armor, she realized that, somehow, it had been melted into his skin. On his arms, chest, and legs the edge of the shell just sunk into his scarred flesh. She shuddered at what kind of madman would do that to himself. "That has to be a beastcaster!" she shouted toward the others.

"Oh, not just another caster, Girl," the ghastly man smirked, "I'm the one that'll be cookin' the lot o' you in a big pot tonight. Though I may toss one o' you to my crabs. You see how hungry they can get?" The caster pointed with his staff to the remains of the crab that Bex had killed. All of them were horrified to see how the other crabs were piling atop the carcass, greedily ripping into it with their claws and stuffing the chunks of flesh into their mouths as fast as they could.

The beastcaster gave another shout. In a mad rush, his monsters surged around the tree trunks that held the young fighters. Skittering wildly upon one another and stacked four rows high, the giant crabs went to work with their pincers. In great gouging slashes all of the tree trunks were being torn to splinters. Even these mighty jungle trees began to sway under the onslaught.

"Jump to the next tree," shouted Tolund. "Use the vines if you have to!" Following his advice, Lindris took a running start upon a long limb and leapt safely to the branches of the next tree.

Seeing Heather's hesitation, Lindris called out to her, "You can do it, Heather! Just fix your eyes upon the next tree and move to that spot." Feeling the tree swaying even more, Heather knew she only had seconds before it fell. With a deep breath for courage, her thin form vaulted over the open air, high above the jungle floor.

She had intended to grab hold of a sturdy limb, but her fingers only brushed upon it. The terrified girl screamed as her body plummeted downward. Desperately, she clawed and scratched at anything to save herself. After a swift drop she managed to grasp a jungle creeper and hold tight. Her body spun around and slammed hard into the side of the next tree. Frantically, Heather scrambled to the nearest large limb and clung to it in a mad panic. Her hands and forearms were bloody from numerous scratches and scrapes, but she was safe for the moment.

Frustrated at his ignorant servants who were still attacking the now-empty tree, the beastcaster ordered his crabs to assault the trees that Lindris and Heather now sought refuge in. In seconds the wave of monsters poured over and around the trunks of these new trees and began to rend and rip at them furiously. Bex squared his jaw. He knew their avenues of escape, and their luck, would eventually run out and a grisly death would find them all. His eyes looked over the sleek black blade of Tolund's sword— the eerie power of this weapon stoked his confidence.

Scampering down to a lower limb, Bex leaped in a straight line for the gigantic crab that bore the beastcaster. It was the last thing the gloating savage expected. Unable to bridge the distance in one leap, Bex landed hard upon the shell of one of the swarming crabs. With a swift jab downward he skewered the crab. Then he moved forward cutting and slashing crabs to his left and right. Realizing the boy's aggressive path, the beastcaster pulled on the reins of his mount to force it to turn in Bex's direction.

So fast was the monster's swipe that Bex had no time to dodge the huge spiked claw. All he could do was try to parry it with Tolund's blade. Though the crab's forearm was the size of a large tree limb, the sword's keen magical edge cut through it like it was cutting through smoke. Using instincts born of hundreds of arena battles, Bex pressed his instant advantage and lopped off the creature's other claw with a swing of his muscled arms.

"Nooo!" bellowed the caster as he slashed Bex across the chest with his staff. Still grasping the sword, Bex caught himself from falling into the swarm of 'smaller' crabs below by clutching the staff-arm of the beastcaster. Luckily, the savage could not dislodge the boy because he too was struggling to maintain his balance with Bex's added weight threatening to pitch him off the great crab's flat back. It was the opening Bex needed.

One quick thrust of Tolund's sword pierced the invulnerable shell-breastplate of the caster. Any other weapon would have bounced off the mystical armor, but Tolund's gift went right through it. With a wide-eyed grunt the beastcaster spilled backward to the ground. Now that his hold over his servants was sundered, the horde of nightmares trembled in place for a moment, stunned and confused. Then, in a clicking, snapping frenzy, they smothered the corpse of their slain master and the wounded crab-giant and began to feed voraciously.

Bex, wisely, had jumped to one side as the crabs were dazed. Now that their own bestial nature was unleashed, he moved away from them as fast and as quietly as he could. A few of the creatures nearest him pursued him with snapping pincers only to be dispatched with just a few quick swipes of Tolund's sword. Again, the crabs nearest the dead ones, feasted upon their fallen brothers. Bex welcomed the distraction and also realized a way for all of them to escape this horde safely.

"All of you, listen up," he called to his friends. "I'll try and kill as many of these things as I can over here. As they move in this direction to feed upon their dead, you can all climb down and head in the opposite direction."

Tolund was furious with Bex even as he had to admire what he'd done to save all of them. It galled him to admit that Bex looked every bit like the muscle-bound hero, like the hero Tolund wished he could be. He wanted to order the older boy to give back his sword, but he knew that was foolishness until they were all safe. They all knew that Bex's plan was a sound one and that they had to act quickly before the mindless swarm renewed its hunt for them.

Bex's brawny arms swung the black blade in vicious arcs as he ran about the thick undergrowth. His friends could hear the grunts and heavy breathing of his efforts. Soon the jungle floor was littered with dead and wounded crabs who were now being devoured by mounds of their hungry brethren. Below each of their trees, Tolund, Heather, and Lindris could see wide openings where the crabs had skittered to the other side to feed. Moving as quickly and as quietly as possible, each of them managed to sneak away to the far side of the jungle clearing.

Far on the other side of the mass of feasting monsters, Bex, sweaty and exhausted, waved a tired arm at them. Not wanting to draw the attention of the swarm, all his friends could do was wave back. Now Bex pointed up toward the interior of the jungle. Lindris nodded and did the same. "He's going to press on and meet up with us once we're all clear of these beasts," she whispered to Tolund and Heather. "We need to hurry; both of you stay close to me."

Following Lindris' instructions, for she was an apprentice-level fighter after all, Tolund and Heather moved quietly through the tangled undergrowth. Tolund was furious. Not only had Bex stolen something that was priceless to him, but then he'd used it to show Tolund up. Now everyone knew that the sword was greater than its bearer, that Tolund lacked the nerve and skill to wield such a magnificent weapon. Tolund was also nervous. Bex was twice his size and stronger than most grown men. Tolund knew that he couldn't force Bex to give the sword back. As he moved on in the increasing light of the coming dawn the emotions were grinding inside of him. More than once, the boy wished that Mr. Pierce was still with them.

As they moved ahead the slope of the ground told them that they were moving uphill. To their left a high wall of thick foliage barred them from turning to meet up with Bex. With the rising of the sun, the air began to warm and all three fighters began to sweat from the close air of this jungle and the effort of their hiking. The sounds of birds in the canopy above and the buzzing of insects grew louder as the morning air grew warmer. Lindris led them on until they found a break in the tangled undergrowth.

Placing a finger over her closed lips, she gestured that silence was still necessary. Once they moved over to the right side of the undergrowth they spied a natural path that moved up the slope which, they assumed, must be the same path that Bex was using. Unsure of whether or not her old friend was in front of them or behind them, Lindris decided to keep marching upward. Just before the ground started to level out again they came upon a small spring to the right of their path. "I think we can rest here for a bit," she whispered. "We held to a brisk pace so I'd wager Bex hasn't passed this way yet. Besides, I can't see any boot prints in this mud so we probably made it here first."

Heather was relieved for the break and for the water. She immediately set to rinsing out her scratched up hands and the cuts she'd received from the crabs' pincers. Tolund stood by the path with a sour look on his face. He was holding on to Bex's discarded axe and still fuming. Noticing this, Lindris started toward him to try and talk to him when both of them heard movement on the trail below them. They could hear footsteps and heavy breathing. Nodding to one another, they took cover beside each side of the trail and readied their weapons.

Lindris breathed a sigh of relief when she saw her old friend Bex stumble into view. "Bex, we're up here," she called out in a quiet voice, still remembering Mr. Pierce's warnings about using stealth in this strange place. Just as Bex smiled and raised a hand to wave at her, Tolund's skinny body exploded from the bushes next to him and tackled the surprised boy.

"I want my sword back, Bex, now!" Tolund growled as he tumbled on top of the larger boy.

"Get off!" Bex shouted as he pushed him aside with little effort.

"You had no right to take it!" Tolund shouted. "Now, give it back!" Tolund charged toward him again.

"Oh, knock it off, you little runt!" Bex swatted Tolund down to the ground with just one swipe of a burly arm. Now, he pinned his smaller companion down with both arms as he sat on top of him. "I had every right, Dellender! If I hadn't taken over we'd have all been torn to shreds. Your sword was the only thing that could have saved us and you didn't have the backbone to use it."

Now angry and humiliated at being tossed about so easily by the older, stronger boy, Tolund was about to shout back when Bex dropped like a stone to the ground beside him. Scrambling to his feet, Tolund looked up to see that Lindris and Heather were also crumpled upon the trail just above him. Instantly the jungle around him came alive with a trio of dark-hued savages, savages bearing the same look as that of the beastcaster Bex had killed. Seeing his sword tucked in Bex's belt, Tolund lunged for its hilt. Something sharp stung his shoulder and his head spun and his sight went black.

CHAPTER 17

THE BEGINNING

Something in the center of the evil circle caught Eli's eye. Almost totally covered in ash, with only a partial corner of it showing, was an unspent smoothstone. "How is it that this one was untouched when all the others were drained for this ritual?" he thought to himself. The Lockslayer's fear was that one of the Fallen One's had indeed crossed over into Vedris by the sorcery of these mad warlocks— warlocks whose blind lust for power foolishly cost them their very lives. "Perhaps this remaining smoothstone will provide the key to what went on here."

Ignoring his own natural instinct to avoid this blasphemous circle, Eli stepped into its center and reached down for the unblemished smoothstone. Crack! The sound of bone striking bone filled the small barn. Strain as he might, even with his supernatural strength, Eli could not move a muscle. Only able to look forward, he saw that the three skeletons within his field of vision had clasped forearms and that their hollow eye sockets now burned with a red light with their heads pointed right at him. He also noticed that the unblemished smoothstone shone now with the same red light.

He silently cursed his own stupidity. He'd known better than to enter into the point of origin for such a vile summoning, but he'd dismissed his own instinctive warnings to satisfy his curiosity. "My enemy knew me well enough to bait the snare for me!" he thought. "Now I'm caught." With his great strength failing him, he tried to summon his wings and weapons hoping that they would break this dark spell. Nothing appeared. All the great Lockslayer could do was stare back at the glowing eyes of the warlocks' skeletons.

Even as his body fought to break free, Eli's mind raced. Whatever came through this portal had planned carefully. It knew that its liberators would become its first meal and that they would provide him with a bounty of smoothstones to feed upon. It also anticipated that its entrance into this world would not go unnoticed by Vedris' most relentless protector and it set the perfect trap. Now all he could do was silently fume and rage at his own foolishness.

Now, beneath him, the ground shifted and shuddered. Tremors shook the earth and a piercing wail rode the wind. Eli's unique gifts now sensed dark power being unleashed in the distance. Chills ran up and down his spine as the lands all about seemed to be screaming in fear. An evil presence greater than anything he'd ever encountered was crying out in hunger. Death was now stalking the world of Vedris.

Cleric Michaels awoke just before midnight. He awoke in a frightful start with his heart pounding and his body soaked in a cold sweat. It was the screaming that woke him. Throwing on his robe, he dashed out into the hallway. All was silent. Puzzled, he knocked upon Cleric Tyziri's door.

"Brother Warren?" answered the drowsy cleric. "What is it? What are you doing up at this hour?"

"Didn't you hear it?"

"Hear what?" Tyziri's eyes narrowed at his old friend's rattled tone.

"The screaming," answered Cleric Michaels as he fought to steady his breathing. "There was screaming coming from all directions, like the whole city was running in terror."

"Hmm, I heard no screaming…, but this is not to be taken lightly," replied Cleric Tyziri. "I will wake the council."

"And I will wake the young Captain. I only hope this was just a random nightmare," said Cleric Michaels.

"We'll know soon enough, I suppose," Tyziri said grimly.

Dressing quickly, Cleric Michaels grabbed his staff and sword and made his way out of the White Sanctuary and down the torchlit streets toward the protectorate barracks. Deep in the night the only souls stirring were the paladins patrolling the streets on foot. Nodding to each one that passed, the cleric was pleased to see that the city was quiet and well-guarded. Despite this, his soul still bristled with a sense of the lull before the thunderstorm. He quickened his pace.

As he moved, his mind shifted back and forth between comforting and fearful thoughts. He was trying to reassure himself that the well-trained paladin officers and protectorate soldiers stationed within the city were alert and ready for anything. Then he began to worry about the numerous innocents, many virtually helpless, who resided inside Ansalion's interior, all pressed in by high walls. Now he pushed those thoughts aside by reminding himself of how formidable the clerics and High clerics of the White Sanctuary were and of how they were now awake and vigilant due to his own warnings. But his courage dwindled again when he worried about the scheming rats hidden about the city—of the reapers, casters, and warlocks who sought to bring calamity and terror to Ansalion from within.

"Enough!" he whispered to himself. He knew that this was no time for doubt and wavering thoughts. Instinctively, he began to pray for a confidence and a clarity that he could not find in reason or logic. "You should know by now that the High King walks far beyond the lands of reason," he said to himself.

As he finally made his way to the block that housed the protectorate barracks, he was surprised to hear voices and the sound of hurried footsteps, horses' hooves, and the hisses of dragons. Protectorate soldiers and paladins were fully awake, armed, and in uniform, and preparing themselves for battle. No one looked surprised when Cleric Michaels strode forward.

"Good evening, Sir," called a protectorate horseman, "we were told to expect you."

"Really?" answered Cleric Michaels. "By whom?"

"By me," the firm voice of Captain Shaw spoke out from the entrance of the barracks. "I thought you'd be joining us soon. I figured that the screams had woken you too."

"We need to talk," said Cleric Michaels, "there isn't much time."

Excusing themselves to a lookout post on the rooftop the two men compared dreams. Captain Shaw, amidst the cries of terror, had seen the older cleric riding a copper-hued dragon up toward the mountains at full speed. He also remembered a swell of black water bubbling up from the lands below and flooding them as the dragon flew over.

The captain also shared that he was running before the walls of Ansalion where huge jars were lined up in neat rows. He saw the oily muck rising in the lands between the foothills and the city. Suddenly, in his dream, the great jars began to tip in the direction of the coming flood and each one poured a steady stream of clean water into the deluge. "I remember shuddering as the clean water mixed with the filth and then was corrupted by it. The jars were causing this black flood to rise and swell even more. I was trying to stop the other jars from tipping over and feeding the flood, but there were too many of them, falling too quickly."

"What does any of that mean?" the cleric asked nervously.

"I don't know."

Cleric Michaels spoke firmly, "The only thing I am sure about right now is that these dreams are important and that you and I have roles yet to play." Before Captain Shaw could respond the beasts all about Ansalion erupted. Dogs howled, horses started and neighed, birds took flight, and dragons roared. In the next second a cold wind rushed in from the foothills and the ground shook in a great tremor. Now a piercing wail echoed in the night, a demonic cry that froze the hearts of all who felt it.

"It's beginning," said Cleric Michaels.

CHAPTER 18

SERPENTS

Tolund awoke to something punching into his ribs. From his right he saw one of the savages jabbing him with the blunt edge of his spear. Now that the boy was awake the same savage went about jabbing the other captives out of their stupor. Tolund's groggy mind struggled to make sense of things.

His own hands were tied together at the wrists with crude ropes woven from jungle vines. He also saw that, running through the center of his bindings was a longer 'rope' that ran to each of his friends, tethering them all together. Looking about, Tolund saw that they were still in the same spot where they were ambushed. Heather, Lindris, and Bex were all bound up in front of him also fighting to regain their wits. Aside from the man who woke them, Tolund saw only two other captors standing guard on each side of them; one of them held a large sack made of animal hide which Tolund assumed held all of their captured weapons. The look of these men was not encouraging.

Obviously of the same tribe as the caster who commanded the horde of crabs, these appeared to be lower-ranking reapers. Tolund guessed this due to their similar skin color, clothing, and weapons;

he figured that they were only reapers because of the absence of the raised, unnatural blood veins that marked casters and warlocks. Oddly, none of the tall thin men spoke a single word to either their captives or to one another. Using only nods and hand gestures, these reapers directed the young fighters to stand and begin marching in a direction that led deeper into the thick jungle. Still dizzy from the drugged darts that felled them, the four friends shambled forward awkwardly.

After almost an hour of silent marching, Lindris ventured a whisper, "We've got to break free before we meet up with more of these—" Crack! The thick wooden shaft of a spear rapped across the back of Lindris' head. The savage who'd struck her pointed his speartip at her and mouthed a soundless warning. This was when Tolund noticed that the man had no tongue. The reaper's open mouth revealed the scarred stump of what used to be a tongue. Looking at the other two he surmised that their silence was because they also had had their tongues cut out. Heather gave Tolund a worried look. They both knew there would be no mercy from creatures who dealt with one another in such a cruel fashion.

Now Tolund gave a look of concern to Lindris. Even after her chastisement she still walked proudly and defiantly with her head upright. The boy was fascinated by how the older girl was so strong and still so elegant and beautiful. He stared at her as she walked for a few seconds more until Bex's bulky form obscured his view.

The four of them plodded on, following the lead of their captors. Lindris was first in line, followed by Bex, then Heather, and, finally, Tolund. One reaper walked in front of Lindris while the other two walked on either side of Bex. Tolund watched carefully as their eyes seem to dart back and forth between the jungle about them and Bex.

They seemed to view the wide-shouldered, muscled boy as their chief threat. Still furious with the thieving Bex, Tolund cared little of his plight at the moment. He was, however, enjoying the fact that his own slight frame warranted less attention from these savages.

Now the boy's mind raced. He realized what Lindris was saying before she was silenced so harshly. Their chances of escape were never going to be better than right now. With only three captors and the heavy cover of the jungle pressing in all around them, escape was a real possibility. However, if more of the barbarians were to arrive or their camp or village was reached a rush to freedom would become virtually impossible. Being at the end of the line gave Tolund the best opportunity to get away and, perhaps, find Mr. Pierce so they might come back to rescue the others.

Oddly, Tolund found himself thinking about the Frog Bleeders. He wondered how one of those crafty tribesmen would get out of this situation. Quickly, he formed a plan. As the small parade tramped through the forest it followed a winding path that led them with many twists and sharp turns. At these points Tolund, being at the back of the line and apparently not perceived as much of a threat, had a moment or so where he could not be seen by the guards walking ahead. He would not waste these moments. With each turn the boy set his strong teeth to one spot on the vine-rope that circled his right wrist. Tolund made sure to gnaw at a point that was beneath his hand so that when his captors did glance back at him they could not spy the fraying of his bonds.

It seemed to take forever. Although it was working and the vine was becoming more and more shredded by Tolund's frantic assault, the tough green fibers of the jungle creeper still refused to snap. Even worse, the ground was beginning to level out as if they were reaching a flat plateau; Tolund was sure this meant that their journey was nearing its end. It made sense that a village or camp would be established on more level ground. Also, the jungle began to give way to more open clearings— this meant less cover for the boy to escape into. His time was running out.

The party was moving in a straight line now. Presently, the savage with the hide sack over his shoulder circled back to inspect Heather and Tolund. Tolund fought to calm his nervous breathing as suspicious eyes glared at him. Heather, who had glanced back throughout the march and understood what Tolund was doing, tripped and stumbled to the ground on purpose. This brought the march to a sudden halt and all eyes upon her. The captor who'd been glaring at Tolund jumped over to her, pulled her up off of the ground by a fistful of her brown hair. As Heather let out a quick scream of pain the savage yanked her hair again drawing her close to the point of his spear. Now he turned her head forward and pointed his spear in the same direction. Heather nodded her head up and down as she blinked back tears. Apparently satisfied with her frightened response and the assertion of their power, the three barbarians resumed their march. After a while Heather stole a glance backwards in Tolund's direction. The boy mouthed the words, "Thank you" to his best friend. She gave a weary smile as both of them realized that her distraction had probably saved Tolund's plan from being discovered.

Now they were being led toward a giant of a tree. Tolund could see that the footpath moved around to the right of the tree's huge trunk. He strained at his bonds, hoping they might bend or stretch even a little. No luck. He could tell that only a few fibers remained, but they still would not surrender. The party curved around the jungle giant now. With his captors just out of sight, Tolund quickly bit at the last few strands. Success! His right hand was free and he used it to help slip his left hand out of the other loop and out of the tether that linked him to his friends. Like a rabbit the lad dashed into the thick foliage to his left.

Almost instantly he heard bodies crashing into the brush behind him. "Run, Tolund!" he heard Heather shout. "Two of them are right behind you! Keep going, keep ru—" something silenced Heather abruptly. Ignoring this, Tolund used his own impressive speed and sprinted ahead to freedom. Even if these reapers matched him in speed he knew that his head start and the smothering green of the jungle worked in his favor. Up ahead an island river moved lazily over the verdant forest floor. Tolund, still hearing his pursuers behind him, improvised a plan. Scooping up a large stone on the run, the lad heaved it as far to the right as he could manage into a deeper part of the river. A loud splash echoed in the jungle air. Now the boy dashed to the left and hid within a massive green bush. Following the sound of the splash in the water the two sleek warriors leaped over the waters and vaulted in the direction that they'd thought Tolund had gone. Allowing himself a wry smile, Tolund now crept like a Frog Bleeder into the cover of the forest on a path that moved safely away from the reapers.

Tolund did not stop until he was a long distance from where he'd pulled his river-trick. He waited and listened intently. Moments passed and there were no sounds of parting brush or stamping feet. More moments passed and he decided to risk a careful look. Scampering up a tree, still hidden by its broad leaves, he spied his friends far ahead. He saw the one man who had remained to guard his friends gestering and waving his arms at his two returning comrades. They seemed to be having a silent argument and all were furious. Now Tolund grinded his teeth in anger as he saw the angry reapers venting their frustration on his three friends by slapping and hitting them repeatedly. "You cowardly snakes! You'll get your due soon enough!" Tolund whispered to himself.

After their tantrum subsided, the three savages carefully inspected each of their captives' bonds. Now positioning each of themselves right next to a captive, they resumed their march with eyes darting all about for signs of Tolund or for signs of more resistance from the three they still held. Now Tolund slipped out of the tree and moved quickly in pursuit while still relying on the cover of the jungle.

He chided himself as he ran. His plan, which had seemed so clever while he was a prisoner, of finding Mr. Pierce and coming to the rescue of his friends seemed ridiculous now. The chance of stumbling across their leader on this strange island even without having to follow his friends was impossible enough. He dare not shout out for him and in this tangle of trees and brush Mr. Pierce could be twenty paces from him and pass by without either of them ever seeing the other. Tolund came quickly to the realization that the fate of his friends was in his hands and his hands alone.

For the better part of a day Tolund followed the procession from a safe distance. The boy took pride in his stealth and caution. Never once did the reapers mark his position. The afternoon was waning now and the shadows began to stretch and lengthen. Tolund was amazed at how much larger this island was than he'd thought when he'd looked at it from the ocean. The lad figured that they must be somewhere near the middle of the island. Just ahead lay the highest stone hilltop. Below that he could see that there was a wide opening or fissure smothered in thick green foliage that formed a tiny valley of some kind. It was here that his friends were being led. As the bright daylight lessened with the setting of the sun, Tolund could make out the shifting glow of campfires at the deepest point within this valley. "This must be their stronghold," he thought to himself.

Suddenly, as the captives were led to the beginning of this valley, they stopped and were greeted by two more savages. Again, these men did not speak, but gestured toward the interior of the valley forest. Tolund followed cautiously.

Moving in a wide arc to the left of where the others had entered the valley, Tolund made sure to use the forest and the deepening shadows to his advantage. He was confident that he entered the side of the valley undetected. Moving like a great cat, he slipped down a rocky slope and into the forest. The boy took great care in moving silently, remembering the advice Mr. Pierce had given earlier and the example of the Frog Bleeders. So it was that he made it to within a stone's throw of the campfires and the crude huts without anyone knowing he was there.

The jungle night had fallen now and everything was blanketed in thick shadow. The weak light of the crescent moon had not emerged yet. Everything worked to Tolund's favor at the moment. Carefully scaling a tree for a better vantage point, the boy got his first look at the enemy's village.

The village was located at the very back of the small valley. There seemed to be almost a half-cave where the stone fissure rose up to meet the rocky peak. Tolund tried to peer into the dark of that spot but could only make out shadow and the tops of the tall jungle trees that ran flush against the cliff wall. Before this grove of giant trees there were a number of domed huts; Tolund counted thirteen of these crude huts. More large trees were scattered amongst the huts and around these were cooking fires, scattered weapons, and numerous bones. It was too far away for Tolund to tell what kind of bones these were, but his instincts feared the worst.

Now the boy spied a new figure coming out to meet his friends and their captors. This was a giant of a man, tall and strong. Even beneath his animal-skin cloak Tolund could make out huge broad shoulders and thick-muscled arms. This man reminded him of the beastlock, Soma. Though not quite as massive as that monster, he was still far too large and fearsome-looking for Tolund's liking. Tolund was surprised to hear actual words come out of the large man's mouth. Though the boy couldn't make out the man's words from this distance, he could tell that his tone was angry. Suddenly the big warrior's fist shot out toward the reaper with the sack of weapons and the smaller man crumpled to the ground. Snatching the hide sack up, the large man turned and strode toward the center of the village. Leaving the chastised reaper on the ground as he spit blood and struggled to regain his wits, the last two reapers led the captives in the same direction.

Tolund's mind fought to come up with a plan to rescue his friends. Just then his concentration was shattered by a hissing sound on the branch right above him. In the silhouette of the starlit sky he made out the form of a large coiled serpent. Stifling the urge to scream, the startled boy leaped to the ground and rolled behind the wide trunk of the tree just in case the savages had heard something. Before Tolund could check to see if the guards had been alerted, another snake hissed from only a few feet to his right. Crawling quickly to his left he was halted by yet another coiled snake. The terrified boy froze, guessing that he'd disturbed a whole nest of serpents.

While he crouched in terror several more snakes slithered up to where he was now surrounded on all sides. The boy did not know what to do. Just as he was about to leap upward to the nearest tree branch, willing to take his chances with the snake in the tree, a loud dragging, sliding sound filled the night air. It sounded like something heavy was being dragged across the thick jungle grasses. Curving around a large tree to his right, emerged the impossible sight of a cloaked man riding atop the back of a dragon-sized serpent. The man bore a staff tipped with a huge serpent skull and the grasses all around the giant serpent was alive with the slithering of hundreds of its smaller brethren. Tolund held his breath.

The stout man on the serpent said nothing and merely pointed his staff in the direction of the village. Skittishly, Tolund stood up slowly and took nervous steps toward the collection of huts. Now the camp guards ran up with spears upraised. Even in his terror, Tolund's heart sank. He had come so far and was hoping that he could find a way to outwit these barbarians and free his friends. The hissing of the serpent-horde grew louder as the lad realized he was being herded by both the giant snake behind him and the swarm of snakes around him.

Quickly, he was captured by the guards. Though tongueless like their fellow reapers, they made their hatred for this impudent child known with numerous kicks to his back as he moved into the village. Just as they reached the light of the first campfire Tolund stole a look in the direction of the beastcaster who'd captured him. The caster had left his giant serpent at the edge of the village and was now on foot, still surrounded by his horde of faithful serpents. The man seemed smaller and stouter than his fellows. Suddenly he turned his head just enough for the firelight to shine upon his cloaked face. In an instant Tolund's mind reeled and his young heart was taken back to that horrible day in a far off swamp where his world shattered like glass. There, with half of his face in shadow and half illuminated by the firelight, was the grim visage of Trainingmaster Pierce.

The dwarf smiled beneath his beastcaster cloak, "Didn't I warn you about trusting too easily?"

CHAPTER 19

THE BEASTWITCH

Tolund was numb. Was betrayal all he could expect in his young life? Could no one be trusted?

Refusing to even look as his treacherous 'leader,' he started to lean forward to gain Heather's ear. This attempt was suddenly interrupted by the loud barking order of the huge savage that seemed to command these tribesmen. The camp grew silent in an instant. Two of their guards moved along the line of prisoners striking the back of their knees with the hafts of their spears until all of the captives were now kneeling on the hard-packed dirt of the village street. Tolund also noted, with disgust, that the beastcaster he had known as Mr. Pierce had voluntarily dropped to one knee and was bowing his hooded head reverently. Now, all of the natives in the village also dropped to their knees and bent low. The boy noticed a slight trembling from each nervous tribesman.

The large man spoke now in the common tongue, "Here now is de last power you will ever look upon, here now is de ancient glory of de greatest beastwitch since de dawning of our world, here now is

Mistress Kuvai!" After speaking, the tall savage also bent as low to the ground as he could in frightened submission.

From the shadowed hut directly in front of them she approached. As she emerged from its entrance the jungle all around them fell silent. No birds, frogs, or insects—indeed nothing living— dared to make a sound in the taut, strained silence. Every shadow seemed to grow darker and even the jungle breezes halted.

Tolund's eyes narrowed and his head tilted to his right in a fearful curiosity. The woman that approached must have been the oldest looking person he'd ever laid eyes upon. Gaunt, withered, and deeply wrinkled, she looked more like a breathing corpse than a living thing. All of her hair had fallen out, save for a few small patches, leaving a weathered bald scalp covered with numerous scars from a lifetime of dealing violence and death. The boy noticed scars all over her arms and legs as well. Even more puzzling was the way she moved. Though her appearance marked her as an ancient creature, her smooth gait was like that of a young strong woman. The closer she strode toward them the more he realized that she also moved like a beast of the jungle— like a lioness or a panther.

Now, almost upon them, the captives were astonished, yet again, by her native 'clothing.' In the shadowed firelight it first looked like the old woman was clad in a simple animal-hide dress like the rest of the women in this horrid village, but as she moved closer they saw that, instead of a piece of cloth covering her wrinkled skin, scales like that of a lizard or snake grew right out of her body. Before she spoke a long forked tongue flicked in and out of her mouth. "Who den might you be, bringing yourselves to de place where you become our food?" she asked in a hissing, croaking voice.

Cowered by the evil that surged out of this eerie old crone, the four young captives exchanged frightened glances. After a moment Bex, angry at his own fear, stood up to look the beastwitch in the eye. He gulped hard as he saw her eyebrows rise in bemusement and her round pupils narrow into the slitted eyes of a serpent.

"We," Bex stammered, trying to find his courage, "...we have come for the stolen people of the Coastland villages."

A hissing chuckle escaped her thin lips. The tribesmen around her grunted in shared amusement. "Have you now?" asked the beastwitch in a mocking tone. "De way I see it, all you cubs be bringing me is food for de cooking pot and new weapons for my reapers." Mistress Kuvai motioned toward the sack of captured weapons. Bex gave a glance to Tolund and then looked back at the sack. Tolund's brow furrowed as he guessed his comrade's covetous thoughts.

"Mmmm," smiled the beastwitch as she pulled Bex's heavy axe out with one scrawny hand as if it weighed less than a leaf or a twig. "We'll put dis one to good use. Dis will lop heads off quick and clean."

Now her hand began to withdraw the hilt of Tolund's sword. As the length of the ebony blade lifted from the sack, her unholy eyes widened in rage. "I know dis knife! All de orders know dis knife!" Kuvai's snake-tongue stretched out and licked the flat of the blade. She coughed violently at the taste and spat the ground in disgust. Instantly, her eyes squinted maliciously and her head snapped in the direction of the young prisoners. "Whose knife is dis?"

Tolund stiffened in fear and felt a shiver crawl up his spine. Mistress Kuvai's eyes smoldered as they glared at the frightened captives. Even her followers shuddered at the tension that filled the air. They knew all too well the sudden wrath that their mistress could inflict. Seeing nothing but fear before her, the old monster closed her eyes and took a deep breath. "Don't need to talk, Cubs," she sneered, "I find tings out on my own."

Now the beastwitch's nose softened like wax and darkened and curved to form a nose like that of a wolf without the long snout. Greedily, she sniffed the air near Bex. As she did this, Tolund caught a strange sight out of the corner of his eye. The traitorous Mr. Pierce was leaning over to Lindris where they both knelt. He seemed to be whispering something in her ear. "I wonder what that lying rat is up to now?" Tolund thought to himself.

Kuvai's interrogation continued. "You smell of its magic, but you are not de one," she scowled at Bex. "Perhaps dis other boy…" Now she moved toward Tolund. Just before she reached him, her sharp eyes noticed Heather's hands. "Hold on now," Reaching down, she examined Heather's melted hands with her own. Instinctively, the terrified girl trembled at the ancient monster's cold touch. The old witch's eyebrows rose in curiosity as she brushed Heather's hood back to inspect the child's scarred scalp and face. "You must be de Bonwell girl, de one dat survived de great Bloodworm. Your skull will make a great trophy for Mistress Kuvai, eh?" Poor Heather's eyes swam with frightened tears.

"Leave her alone!" Tolund growled, finally finding his courage at the sight of his terrified friend. "The sword is mine. I'm the one you want."

"Ahhh," smiled the beastwitch, "dat must make you de Dellender boy. Old Kuvai must have de Fallen Ones smiling up at her from de Abyss to have you come sneaking up to my island, all ready for de killing! My hut will be full of many great trophies after tonight!"

The pleased creature ran her palm over Tolund's head greedily like he was a prized goat about to be slaughtered. Suddenly, her nostrils constricted as a jungle breeze blew across her. Her wicked tongue whipped in and out of her mouth rapidly. "Wait!" she shouted as her head snapped in Mr. Pierce's direction, "you don't smell right! You are not K'shula!"

"Now!" bellowed Mr. Pierce as he jumped to his feet and held the serpent-staff up high. In a coiled strike the giant snake that Mr. Pierce commanded burst forward and engulfed Mistress Kuvai in its huge yellow and black jaws. The old witch gave a shrill wail of surprise as she disappeared inside the behemoth's gullet. At that same moment a horde of smaller serpents thrust up from the jungle grasses and assaulted the startled tribesmen.

The reapers near the captives went down flailing with their arms, legs, and bodies covered with slashing vipers. The large beastcaster who commanded the savages bolted back toward the middle of the village screaming orders to the remaining warriors.

Suddenly, the giant snake rose and stiffened with frantic hisses. Tearing and clawing her way out of its center, the enraged beastwitch screamed as she burst from the snake's body in a slashing frenzy. Unharmed and undaunted, she shook the snake's blood from her powerful body.

"The witch is mine!" shouted Mr. Pierce as he freed his fighters with his dagger. "You four get your weapons and find the villagers. Remember your training and do not hesitate because now you are fighting for your lives and theirs!" Now that he'd cut everyone's bonds, he tossed the serpent-staff to Lindris. "Do as I've told you, Lindris. Your new army should more than even the odds. You can do this!" The brave girl nodded confidently even as she felt the magic of the staff reach out to her mind, connecting her to all the serpents around her.

"Fighters," Lindris ordered, "arm yourselves and follow me." She tossed the weapons sack toward her friends. Ignoring this, Bex dashed up quickly and grabbed Tolund's sword from where the beastwitch had dropped it.

"Bex!" shouted an outraged Tolund, "you know that's mine. Give it back!"

"Sorry," the older boy smirked, "no time for good manners. Talk to me after we survive this." Turning his back on Tolund, the burly lad sprinted after Lindris who was pursuing the beastcaster into the village.

"Here, Tol," Heather called as she tossed Bex's axe at him. "You can fight with anything, and we have to keep up with them." Gripping the haft of the axe with angry white knuckles, Tolund scowled in disgust and charged with Heather into the fray.

Behind them, Mr. Pierce threw off the cloak he'd stolen from the beastcaster he'd ambushed earlier. "I hated the stink of that thing anyway," he quipped to himself. Now he drew his own fabled axe from its backsheath. His own trial was about to begin.

With a sickening thump the giant snake had fallen to the dirt. Even in its death-throes the brute was devastating for its twisting coils were thrashing the nearby huts, sending debris flying in all directions. In the midst of this the beastwitch stalked forward with murderous hate burning in her eyes. "I don't know you, little dwarf," she snarled, "but I will be tasting your blood tonight!"

With frightening speed, Mistress Kuvai's body writhed and shook and shifted as dark sorcery, honed over three centuries, molded her shape. Swelling in size, her form was now as large as the monstrous serpent that she'd just slain. Her lower half turned to thick green scales as four clawed legs, like those of a giant landdragon, twisted outward. Down her back, along the bottom of her spine, she grew a tail the size of a thick tree that sprouted razored spikes at its end. The witch's torso and chest hardened into the red shell of a huge insect. Finally, her arms, now long and sinewy, melted into her most lethal weapons. On her left arm her aged fingers separated in the middle and sculpted themselves into a gigantic red scorpion pincer with cruel spines along the inner edges to grasp and hold her prey. Her right fingers drew together and folded and formed into a giant venom-laced scorpion tail— the bulbous end swelled with milky poison which dripped from the barbed stinger at its point. Long black hairs pushed out from her new insect limbs. "Are you ready for de dance, little dwarf?" she sneered.

Pierce's only reply was a roaring shout as he hurtled his axe up toward Kuvai, putting all of his weight and strength of his muscled arms into the throw. His ferocity and direct assault took the beastwitch by surprise. There was a cracking sound as his axe bounced off of the insect shell that protected the center of her chest and fell to the dirt.

"Heh," she laughed, "a bold strike, but my armor is too great for a speck like you to get through." Even as she mocked his attack, the witch's giant pincer shot toward him, but the wily dwarf had rolled to one side as soon as his axe left his hands.

"I had to try," laughed the dwarf as he dashed for cover of ruined huts and downed trees. The quick taloned legs of the beastwitch clawed the dirt in a rush of dust as she bolted after her prey.

The four young arena fighters sprinted after the fleeing beastcaster. Slithering behind them came the horde of serpents now commanded by Lindris. "Hold up!" the girl snapped. "We have to let the snakes catch up; we won't have a chance without them. And, you…" she gave Bex a hard stare, "you give Tolund his sword back!"

"Why?" sneered Bex. "We already know that it's too much weapon for him."

An angry Heather now chimed in, "It doesn't matter what you think, Bex! The sword was meant for Tolund, not you."

"I don't need them to speak for me," Tolund said firmly as he stepped up to Bex defiantly. "Now, give it back or we'll cross blades over it!" As the smaller boy threw out this challenge he raised Bex's own axe up in a fighting stance.

The larger boy's lips clenched into a tight line as he looked first at Tolund and then at the angry faces of the two girls. A harsh sigh of exasperation blew from his nostrils, "Fine! But we all know that this is a mistake. I only hope it isn't a fatal one." With one brawny arm Bex easily ripped the axe from Tolund's hands. Now, with the other arm, he stuck the ebony sword into the dirt. Without another word, he turned and stalked in the direction of their quarry.

Tolund pulled his blade from the ground and held it up with both hands. "Thanks for that," he smiled as he nodded to both girls.

"What Bex said may have made a lot of sense," Lindris replied, "but something can make sense and still be wrong. This is your sword, no one else's." Before Tolund could respond, the grasses and dust all around them came alive with the writhing forms of hundreds of snakes.

"Our army's arrived," smiled Lindris as she held up one of her own swords along with the serpent-staff. "Let's get this job done."

At an urgent march they followed the fuming Bex on the path towards the interior of the foul village. The last of the fleeing women and children were making their way out of the village through side paths that led out to the deep jungle that bordered their huts. Tolund was certain that it was the multitude of serpents that terrified them most, but he also surmised that they must have been in shock from being invaded in their very own stronghold. Over the long ages, he was sure that no one had ever dared to come looking for this deadly beastlock tribe. The design of their village neglected the very idea of defense for there were no walls or barriers to repel attackers. So arrogant were they in their dark power that the thought of anyone ever seeking them out, let alone invading them, seemed absolutely impossible. The four fighters moved through the empty huts without incident for no ambush or defense had been rallied to stop them. Moving past the last row of skull-lined huts, they discovered why.

The savages' defense was before them. Tolund figured that almost two dozen warriors were holding the line behind a fence of sharpened wooden poles that prefaced a small tunnel behind them. The beastcaster stood behind his men, also barring entry to this dark tunnel. These reapers were armed with razored swords cut crudely from a black glassy stone found on the island; a remnant of the great fires that formed this small island long, long ago. They also bore shields made of the giant ebony crab shells and adorned with the grinning skulls of people they'd slain over the years. Determined and ready to fight, they awaited their brutal master's command.

The four fighters lined up side-by-side with one another with Bex and Lindris at each end and Tolund and Heather in the middle. Tolund was nervous for himself, but he was even more anxious for Heather who was even less experienced at true warfare than he was. Before he could give her a word of encouragement the beastcaster howled like a mad dog and his ruthless warriors charged.

This all seemed like a great game to Mr. Pierce. Even though it was taking all of his skill and cunning to stay just ahead of her slashing claw and lethal stinger, a savage smile spread across his face. "Hah!" he exclaimed as he slipped between huts to escape her last attack.

The beastwitch's frenzied pursuit had decimated most of her village. Huts were crushed and trampled, trees were splintered, and one of the disturbed cooking fires had ignited the debris and now a large wildfire was burning out of control. All of this served Mr. Pierce's strategy perfectly. Using anything before him as cover, he moved like a cat over, under, and around things. His only remaining weapon was his dagger, which he held in his right hand as he weaved and scurried to stay ahead of the behemoth that was always just behind him.

"Yesss!" hissed Mistress Kuvai as she saw the dwarf stumble over an upended cooking pot that slipped underneath his boot as he tried to use it to vault over a mangled hut. Her cruel pincer shot toward his left leg and managed to snag the side of his boot. Instantly her poisonous stinger snapped forward, moving like an arrow toward Mr. Pierce's chest. SKREET! The point of the stinger scraped off of the iron cooking pot as the dwarf deflected her strike with the only shield at hand. SKRIT! Another stab of the stinger was warded off.

Infuriated, the witch-monster latched onto the cooking pot with her clawed foreleg and crumpled the black iron like it was made of wet clay. "Aiee!" she shrieked in pain as the crafty Mr. Pierce thrust his dagger deep into the foot of her other foreleg. The beastwitch's massive pincer thrashed the dwarf aside, its spines drawing blood as it sent his body flying into the jungle brush. Kuvai spat evil curses in an unknown language as she used her pincer to wrench out the dagger.

Mistress Kuvai could hear the dwarf's mocking laughter as he moved deeper into the thick foliage. With a murderous roar she rushed into the wide thicket after him, "All your weapons are gone now. De jungle won't hide you from me!" The instant reply to her threat was a sharp pain across her eyes and face as a tree branch slapped into her like a bullwhip.

"I'm the only weapon I ever need!" barked Mr. Pierce. True to his word, he'd led her into the heavy foliage and drew back a stout branch like a bowstring. The beastwitch's huge form was easily marked and a simple target for his improvised trap to hit. Fighting off the stinging pain, Kuvai shook her head and blinked her eyes furiously.

Making full use of the brief respite, Mr. Pierce wound back stealthily in the direction of the ruined village. In just a few quick moments the wily dwarf heard the witch-beast take up the chase again, following his exact path back toward the village.

Reaching the fiery ruins of her own hut, Mistress Kuvai rose up to her full height to spy out her elusive prey. The trees and brush around her roared and snapped as did the burning remains of the village. She scowled in anger as she saw that the blaze was engulfing the rest of her village and spreading into the surrounding forest.

"Looks like we've made a bit of a mess, eh, Witch?" sounded the mocking voice of Mr. Pierce.

"Brush and sticks are nothing," she snapped back. The beast-witch's hateful eyes shifted back and forth furiously, trying to find her quarry. "I'll use your blood and de blood of your cubs to douse dese fires!"

Suddenly she charged at the last tangle of debris that wasn't ablaze, knowing that this was the only nearby place that the dwarf could safely hide. With her powerful forelegs and her one great claw she shredded his hiding place while her poisonous barb was poised and ready to spear the dwarf the second she uncovered him.

"Ha-hah!" Mr. Pierce laughed from behind the witch as he launched a burning branch that hit her between her huge shoulder blades.

"Very clever," she seethed, "using de fire as cover. You are a most clever dwarf."

"Oh, I'm like no dwarf you've ever met!" he bellowed. Mistress Kuvai's head snapped back to her right in frustration for the place where he called out now was not the place he'd attacked from a second ago.

The old witch was furious. She could not see or smell him out due to the heavy smoke in the air and it was difficult to hear his footsteps over the snapping of the flames. Her prey was proving to be an expert at concealing himself.

"Hmm," she grinned malevolently, "you'll find dat old Kuvai is clever too." Holding herself in place amidst the rubble, the ancient beastwitch lowered her head and grimaced. Instantly her head began to twitch and thrash about. Her eyes were shut tight and she hissed in pain with spittle shooting out between her clenched teeth. Even as he moved to his next hiding spot Mr. Pierce's heart chilled at her dark power. In just a few moments her head shot upright again.

Mr. Pierce gasped at her new visage. "De Fallen Ones teach us many tricks, clever Dwarf!" she howled. Where once she had two human eyes she now had many eyes. They were round, black as coal, and of different sizes. They were scattered all about her face and head, both in front, to the sides, and in back. "I see de hearts of things now. I see like de dread hunters of de Abyss." Mr. Pierce did not know what she meant by this last boast, but his instincts told him that the endgame was upon them. He winced in pain as he prepared his last gambit.

The beastwitch's world was a different sight now. Instead of the bright firelight against the black of night, now the flames were a dull grey in color and the night sky a darker veil of grey. The ground, rocks, tree trunks, and other solid things were a solid black. Now, to Kuvai's delight, only one color stood out. Marking him clearer than the moon itself, the beating heart of the dwarf now shone forth in glowing, pulsating crimson. His time of hiding had come to an end.

With a great roar she charged in a straight line toward her prey. The dwarf had crouched low behind a small boulder, matching its shape perfectly to avoid detection. Oddly, as she thundered forward with her pincer snapping and her stinger raised, he did not try to run. He did not move until she was a mere seven feet from him.

Smoothly, he jumped to his feet and brought his right hand around in one swift motion. Suddenly, over the sounds of the wind and the wildfire, the nightmarish screams of the beastwitch echoed across the cursed valley. Mistress Kuvai thrashed her head about in agony, trying to dislodge the white-hot coals and cinders that now blanketed her face. Several of her demonic eyes were seared shut by Mr. Pierce's shocking attack. Her pain was so great that she was trying desperately to shapeshift her hands back into their human form so she could wipe the fire from her face. The vengeful dwarf did not hesitate.

As her gigantic form rolled and writhed upon the ground he picked up his fallen axe and stood proudly. As planned, he had led her all the way back to where his axe had landed after its first strike. With his right hand still blistering from the coals he'd just grasped and flung, he joined it with his left hand and, ignoring the intense pain, gripped the haft of the axe tightly.

"I am Volindor Pierce," he shouted, "and I am your death!" In one savage strike he brought the heavy axe down upon her heart with all of his weight and strength, right upon the spot where he'd already cracked her armored shell. This time the crescent blade sunk deep to the axe haft. With her heart pierced, Kuvai's monstrous form shuddered in her death-throes as she screeched and screamed. With her last desperate breath she swiped at the dwarf with her poisonous barb, but her foe was too wily and ducked under it safely. Grimly, Mr. Pierce slashed the axe down once more upon her skull, "That was for the innocents of the Coastlands and all of your victims over the ages!" In one gurgling hiss the ancient evil of Kuvai breathed its last.

CHAPTER 20

FREEDOM

Tolund didn't want to admit it, but his training and prowess were not the reason he was still alive. At the first rush of the enemy it was all he and his fellow arena fighters could do to stave off the jagged glass blades of the savages. All four of them, even Bex with his great strength, were forced back by the ferocity and greater numbers of the reapers. The only things that saved them were also the things that terrified them.

Without even a word from their new 'master,' the serpents exploded out of the grass and dust to instinctively protect the bearer of the beastcaster's staff. All around him Tolund jumped at the sight of coiled snakes of all sizes striking to their full length at the horrified tribesmen. More than half of the attackers fell to the ground in agony with numerous snakes latched on to their legs. The poison of those deadly fangs worked quickly.

In mere moments the tribesmen were in full retreat to the wooden barricade. Lindris ordered her serpents to pursue the enemy and to protect her three friends who followed close behind. To their dismay, the reapers had regrouped in a defensive position at the scathing commands of their beastcaster lord who barked those orders from the other side of the great fence.

The surviving nine warriors were determined to hold the line as much out of fear from the serpents as the terror of failing their ruthless overlord. Driving their shields into the ground side-by-side, they created a makeshift wall to fend off the snakes. Now, they frantically hacked and slashed at the snakes before they could slither past the shield-barrier to strike at them. Soon, there were dozens of serpent carcasses covering the dusty ground. Even so, four of the tribesmen had died under the fangs of snakes that had been too fast for their blades. Lindris scowled at the sight of her newfound 'army' being thwarted. With a shout she charged in. Following her lead, her three companions joined in the final assault.

Tolund vaulted over the shield-wall and closed in on the nearest savage. Though thin and wiry, he was a tall warrior with good reach and more than ready to fight to the death. In furious swipes the two clashed blade-to-blade. Tolund's training moved his sword instinctively. Slash after vicious slash, the warrior's blade could not penetrate the boy's defenses, but the sheer strength of the larger man was too great for Tolund. Adding greater weight to each strike, the savage was able to force the boy back. In one grunting slash the reaper pushed Tolund back over the shield-wall and onto the dirt.

Frantic speed saved Tolund's life. In the very second that he landed hard upon the ground he rolled to his left anticipating the reaper's next strike. The blow, intended for the center of the boy's chest, stabbed into the dirt. Quickly, he was up on his feet to block the next slash which was leveled at his head. However, so strong was the cut that although Tolund's ebony sword blocked the savage's stone blade, the top edge pressed his own blade back hard enough to clip the lad's scalp. Pain screamed at Tolund just above his right ear as he stepped back to better defend himself.

Anger overcame fear as his scalp burned and he felt his own blood streaming down the side of his neck. Tolund went on the attack. With his feather-light sword leading the way, he loosed a flurry of aggressive strikes at the savage. The tribesman was unimpressed and defended the lad's barrage easily. In a brief moment the two now circled each other, trying to catch their breath. In a flash of insight honed by countless arena sessions, Tolund realized that his attacks were too centered. He'd been trained to aim for his opponent's crest which hung in the center of the chest. The savage seemed to have no trouble blocking these attacks. Tolund moved in with another strategy in mind.

As Tolund's magical sword was lighter and, therefore, faster to the mark than the heavier glassy stone weapon of the reaper, he could put the reaper on the defensive. With a high-to-low cut, Tolund forced his enemy to block with his forearm angled upward. Instantly, the gleaming black edge of the lad's sword curved in a half-slash into that forearm. With a grunt of pain the reaper dropped his sword.

Desperately the warrior reached down to retrieve his blade. Erupting from the dust, a brown-speckled sand viper latched its fangs into the reaper's already bloodied arm. The savage cried out and stumbled in the direction of his burning village, trying frantically to pull the snake from his arm with his other hand. Before the viper's hold could be broken, the savage's body crumpled to the jungle grass and stopped moving.

Before Tolund could think about his victory he heard Heather cry out from behind him. Wheeling about, he could see that she was desperate. Lying flat on the ground with her spear held up across her, she was blocking the sword cuts of her ruthless attacker with the haft of her spear. The enchanted wood of her spear was not buckling, or even splintering, but her meager strength was being overwhelmed. Knocking the spear from her hands with an upward stroke, the cruel reaper coiled for the fatal strike.

Tolund saw red and attacked. In a straight lunge, using both of his arms, he buried half of his magic blade into the side of the large tribesman. With widened eyes the savage grunted only once and fell to the dust. Grasping Heather's hand, Tolund pulled her up and away from the dying reaper. After a few gasping breaths the man ceased to move. Not since the Nidolzyn hunter from the Wastelands long ago had Tolund directly taken the life of another— this time, though still troubled by the act, the boy gritted his teeth and kept his wits about him. Defending his friend felt right to him, even more than defending himself.

Now, back-to-back, Heather and Tolund held their weapons up and surveyed the area. Bex and Lindris had each dispatched a reaper, but the serpents had won the battle. The nine tribesmen who had held the line before the great fence all lay dead upon the ground. Over the heavy breathing of the young fighters and the roar of the village fire behind them they all heard the wild laughter and heavy steps of the beastcaster as he retreated back into the tunnel. "De battle is not done yet!" he taunted.

"No, it is not," answered the bellow of Mr. Pierce who was arriving from the direction of the ruined village, "of that you can be sure!"

With a quick glance the dwarf surmised that none of his charges had taken serious wounds. "Form on me, Fighters. We cannot let him get away. Lindris, order the serpents back. If I'm right, that blackguard is leading us to the captive villagers and we don't need an army of vipers around hostages. Are all of you ready?" The steely looks from his fighters gave him his answer. "Good, then follow me!"

At Mr. Pierce's urgent command, and with him leading the way, they all sprinted down the dark tunnel. Emerging from the end of it they were met by torchlight and the grinning beastcaster. "I guess de celebration will be starting early, won't it?"

The large savage stood tall before them about ten strides back from where the tunnel ended. Behind him, up against the back of the rocky chamber was a monstrous grey egg. Small dark cracks streaked along its surface and a foul black mist curled up from each one.

"You're hatching a dragon?" questioned Mr. Pierce.

"Aye," smirked the beastcaster. "And guess what its first meal is going to be?" The brute gestured to two large pits on the far left and far right of the chamber, each one covered with thick wooden bars. Tolund saw Mr. Pierce tense up and grip his axe tighter as the moans of the prisoners could be heard.

"The stolen villagers?"

"Hah!" grunted the caster, "Dey will serve a great purpose for dere worthless lives!"

Mr. Pierce held his axe up in his right hand, pointing it directly at the beastcaster, "Tonight's the night they go free! Your beastwitch is dead, your reapers are dead, and you're all alone." The dwarf's tone was threatening and final.

"Am I?" In a swift motion the beastcaster wheeled about and smashed the flat of his stone blade upon the center of the dragon egg. The huge shell began to split apart and the creature within, easily the size of a large oxen, moved and hissed furiously while more black steam poured out of the widening cracks.

"No!" cried Mr. Pierce as he hurled his axe at the vile savage. Down went the beastcaster with the dwarf's axe lodged in his left shoulder. Without hesitation Mr. Pierce bolted toward him to finish the job. "Fighters," he called out as he charged, "kill that hatchling before it frees itself or we are all dead!"

After a quick inward breath to steady herself, Lindris dashed forward, "Come on!"

Her companions followed with Bex right alongside her and Tolund and Heather a few strides behind them. They were halfway across the chamber when the new dragon's snout smashed through the thick shell of its egg and its screeching head emerged.

Though its body was still struggling to free itself, the long neck curled toward them and the black fangs of the ebony hatchling were bared at the advancing fighters.

"It's too late!" warned Mr. Pierce who was now grappling with the giant beastcaster.

"Run! Get back up the tunnel!"

Before a single step could be made in retreat, the shrieking hatchling spewed a deadly stream of black mist in the direction of the young fighters. Even as he threw himself upon the ground to avoid the dragon's breath, Tolund realized that this was the same mist that he'd seen steaming off of the Tailor's ebony dragon, Descent, long ago.

Tolund was lucky. Only some of the clinging spray had touched him. Even so, his head began to spin and his stomach twisted. He was trying to push himself up to his feet so he could get himself and Heather up the tunnel and out to safety. Now he heard screaming.

Stumbling to his feet, he saw poor Lindris rolling around the dirt and clutching her head with both hands. Her anguished screams terrified him. Suddenly, from his left side, two strong hands clamped hard upon his neck. Bex, with madness in his eyes, began throttling him and spouting crazed nonsense, "Fire! Blood! Arrows! Worms! Lightning! Worms, worms, worms!" The words flew from the boy's foaming mouth while his head twitched back and forth furiously.

Tolund was desperate. As best he could, he was trying to pry Bex's grip from his throat, but the larger boy, already renowned for his brawny strength, seemed even more powerful in this madness. Tolund could not move those iron fingers from around his neck.

"Rip, snap, rip!" shouted Bex who, it seemed, was trying to separate Tolund's head from his body. Now Tolund's air was completely cut off and his vision started to blur. A loud crack sounded. Bex's murderous grip relaxed a bit. Again the crack sounded— from far away Tolund heard Heather's voice shouting something in a stern tone. Bex's hands fell away from the boy's throat. Tolund collapsed, gasping and coughing for breath. He heard another crack and saw Bex's body slam to the ground next to him. Now someone was shaking him.

"Tol, are you all right?!?" Heather shouted in concern. As his breath returned and his vision cleared, he saw the soft brown eyes of his best friend. He realized that Heather had cracked Bex upon the head with her spear until he let Tolund go. Her eyes, face, and even her scars looked lovely to him at this moment. "Are you all right?" she repeated.

"I'm fine, I..." he coughed again, fighting to steady himself. "I just...I just need to get my breath back," he mumbled.

"We don't have time for that!" Heather barked. "The sounds of cracking shell and dragon hisses echoed around them, confirming her words. Tolund shook his head firmly to clear his vision. He saw that the beast had worked one of its shiny black wings out of the egg and was thrashing about furiously to free the rest of its body. Tolund instantly realized what he had to do.

"This will be my only chance to kill it!" he shouted to Heather. "You need to get out of here! Run up the tunnel and just keep running!" Tolund lifted himself to a crouch and gripped his sword.

"But..." Heather began to protest.

"Just go!" Tolund ordered. "Now!"

With a conflicted heart, Heather stumbled back in the direction of the tunnel. Tolund dashed in the other direction, toward the dragon. Once again, the lad's quick feet saved his life.

The hatchling heard Tolund's footsteps upon the dusty ground and reacted instinctively. Curling its long neck in the charging boy's direction, it took a deep breath to gather its vile fog from its lungs. Just as the sprinting boy was upon it, it spewed forth a thick stream of the demonic mist. With both hands firm upon the hilt of his sword,

Tolund felt the blade drive deep into the hatchling's leathery chest. He heard a high, piercing screech and the left side of his face went black, wet, and numb.

Tolund was thrashing about in a whirlwind. His body seemed to fly and then tumble.

His skin seemed to burn white-hot and then freeze solid. He could hear voices shouting from far, far away, but he could not make out what they were saying. The last thing he remembered was attacking some shadowy figure in front of him and then the sight of thick, bony knuckles. Everything went black.

CHAPTER 21

STRANGE TRAVELS

Tolund felt a light touch upon his brow. Gentle hands moved the hair from his forehead. Heather's voice seemed to call him from a distance. Now it echoed closer and clearer and he could make out the words.

"You're going to be all right, Tol," Heather's soft words beckoned. "Just take deep breaths. Everything's all right now, everyone's safe."

Rising up on one arm, with his head still spinning, Tolund saw that his friend's words were true. He was lying on the thick green grass of a meadow that was just before the entrance of the beastwitch's village. All about him rested the liberated captives from Ibago and Berbago. With every deep breath the boy was pleased to feel the threads of the dragon's madness clear away a little more. Soon he could focus more on the sights around him.

Most of the freed captives were comforting one another and weeping tears of relief and joy. Even though they seemed to ignore his presence, Tolund still felt awkward and out of place among their emotional outpouring. The boy was relieved to notice that they all looked to be in good health. Tolund would learn later that their captors had kept them well-fed so they could better serve the hatchling's appetite. Still, having come so close to a horrible death and having to endure the nightmares of captivity and helplessness forced upon them, it was more than understandable that they clung to one another in the face of this new dawn.

Tolund could not help but be moved by this moment and he noticed that Heather, Bex, and Lindris were no different. All of the young fighters blinked back tears of emotion. Heather took it all in and just wiped her happy tears away with her sleeve. Bex and Lindris, trying to carry on like older, stoic warriors, fixed their eyes on other things and feigned disinterest. Tolund told himself to never forget this moment— to never forget the value of freedom, family, and life as he read it in the joyous faces of the rescued people. It was a scene that he wanted to hold in his heart and mind forever.

Tolund's musings were gently interrupted by a question from Lindris, "When do you think Mr. Pierce will be back?"

"Where did he go?" asked a curious Tolund.

"Ah, that's right," the older girl answered, "you weren't awake when they left."

"Mr. Pierce and the two chiefs went to oversee the final ruin of the village," Heather interjected. "They wanted to make sure that no other threats were hidden in this valley. The fire that the beastwitch started burned the village to the ground, but they had to be certain that no other tunnels or hiding places held weapons or any other monsters."

"He said that we could not leave until he was sure that this tribe's fangs had been removed," added Bex. Oddly, Tolund noticed that Bex would not look him in the eye when he spoke.

Satisfied with his friend's explanation of things, Tolund rose to his feet with a groan. His head ached and the left side of his face felt bruised and swollen. As he carefully rubbed his hurting face he heard Lindris let out a small laugh. "Pretty strong for an old dwarf, isn't he? You lost your mind when that dragon breathed its mist on you. Mr. Pierce dropped you with one blow to keep you from hurting anyone, or yourself."

"I suppose I should thank him," Tolund quipped, "but part of me wants to hit him back."

"Good luck with that," Lindris laughed, "even with Bex on our side, I'm pretty sure the old brute could out-brawl all of us." All of the friends joined in Lindris' amusement and Tolund was relieved to hear them all laughing after what they'd just been through.

"How's your throat?" Bex asked timidly. Tolund now realized that his throat and neck were also sore from Bex's mad attempt at strangling him. He also noticed the tone of remorse in the older boy's question. As a fellow victim of the dragon's mind-twisting breath, Tolund knew that Bex did not mean to attack him.

"It hurts a bit," he said with a smile to Bex. "I wish you weren't so strong."

"Hmm," grunted the older boy as he looked down at his own feet. It seemed that Bex was struggling with his own thoughts as he hesitated to speak. After a few heavy breaths the stout lad spoke again, "I guess I'm sorry for more than just the dragon-madness, Dellender. Now that I've had a chance to think about it, I've realized that it was wrong of me to take your sword like that. It wasn't mine to covet under any circumstances."

Tolund's only reply was the lifting of his eyebrows in mild surprise. Bex continued, "I mean, I still think it's probably too much weapon for you right now, but maybe that's my father talking. In any case, I'm no thief and I never should have done that to you. I really am sorry and I promise that it will never happen again."

For a moment Tolund stared hard at Bex, trying to determine if his words were heartfelt and genuine. Hoping that they were, Tolund decided to take the boy at his word. Offering his hand, Tolund gave Bex a firm handshake. "It's better off this way for both of us," Tolund smiled, "your axe is too heavy for me anyway."

With a new understanding between them, the mood seemed to lift immediately. However, as Tolund turned to walk toward Heather, he had the nagging feeling that Bex was still staring at the sword sheathed upon Tolund's back. "Real trust must be as scarce as Mr. Pierce warned," the boy thought to himself.

After an uneventful night of rest the chiefs ordered their people to move out. The sun would be rising soon which would give them the best chance to reach the boats along the coastline before nightfall. As word of their leaving went out among the liberated villagers a marvelous transformation occurred. Faces lit up and weary spirits lifted at the thought of leaving this accursed island and heading for their homes.

In a single line they all tramped down the path that led away from the beastwitch valley and toward the ocean. Mr. Pierce led the way with his axe at the ready and with each chieftain alongside him. The wily old dwarf had Tolund cover the left flank of the line, Heather the right flank, and the older apprentice fighters protected the end of the procession. Joining each of the young fighters were villagers from both Ibago and Berbago who had armed themselves with the weapons of the fallen beastcasters. All of them were eager to help protect their own people in the march to freedom.

As the procession moved out, Tolund could feel the presence of others in the surrounding jungle—it felt to him like angry eyes watched their every step. Scanning the thick jungle carefully, the lad spotted survivors of the beastwitch clan spying on them. With their great witch, warriors, and dragon-god vanquished, as well as their village decimated, they had taken to the jungle for refuge.

Suddenly, Mr. Pierce, who had also caught sight of them, called out in a thunderous tone, "People of this island, you have brought great pain to us and we have brought great pain to you. It is our wish that all of that ends here, today!" Now his tone intensified, "But…if you ever dare to come near to our shores and our villages again to threaten us in any way, we will stand ready to defend ourselves and we will end you once and for all. This is both a warning and a promise; live in peace on your own or threaten us and die!"

In one mighty swipe of his axe the brawny dwarf struck down a small tree and then cut off its branches to form a crude pole. Stabbing it into the ground, he stepped aside as the chief of Ibago and the chief of Berbago lifted up the charred skulls of both the beastwitch and the dragon-hatchling and skewered them on the pole, one on top of the other.

"This will remind you that we are also powerful," cried the dwarf, "and that we are a fierce people that will protect our own!" Without a backward glance, the three leaders resumed their march, walking proudly with heads held high.

Heather called over to Tolund, "He's my own trainingmaster and even I'm a little scared of him right now!"

"Let's hope this threat works," Tolund answered with a slight smile. "If these people have any sense at all they'll just stay on their own island and leave the rest of the world alone. Maybe they'll figure out the insanity of following wicked leaders and change their ways."

Once their party resumed its march to the coast few words were spoken. All of them traveled as quietly and as quickly as they could manage. Each of the chiefs warned their villagers that this island was still inhabited by dangerous beasts and, therefore, they should be careful not to draw attention to themselves. Fortunately, without the beastcasters enslaving their minds, the creatures of the island gave this large group of walkers a wide berth and the trip carried on without incident through the hot tropical morning.

Finally, in the waning afternoon hours, the elated villagers were once again dipping their tired feet in their beloved ocean. Though hungry, no one complained of food except for the very young children. Mr. Pierce called his young fighters and any willing villagers to his side to help him retrieve the boats,

The dwarf explained to all of them that before, when they first landed upon this dark isle, he had slipped into the jungle to take out two sentries that he'd spotted as they'd made their landing upon the beach. Tolund's brow furrowed in annoyance at this revelation. Mr. Pierce noticed this immediately.

"I did not tell you young fighters of my side quest because I thought it was as good a time as any to test your mettle," he said with a wry grin. "If all you pups do is depend upon me then I've been of no use to you at all as a mentor." Mr. Pierce could tell by Tolund's dour expression that that did not sit well with the boy, but if that reaction bothered the dwarf he gave no evidence of it.

Mr. Pierce continued to explain that, after successfully ambushing and dispatching the sentries, he'd discovered a line of boats with strange markings carved into the bottom of them that glowed faintly with mystic power. He'd deduced that these witch-markings allowed these boats to move over the waters without disturbing or attracting the firewhip beasts that lurked below. The unblemished wood of the hulls bore the proof that no firewhips had so much as laid a single ghostlike tendril upon them.

With little effort, the work party retrieved the boats and anchored them upon the beach before the weary villagers. After a night's rest the chiefs instructed them that they would all set out for the mainland at first light. Fires were stoked and volunteers set out to forage for food while the rest prepared to camp for the night.

As Tolund helped search for fruit and berries in the jungle he was surprised by a tight grip upon his shoulder. The boy winced as he felt Heather's fingernails clamp down harshly upon him. "We cannot tarry!" she snapped in an eerie whisper. Tolund saw that she was staring off into the thick foliage with her other hand clutching her pendant.

"Wait, what are you...?"

"We cannot tarry!" she whispered again with more urgency. Now she began to drag Tolund toward the darkening jungle with a strength she should not have possessed.

"Heather! Let go!" the boy barked. "What's the matter with you?" Ignoring him completely, the frail girl dragged her friend along like a bull dragging a feather. Try as he might, the lad could not break her grip or snap her out of her trance. Surprise turned to panic.

Unsure of what to do, Tolund called out for help, "Mr. Pierce!" From far off he heard his trainingmaster shout something back. Heather quickened her pace to a sprint. Tolund fought to dig his heels into the earth to slow them, but nothing he did seemed to make a difference. Soon, they came to an abrupt stop. Tolund was surprised to see that they'd stopped at a small jungle pool that was fed by a humble waterfall pouring down from the slope above it.

Before he could question Heather again or try to break this spell, he heard crashing in the brush behind them and the shouts of Mr. Pierce, Lindris, and Bex. "There's something wrong with Heathe—" before Tolund could finish his warning he was plunged under the surface of the pool.

Beneath the water Tolund heard the cries of his friends and saw their bodies splash into the pool. He could see them swimming underwater to catch up to them with looks of astonishment on their faces. Suddenly the boy clenched his eyes as a bright white light filled the water. The shining pool lit up the jungle around them in an unnatural display of power. Seconds later, the light faded. Soon, the ripples upon the surface of the pool stilled in deathly silence. None who went into the spring surfaced again. The trickle of the little waterfall mingled with the sounds of the sea breezes and the jungle birds all around. In this new stillness of the now empty pool, it was as if no travelers had ever been there at all.

CHAPTER 22

DARK SIEGE

It was just before dawn at the great city of Ansalion, but no sunrise would be welcomed this morning. Impossibly, a thick dark mist, which had been streaming out of the bordering forest during the night, now smothered the skies above and around Ansalion.

"Have the scouts returned?" questioned Captain Shaw.

"No, Sir," answered the watchman from the front gates. "We sent them to investigate this strange mist hours ago. Of the seven we sent, not one has returned."

The young captain breathed deep as he grimaced, "Then we must assume they are lost. We have to fully secure the city. Set our full guard before the walls, I will give the word within the city and then join you in front of the main gates."

"We'll be ready, Captain," nodded the soldier as he turned to carry out his orders.

Captain Shaw moved quickly to the lookout post above the protectorate halls. After informing his superiors, he ignited the signal fires that warned the city and rang the Protectorate bell three times. Dust scattered from the ancient bell as it echoed across the dark city.

Almost immediately, three bells sounded from the Paladin bell and then another three sounded from the bell of the White Sanctuary—the alarm had been heard and acknowledged. Ansalion was now on full alert.

In moments, the Paladins, gliding over each quarter on their patrol dragons, ordered all citizens to remain in their homes and halls and to stay off of the streets. Protectorate soldiers began to reinforce the wall towers and gate entrances. Paladins on horseback now moved along the streets in full armor, with spears and shields at the ready. As the streets were being secured, the White Sanctuary also made preparations.

Inside the shining halls, clerics of all levels prepared themselves with prayer. All of them could feel a creeping malevolence approaching the city and each feared that even the combined protectorate and paladin forces would be hard-pressed to withstand this dark siege. "Remember, Sisters and Brothers, that steel and sinew have limits," advised Cleric Kellesh, "limits that do not apply to faith and wisdom! If our suspicions are correct, Ansalion, indeed all of Vedris, will need all that we can provide. We will not be found negligent in this desperate hour!" So it was that prayer and preparations continued in the White Sanctuary.

Across the city, at the dragon stables of the Protectorate, Cleric Warren Michaels tightened his saddle harness and called out to Captain Shaw, "I suppose I'm as ready as I'll ever be."

"This makes no sense," answered the younger man.

"I know, but I also know, as you do from what we both dreamed, that I must fly past this invading evil and complete some unknown task."

"Yes, I feel the urgency of it too," frowned Captain Shaw, "I didn't say that it's the wrong move, I just said it didn't make any sense."

"Well, my young friend," smiled the older cleric, "sensible or not, that is my course and I can't shake the feeling that time is crucial." With that, the cleric gave his ally a quick nod and spurred his dragon to take flight. In just a few moments he was over the city walls and out of sight.

"Hmph, sometimes it's hard to tell fools from men of faith," Captain Shaw said softly to himself.

Early dawn stretched on to mid-morning. The mood of the city remained hushed and taut. Inside the high walls, the paladins surveyed the streets for any signs of treachery or trespass. Outside the walls, the Protectorate maintained their presence with archers all along the top of the gates and infantry skirting its base. All available dragon riders patrolled the skies above with vigilant eyes. The city seemed determined and invincible— then it began.

Soundlessly, a monstrous tremor shook all of Ansalion and the lands around it. From the misty forest, just before the main gates, a surge of dark power burst forth like a mighty wave. Birds and beasts in all directions fled in terror, moving as fast as they could from whatever was approaching the city. Even the well-trained dragons and steeds started and were only prevented from bolting by the efforts of their riders.

"This is it, men," bellowed Captain Derrus who was commanding the infantry before the main gates. "Stand fast and keep your wits about you!" In response, his spearman lifted their spears and his archers notched arrows in their bows.

"Riders to the front," ordered the staunch voice of Captain Shaw. Following his lead, his cavalry trotted over the grassy plain to the edge of the now-haunted forest. With their lances before them and their shining armor reflecting the light of the dancing flames from the watchfires, they stood as a proud barrier between the cursed black fog and the anxious city.

Agonizing moments pressed down upon the defenders. Brave soldiers felt the weight of each heartbeat increase and each nervous breath grow shorter in anticipation. Finally, the black mist stirred.

A voice, jagged and grating, breathed out a challenge, "Is your time at hand, great city of sheep?" Impossibly, the voice carried forth to terrify every soul it threatened— every soldier, paladin, and citizen no matter how far they were from its point of origin felt its touch. Boring into both mind and soul, even the most valiant trembled at the horror of it. "Is my feast before me at last?"

The gentle-folk of the city and the very young failed this first test of courage. Many sought places to hide in their homes, weeping openly, and some even crumpled to the ground overwhelmed by fear. While those around them sought to comfort and reassure them, the macabre voice spoke again. "Do you think I'm blind to your trembling? That I'm deaf to your shrieks?" it scoffed. "Can you appreciate how delicious your agony is?"

Now, the ebony fog about the forest parted just enough to bring an unexpected sight. Captain Shaw and Captain Derrus and their troops were amazed to see a single frail form stride forth from the shadowy mists. What emerged was a simple-looking farmer in a tattered tunic, unarmed and unimpressive, bearing an eerie smirk upon his face.

With his head creaked to one side like a broken puppet, his thin form and ragged appearance still radiated palpable evil outward. "A demon is still a demon no matter what mask he wears," warned Captain Derrus. As if in response to the bold captain's words, the ground shook again. Small cracks and fissures broke in all directions with the 'farmer' at their center. More black mist spewed upward from these cracks and, within it, flies and beetles from the Abyss itself, streamed up into the air.

The farmer laughed a blasphemous laugh, "Will you love my pets as I do? Will you not welcome their affections?" Before a single soldier could turn to flee the swarm was upon them. While the flies' stings were vile and painful, they could be withstood by the stout-hearted defenders— the beetles were another threat entirely.

Each the size of a man's thumb, the voracious insects flew ruthlessly toward their victim and, finding an unprotected target, clawed and burrowed on to their foreheads. Once a beetle bored its way into a soldier's forehead even the strongest warrior instantly went limp and collapsed upon the ground.

In this chaos, Captain Shaw, protected by his cavalry helm, was unaffected by this pestilence. He did not hesitate. "Arrows upon this creature, now!" he commanded. Even amidst the furor of this mad scene, Shaw's fierce order was heard by the protectorate archers and obeyed immediately. A rain of barbed-iron poured down upon the 'farmer.' Impaled from head to toe, the thin figure did not even take a step backward or hold its arms up in defense. Stuck with dozens of shafts, no blood issued forth from his flesh and neither did a cry of pain or alarm escape its lips. The skewered form just stood there as if he'd been sprinkled with dust from a sudden gust of wind.

"This cannot be!" exclaimed Captain Shaw. Looking about quickly, he could see his horsemen shaken by this horrific sight. Now, before he could order a second volley upon the enemy, he heard the cries upon the tower walls as the swarming beetles had reached the archers. Fighting for their own lives and falling easily to the pestilence, he could see the archers would be of no more use in this fight. Young as he was, Captain Shaw knew that this was a crucial moment. He knew his forces were on the edge of panic— he could not allow that to happen.

"Protectorate, form on me!" he cried savagely. "For the High King! For Ansalion!" Spurring his mount to a gallop, he charged forward. Suddenly snapped to attention by training and loyalty, his horsemen followed right behind him. The armored cavalry now thundered toward the 'farmer.'

"Am I a dog to be trampled?" the creature mocked with an arrow stuck through its lower lip. Casually, it raised its left arm which was also pierced by several arrows. A hard rush of black mist crashed forward like a wave from a great ocean storm. Men screamed and horses neighed as the evil wave slammed into them, sending them backwards, rolling end over end. Captain Shaw, once he'd pulled himself to one knee, could not believe what he was seeing.

In a single attack his cavalry was decimated. Most of the horses and men lay dead all about him. Reeling and grasping for his own courage, the young captain looked on as the 'farmer' smiled a ghoulish smile and then burst into flames as black as night. The form of the lost fool who had dared to call forth a Fallen One seemed to harden and crack, as if its flesh was solidifying into scorched stone. All of the impaled arrows burned to ash and the iron of the arrowheads melted and dripped molten iron at his feet. Now the thin body crumbled away leaving only a form of blood-red smoke and black fire.

A low call sounded from the monster's throat and, at once, all of the flies and beetles hurtled back to their master directly into his fiery aura. Captain Shaw, frozen in horror, watched in terrified awe as the burning form grew larger and thicker as the pestilence fed its pyre.

"Now, will you not welcome the magnificent 'Hsryliath' to his new kingdom?" the demon cried out triumphantly.

Before a defiant Captain Shaw could unsheathe his sword to answer the beast, more arrows shot down from Ansalion's towers. Again, both shaft and arrowhead withered in the unworldly flames. The Fallen One, who had grown five times larger than the diminutive farmer it had consumed, took a long, deliberate stride toward Ansalion's front gate.

Vowing silently to waylay this beast while it was still far enough from the gates, Shaw drew his sword and held it firmly in his brawny arms. Suddenly, the young warrior was struck from behind. Rolling with the impact, he turned to see what had slammed into his armor. Lurching toward him awkwardly was Captain Derrus with a beetle stuck firmly in his forehead. His eyes now wept oily black tears and his visage was entranced and ghostly. Gripping his warhammer with both hands, he stalked forward. Behind the possessed captain, Shaw saw that all of the soldiers who'd been infected with beetles were attacking their unaffected allies. With gritted teeth, Captain Shaw was forced to take arms against his own comrades while the demon, Hsryliath, smiled in sadistic delight.

CHAPTER 23

A SHIFT IN THE WIND

Cleric Michaels steered his borrowed dragon over the shrouded forest awkwardly. It had been eleven years since he'd last flown a patrol dragon and his 'rust' was showing. Fortunately, the copper and black flier he'd borrowed was a steady, well-experienced dragon. In spite of the cleric's twisting and shifting in the saddle, the leatherback quickly adjusted to his rider's movements and maintained a smooth course of flight.

"Thanks, Old Fellow," Cleric Michaels said with a friendly pat upon the beast's neck. "It seems they gave me the right mount after all." A relaxed rumble issued from the dragon's throat.

Cleric Michaels, feeling a strange urging, pulled the reins to the right of the mist-covered forest. The patrol dragon veered cleanly in that direction and, at his rider's command, increased his speed. Now they were bolting past the wooded valley and up the hillside toward a higher plateau. Something odd caught the cleric's eye.

Though the sky was dark in all directions, the morning sun had risen and brought some light to the hazy sky. Cleric Michaels directed his flier downward. What had caught his eye was a strange trail cutting through the brush and trees. Now low enough for a better view, he saw that the path looked like it had been burned into the landscape. Oddly, the ground and trees were blackened, as if by fire, but there was no evidence of smoke, ash, or soot. A shudder rippled up the cleric's spine. What he could not have known was that this was the very path that Hsryliath had taken earlier. He did not know that a Fallen One of the Abyss now stalked Vedris and was on its way to laying siege to Ansalion.

Curiously, his strange urging tugged at him to follow this trail upward to its source. On the swift wings of his dragon this did not take long. In moments he was closing in on what looked like a simple farm in the distance. Suddenly, a stinging pain stabbed into his forehead. Cleric Michaels lunged back instinctively using both of his hands to claw at the buzzing, chittering thing that was burning his skin. This violent reaction wrenched him backwards with such force that, when combined with the full weight of his body, the cleric was completely unsaddled and was hanging only by the leather strap about his waist. This was an unexpected shock to his dragon.

While Cleric Michaels sought to tear the burrowing Abyss-beetle from his forehead, his dragon was flapping and twisting furiously to keep them both aloft. With the cleric's body hanging and pulling on the saddle while he thrashed about, it was all his dragon could do to maintain flight. Now both of their bodies spiraled down toward the ground at a frantic speed. The dragon's roars mixed with the man's defiant shouts as both of them fought their own desperate battle.

Roaring fearfully, the patrol dragon poured all of its magical strength into a final sweep of its wings. Only ten feet above the hard ground the gambit succeeded and the beast leveled its flight path.

Though it saved them from certain death, they were far from safe. Such was their speed that the best the leatherback could manage was to avoid directly crashing into the ground for they were going too fast to land safely.

Diving to its side, the faithful dragon bore the force of the landing by keeping its rider's body above its own. In a cloud of dust a screech of pain cut the morning air. When the two bodies stopped skidding, the copper and black form did not move. In a valiant act of loyalty, the old patrol dragon saved his rider at the cost of its own life. Had he been able to, Cleric Michaels would have wept at this courageous beast's sacrifice. Due to his own plight, he was barely aware that he'd even stopped flying.

With his struggling body cushioned by the dragon's huge form, the cleric managed to survive the brutal landing. If he was injured he was unaware for all he could focus on was the bloodthirsty insect that was trying to dig into his skull.

Using both of his hands, Cleric Michaels was trying to rip the beetle from his scalp, but its four spiny legs, with their barbed ends, were hooked too tightly under his skin. The pain was excruciating and his warm blood was streaming down his face. From sheer panic, the man had managed to hold the invader at bay, but he could not dislodge it completely.

In the midst of this great struggle, Warren Michaels felt flashes of madness streak into his thoughts. Dark, knifing thoughts slashed into his soul. Black and evil, they blurred his vision with shadow and nightmare and hate. An insistent thought kept shrieking at him to let go of the beetle and let it soothe his pain by becoming one with its mind. The thought promised that this pain and all future pain would disappear forever.

Somehow, someway, as his mind was drowning in this evil, the cleric heard one word echoing in his mind: 'faith.' Like the ringing of a great bell that rang out clear and strong, the word 'faith' cut through the spider webs of madness in his mind. He heard it even over the beating of his own frightened heart and the clicking and buzzing of the vicious insect.

"No!" shouted the cleric aloud. Forcing a quick prayer, he asked the High King for deliverance and then he spoke at the evil that was trying to smother his soul. "I-do-not-belong-to-you!" Feeling a rushing warmth from deep down, he repeated those words with more conviction, "I-DO-NOT-BELONG-TO-YOU!!"

In a screech of sudden pain the beetle released its grip from his forehead. A relieved Cleric Michaels shook his head from side to side to free his mind and wiped the blood from his face. As he squinted again and again to clear his vision, he heard a strange sound on the ground to his left. Looking downward in the direction of the chittering noises, he was pleased to see the oil-black beetle in its death-throes. He realized that the purity and urgency of his prayer pierced this thing like the razored tip of a spear.

How long he took to recover his wits and breath he did not know. After he stemmed the bleeding on his forehead by pressing his sleeve hard upon the wound, he looked around to catch his bearings. His sore waist was still tethered to the dragon's unmoving body by the leather saddle strap. Severing the strap with his blade, he felt a great swell of gratitude and pity for the poor dead beast that had saved his life. Before he could do anything else, his thoughts were interrupted by a loud grunting sound coming from behind him. Turning about with his sword held high, he saw that he was only a short distance from the farm he'd been flying toward.

The grunting sound broke the silence again. It seemed to be coming from the stone and thatch barn. Before he left to investigate this new sound, he pressed his palm gently on the fallen dragon's scaly hide. "Rest easy, Old Boy," he said kindly, "you will never be forgotten…not by me."

The short walk to the barn seemed to take forever. Cleric Michaels was so worn from his ordeal that he felt like he would collapse at every step. Still, the grunting sound that continued from within the barn compelled him to keep going.

Littered about the barnyard were the strangely blackened carcasses of all of the farm animals. The cleric recognized the stench of evil that clung to this now-poisoned ground. He'd smelled it in the Boglands months ago and he'd smelled it on the vile beetle that he'd just fought off. He gripped his sword tighter as he approached the doorway of the barn.

Strangely, the door for the barn was splintered upon the ground and someone with huge boots had tramped over the dirt floor. Now Cleric Michaels squinted at the unbelievable sight before him. Frozen in place, amidst a circle of blackened skeletons was a massive armored figure that was hard to make out. The shadows and sides of the barn's interior reflected so perfectly off of this warrior's armor that it was hard to see him clearly. The eyes of the skeletons burned red and bright with unholy power and their arms were locked together, forming a complete circle around the armored one. He also spied a smoothstone in the center of the circle that burned the same red light. He heard a grunting sound again.

Now that he was close to its source, the cleric knew that it came from the great brute hunched down in the center of the circle. He seemed to be grunting in an effort to move or to stand up, but could not. The warrior ceased his grunting and his futile struggle and addressed the cleric, "Are you going to just stand there and stare or are you going to do something?" The deep growling voice was quite intimidating.

"How do you know that I'm not here to inspect my trap?" asked the cleric.

"You are not evil," said the warrior flatly. "I can tell."

"Hmm," mused Cleric Michaels. Although the warrior's back was to him, his heart soared at the possibility of who this creature might actually be. "I'll do what I can, but I've never seen anything like this before."

With a nervous swipe of his sword the cleric brought his blade down upon the nearest skeleton's skull. Shattering like a clay pot, the shiny black pieces fell to the dusty ground. Instantly, a hissing erupted from the grinning mouths of the remaining skeletons. "Defend yourself," barked the warrior who was still straining to break free from this invisible prison.

With surprising agility, the skeletons leaped up and skittered toward the cleric. Cleric Michaels stepped backward and swiped with his blade to fend off their snapping teeth and bony fingers. In his first attack the cleric managed to lop off one of the skeleton's arms and then another skeleton's legs. Oblivious to this, these nightmares pressed toward him— one clawing with one arm and the other crawling upon the ground toward him.

A veteran of many battles over the years, the old cleric instantly formed a plan. Backing all the way to the barn's doorway, he prevented them from piling onto him with their superior numbers or flanking him on either side. He also ensured that he would have a single target assaulting him through the narrow doorway. Now, as each undead horror shambled through the doorway, the cleric took great care to shatter their skulls. This had vanquished the first skeleton easily enough and now proved to be just as effective against the rest. In five deliberate cuts all the skeletons fell to dust and stopped moving.

"Ah!!" shouted the large figure in the center of the cursed barn. The giant warrior stood upright with his arms stretched outward. "With the creatures down the holding spell is broken!" Using his heel, he crushed the smoothstone that had fueled the trap.

Cleric Michaels gasped at the size of this hulking warrior. Once he stood upright, his armor and stature all but confirmed the cleric's suspicions. "You simply have to be the great Lockslayer," said the cleric brightly.

"Hmph," Eli grunted scornfully, "hardly the 'great' anything right now. How could I have been so stupid to walk into this trap like some drunken fool!" The brawny warrior took a deep breath to dismiss his own fuming.

"Forgive me," he said more cordially to Cleric Michaels, "you have my thanks. I might have been trapped there forever if not for you."

"We've no time for conversation," replied the grateful cleric. "All of Vedris is in danger and you are needed now more than ever before!"

Quickly, the two of them shared what they had learned about this encroaching threat with one another. Summoning his wings of speed, Eli lifted the cleric with him as they both sped to Ansalion. In their wake, a still, disturbing silence hung over the dead farm and all of its many victims.

CHAPTER 24

WAR

"Farewell, Good Cleric," the Lockslayer called as he dropped his new comrade successfully to the ground. "Try to keep yourself hidden and give this battleground a wide berth!" Without looking back, the warrior lifted himself to a greater height and rushed away. He was out of earshot before Cleric Michaels could thank him.

With a wave and a worried smile, the cleric spoke softly, "Go with the High King's blessing, my Son. May He guide and protect you this day." Now, anxiously, Cleric Michaels started down the wooded hillside. The Lockslayer made sure to set him down far to one side of the conflict, but the old cleric knew he had to get a closer look so he continued to move in the direction of the great city.

Flying high over the misty forest, Eli's sharp eyes saw the turmoil at the city's gates and saw how a single dark shape stalked toward Ansalion's beleaguered defenders. Gritting his teeth, he summoned his wings of speed and his longsword and began to dive. Even as his nerve was tested at facing an enemy greater than any before, his heart pounded at the thought of hot-blooded conflict. It was what he was born for.

The battlefield, dark with the swirling pestilence, rang out from the clamor of battle. A horrified Captain Shaw was living up to his young reputation and ably defending the area before the front gate—though it was all he and his remaining allies could do to fight off their entranced comrades without causing serious harm to them. This brave defense was clearly over-matched and the small band of fourteen was being pushed back to the great wooden gate itself.

"Now, now, Great Captain," mocked Hsyriliath, "how does one fight to the death with his own brothers? How do you cut down your own comrades and walk away unchanged?" Cruel laughter rumbled out of the demon's throat. A gloating smile spread across his face with its splitting skin and tongues of black fire dancing over his ruined flesh. Even the beetles and flies that flitted about him seemed to be moving more quickly as if they were celebrating with their master.

"SWIP!" A great hulking form and a flash of silver streaked in front of the demon. Hsyriliath screeched and slumped to its hands and knees. It was cut almost in half just below the ribcage.

Turning its head to see the mighty form of the Lockslayer soaring upward to one side, the abomination chuckled again. "Do I get to play with my food after all?" Hsyriliath stood up, oblivious to the fatal wound it had just received. Instantly, his horde of beetles and flies swarmed into the gaping cut, their bodies steaming and melting into the demon's flesh to heal it and make it whole.

Without pause, the Lockslayer rolled over in the sky and shot down like an arrow, straight for the monster again. Even if the creature had tried to evade this second attack, it would have been impossible due to Eli's great speed. Now the Fallen One let out an amusing grunt as the shining sword lopped off his right arm just below the shoulder. Moving with indifference, it stumbled over to retrieve its severed arm.

"Would I not disappoint you if I were so easily put down?" its deep voice mocked. Using its left arm, the creature lifted the severed arm back to where it belonged and, again, his little servants crawled upon the place where the flesh had been sundered. Burning and melting once more, the arm was restored in mere seconds. After two devastating attacks the demon now stood there, unharmed, with a brazen smile upon its face.

Eli wasted no time on shock or dismay— war must be decisive. Diving again, he now summoned his flawless spear. At full speed, with beetles and flies pelting his armor as he dove, the Lockslayer skewered the demon's great body. Impaling the beast straight through its chest, he lifted it up into the sky with him.

Surprisingly, the demon did not struggle or even cry out in pain. Tilting his head to one side, he taunted his attacker, "Did you know that Hsyriliath has long wanted to test your vaunted reputation?"

Ignoring the monster, Eli used both of his powerful arms to hurtle the spear, with its trapped victim, into a huge granite boulder that sat in a clearing up on the hillside. The spear-tip pierced the rock with a sound like screeching thunder. Angling his wings so that he banked back around, the Lockslayer smiled grimly at the sight of the demon's huge form stuck into the boulder like an insect pinned to a board. Disturbingly, Hsyriliath did not struggle to dislodge the spear from its chest or try to wriggle free—it simply hung there with its arms outstretched, waiting for his attacker's next move.

Eli did not hesitate. His longsword faded and now a shining silver bow and a quiver of arrows appeared. "It's past time you were returned to the Abyss!" he growled.

In a clean, straight line his ruby arrow whistled toward its target. The ebony mist suddenly dispersed as the demon's body exploded in a great burst of magical flame. The onslaught continued as fast as the Lockslayer could loose his arrows. Storm, darkness, light, and more rained down upon Hsyriliath's ravaged form. Arrow after arrow smashed into it, causing a great noise that echoed over the countryside. Amid the smoke and fury the demon could not be seen. Satisfied after two waves of mystic arrows, the great warrior circled above waiting for the smoke to clear.

A deep rumbling laughter could be heard from below. "How could I be disappointed with that effort, Great Slayer of Little Warlocks?" Hsyriliath taunted. As the smoke cleared, Eli was pleased to see the broken and shredded body of the monster hanging limply upon the silver spear. So great was his assault that all the trees and brush around the beast had been destroyed and even the edges of the boulder had melted. Eli's satisfaction instantly came to an end.

"No!" he cried out as he saw Hsyriliath's swarm rush in again to heal their master. Eli brought forth his brown wings of strength to push away the insects, but he was too late. Smiling, the demon rose up with renewed power, his form even larger than before. With a smirk the monster ripped the spear from the boulder and its chest and cast it aside.

Quiver and bow disappeared. Now a two-bladed battle axe shimmered in his right hand and a silver mace shimmered in his left. Eli dove straight at Hsyriliath with a savage cry. The glade shook with the force of the great warrior's attack. With both of his mighty arms striking viciously, he brought axe and mace down upon the demon's giant skull in an avalanche of wrath.

For what seemed an eternity, the Lockslayer's fury slashed faster and faster. Lost in his own bloodlust, he knew nothing of fatigue or relenting. Black ichor sprayed from the demon's form and even the boulder behind it cracked and splintered beneath this ruthless storm.

"THOOM!" an explosion of dark power blasted the Lockslayer's body back into the treetops far behind him. Righting himself on his great wings, Eli winced in pain from the demon's attack.

"Am I to let you have all of the sport?" cackled Hsyriliath. Once again smothered by his beloved swarm, the Fallen One now shone with a seething, shadowy aura of power. Rising to his feet, the beast had now enlarged to thrice the Lockslayer's size. Red smoke and black fire poured from his form as he stood as a lord of the Abyss in all of his blasphemous 'glory.'

"Did you truly think you were the only one who craved blood and conflict?" With a grin the Fallen One charged toward a disbelieving Eli.

Cleric Michaels gasped as he rounded a grove of trees and looked upon the siege of pestilence and madness that stormed the gates of Ansalion. Now his head snapped to his left when he heard the thunderclap of the Lockslayer's assault upon the demon on the upper hillside. He looked about him as the ground trembled and the trees shuddered from the forces unleashed nearby. "High King, protect us!" he whispered reverently.

Moving down the hillside, he double-checked his brow. As a precaution against the vampiric-beetles, he'd torn off one of his sleeves and wrapped it firmly over his scalp and forehead. After that, he'd donned his hooded cloak and drew the hood as tight as he could. Finally, he unsheathed his sword and held it ready for whatever he may encounter on the valley floor.

Cleric Michaels had to steady his nerves again as the ground shook once more from the war being waged. Now another sound moved through the shrouded air, it was the bell of the White Sanctuary. The cleric recognized this sound clearly as this great bell had a very distinct tone, as did the bells of the Paladins and the Protectorate. This one was sounding continuously, which was a signal for the people of the city to seek refuge in the White Sanctuary itself. Never in his long life had he heard this call go out. Never did he imagine that things could become so desperate that only the High clerics and their stronghold could defend the people. For this alarm to sound Warren Michaels knew that the combined might of the Protectorate and the Paladins had failed.

Peering more intently at the city, he could hear far off echoes of people crying out and the neighing of horses and the roaring of patrol dragons. Also, he spied great orange glows that shifted in the black air all about the city. "Fire…," he whispered numbly, "the city is on fire."

Inside Ansalion chaos reigned. Undeterred by the thick stone walls or massive gates, the pestilence from the Abyss had streamed over the high walls and engulfed the city. Everywhere, the hellish beetles were boring into the scalps of the unprotected populace, transforming them into more slaves of Hsyriliath.

Though the paladins on horseback and dragonback wore helms that protected them from the beetles, their mounts did not. Soon, in a scene of madness, the paladins were forced to fight off their own possessed steeds and dragons as well as the possessed townsfolk. Yet, that still was not the final threat that hastened the fall of Ansalion.

In their own dark councils the warlock orders had planned for months for the Fallen One's great summoning. This was the first half of their shared plan. When the demon finally unleashed its power before Ansalion's gates, they knew it was their time to strike from within the city walls. Reapers and casters from every order took to the streets when the black swarms filled the air. With heads covered, for even they did not trust their free will to one of the Fallen Ones, they gleefully joined the fray.

Striking treacherously, they set about ambushing the paladins and any citizens not enslaved. Some they murdered through cowardly attacks from behind, but most they subdued so they could uncover their foreheads to add another slave to serve their cause.

In less than an hour since the swarms first invaded, Ansalion's streets were empty of protectors leaving only the wicked and their thralls moving about unchallenged. Next, the casters barked orders and their ruthless mobs set upon the dwellings.

Roaming about, they battered down doors and stormed any home or building where people sought refuge. Dragging their victims out into the street, they again let the vile insects transform the innocent into more soldiers for the wicked cause. The great multitude of free folk in Ansalion were quickly becoming the city's conquering army. Street by street, block by block, the raiding continued until the army of Hsyriliath swelled up to staggering numbers. However, even in this madness, hope lingered.

Despite the sorcerous invasion, there were two areas of the city that remained free. The Grey Quarter, with its traditionally stubborn and suspicious dwarves, proved to be too great an obstacle for the raiders to overcome. Also, the White Sanctuary, which now sounded the call for refuge within its holy walls, remained inviolate.

The dwarves, upon hearing the first alarm in the morning, naturally withdrew to their underground vaults. Generations of fierce territoriality served them well on this day. Their numerous granite vaults now became personal fortresses which mere reapers and casters could not breach. Stone slabs or thick iron bars blocked entrances and many of these held deadly traps created to protect their wealth from thieves at all costs. Dozens of foolish raiders died this day by spikes, poison, fire, and more when they tried to force their way into the vaults. Though unable to help their fellow citizens, the dwarves of Ansalion would not become victims this day.

The White Sanctuary had its own means of defense. When the demon launched its assault, the High Clerics, already alerted by their prayerful councils, stood ready. Finding even greater power together, the clerics called forth a great ward of protection. In moments, a nimbus of supernatural light blanketed the sanctuary, itself, until it burned bright and clean from the lowest walls to the highest spire. Though the light served to soothe and calm the refugees that fled toward it, it also stung the eyes of the wicked that pursued them. Furthermore, fleeing citizens were able to pass through the threshold of the great church safely, but those that hunted them found a different greeting. When the first reaper dared to touch the light, he burst into cleansing flames and was consumed where he fell. Finally, the holy light was such that the beetles and flies of the Abyss could not even approach the great church. Once the innocent were within a hundred paces of the sanctuary, the pestilence recoiled in fear.

So it was that in Ansalion's hour of desperation hope was not entirely lost.

Shaken by the plight of the great city, Cleric Michaels continued across the flat lands that lay between Ansalion and the valleys that preceded the fabled Mountains of Life. The black mist brought on by the demon still shrouded his path so the cleric had to take great care with his footsteps. Several beetles sought to reach his scalp, but they were foiled by his head coverings and then chased away with his blade. The tired man walked on, unsure of what his next step would be.

His first plan was to head for the city and hope to provide some aid to the people within. He thought he might make his way to one of the lesser gates and gain entrance there. After that, he would try to help out any way that he could. However, after hearing the madness from within the city walls, he was unsure that he could even get there in time to make a difference to anyone. He feared that the city would be conquered before the next sunrise, perhaps sooner if the Lockslayer fell.

Still, he could not help himself, he had to try to do something for the poor folk under siege. Cleric Michaels resolved to make for the northwestern corner as swiftly as possible no matter what the outcome. His pace quickened.

Two moments of clarity would change his plans entirely. First off, as he moved closer to the Jorlavar river which was only a short distance from his current position, a clean breeze moved over him from the direction of the Mountains of Life. Instantly the cleric appreciated how the fresh air pushed aside the black mist and the flies and beetles that still harassed him. He took a long, deep breath. As he did this his heart beat a little faster and something stirred inside of him. Now he felt an urgent longing to follow the path of the breeze.

Warren Michaels was no novice cleric or foolhardy skeptic, he knew there was something special about this new breeze. He knew the feel of his own soul and how it could sometimes speak to him in a way his mind could not fathom. Deliberately, he turned about and started walking in the direction of the mountain wind.

After walking only a short time, the second moment of clarity caught him by complete surprise. The veteran cleric let out a startled gasp as he saw the impossible occur. A small pond, halfway between the Jorlavar river and himself, suddenly lit up with a lovely silver light. It was so bright that it looked as if a full moon had settled to the bottom of this humble pond. Peering intently, he was shocked again to see that people were emerging from these shallow waters. Although he could not make them out from this distance, he was still certain of what he saw. With sword in hand and his heart beating rapidly, he rushed forward to investigate.

The first two figures that stepped from the eerie pond were two youths, one lad and one lass, that he did not recognize. Though sopping wet, they did not seem cold in the chilly air; they did not shiver and they did not even seek to dry themselves. Oddly, the water that soaked them still glowed faintly with the silvery light.

The puzzled cleric was about to shout out a greeting when a dwarf suddenly surfaced in a fit of splashing and coughing. This figure he instantly recognized. "Trainingmaster Pierce?" he called out. "Is that you?"

Shaking his head to clear the water from his eyes and ears, the dwarf squinted in the cleric's direction. "Warren Michaels? What in blazes are doing on this islan—" Mr. Pierce was going to say 'island,' but looking about he could see that this was not the island he was on just a few moments ago. "Where are we, Michaels!" he demanded in a surly tone. Before the cleric could answer him two more figures burst from the waters.

"Tolund? Heather?" cried the delighted and stupefied cleric. "What are all of you doing jumping out of a glowing pond on the borders of the city?"

"City?!?" barked Mr. Pierce who scrunched his face in confusion. "Ansalion? That makes no sense! We were all in the Coastlands just a moment ago! How did we dive into a pool in the Coastlands and surface in a pool near the great city?!?"

Before the cleric could reply to the dwarf's baffling question, a sound like a boulder crashing from on high exploded in the distance. Drawing everyone's attention they all peered through the strange black fog. A figure clad in silver armor struggled to his feet and then, igniting wings of bright fire, took to the air.

"Eli!" cried Heather.

Instantly, the forest before the silver warrior splintered as a hulking monstrosity charged forward. In a furious rush the Lockslayer dove down to meet the demon with mace and axe. The two now disappeared into a writhing cloud of pestilence and flame as they slashed into one another.

"Tolund, " Heather pleaded, "it's Eli. We have to help him— it's Eli!" Even as she'd shouted this her feet were flying over the grassy terrain toward the carnage in the distance.

"Heather! Wait!" Tolund shouted. Now, not thinking clearly himself, the lad dashed after his friend, drawing his ebony sword as he ran.

"Fighters," commanded Mr. Pierce, "get back here now!" If they'd heard their trainingmaster's orders they gave no sign of it. Neither Heather nor Tolund slowed their pace or even looked back at their comrades. Fortunately, the faint glow that still clung to their wet clothes made them easy to track in this fog.

Mr. Pierce let out an exasperated growl as he looked to Bex and Lindris. "Well, get your weapons out and let's get after them!" Before the two confused fighters could comply, everyone was startled by yet another figure splashing up from the waters in the pond. To their amazement, an obviously rattled dwarf clad in dented and ruined armor and a shredded bearskin cloak shambled out of the pond.

"Run! Flee!" he screamed in a mad panic. "They're coming! They're going to slaughter us all!"

CHAPTER 25

THE BEGINNING OF THE END

It was hard for Heather to see clearly as she sprinted forward through the shadowy mist. She could feel the bodies of the huge beetles and flies pelting her cloak and face as she ran, but all they seemed to do was buzz away from her as fast as they could. She was more concerned with the savage battle raging before her.

Though terrified by what she heard in front of her, the girl could not stop running. Along with Eli's grunts and shouts, she heard the horrible screeching of the monster and heard its great claws scraping over his armor. She did not know what she would do when she got to them— she didn't even have her spear anymore. Still, she could not stop her feet from moving.

"Heather!" called Tolund from just behind her. "Wait for me, I'm with you!" Before the lass could even turn her head to answer him, another thunderous crash shook the ground. The force of this was so great that it knocked both of them off their feet. Struggling to their knees, the two friends saw the fiery wings of the Lockslayer Illuminating an impact crater off to their left.

"Eli?" Heather called as her eyes welled up. No voice called back. The only reply to her was a weak flickering from his wings which suddenly disappeared. "Eli!" Heather scrambled to the edge of the earthen crater with Tolund right behind her. Both of them lost their breath when they saw him.

The mighty Lockslayer did not move. Face down in the dirt, his invincible armor was rent with gashes where the giant beast's talons had slashed through and dents where its fists had crumpled it. Blood streamed from numerous places in his armor.

"What is this?" interrupted a demonic voice from behind them. Tolund and Heather turned. Tilting its head to one side, Hsyriliath grinned, displaying its rows of black razored teeth over blood-red gums. "Are you my new playthings?"

"No!" Heather screamed defiantly. "Strangely, as if she were someone else, the girl's eyes glowed with supernatural power and her right arm pointed straight toward the Fallen One. Speaking ancient words in the elvish tongue, words Heather herself had never heard before, she gave a command. Suddenly, the cloud of pestilence that clung to the demon dispersed in all directions in abject fear of these words.

"How did a mortal worm, like you, manage that?" Hsyriliath exclaimed in a tone mixed with surprise and annoyance.

The only reply Heather gave was to make a fist with her outstretched hand and to speak more haunting words in elvish. Instantly, impossibly, Hsyriliath's massive form was engulfed in flames that burned white-hot and pure. All the lands before Ansalion echoed with the anguished shrieks of the monster. Though thrashing about in agony trying to fend off the ghostly flames, the great demon still remained on its feet.

"Will this spare you my wrath?" it screeched. "Will this prevent my snapping your bones and ripping your limbs from your body?" Now ignoring the torturous fire, Hsyriliath smashed two great fists down upon Heather.

"Where am I?" called the newly arrived dwarf as he fought to steady his breath and get his bearings.

"Hmph," grunted Mr. Pierce, "we've no time for this! Bex, Lindris see to whoever this is. Cleric, you're with me!"

"Wait!" demanded the newcomer. "We must find cover! You don't know what's coming." Mr. Pierce wanted to rush to Tolund and Heather, but a nagging instinct inside of him told him to listen to this strange dwarf.

"Enough," snapped Mr. Pierce as he grasped the dwarf's burly shoulders with both hands. "Explain yourself, now!"

"I...I am Lord Gresk, a clan leader from the Frostlands. How I got here I don't know. I was drowning in an icy sea, but somehow surfaced here...here with you." Squinting through the black mist about the countryside, past the battle raging before them he spied Ansalion's walls. "Is that the Great City?"

"It is, but enough babbling. What is coming?"

"We've got to warn Ansalion!" cried Lord Gresk. "Dragons, there are dragons on the wind. They've been unleashed across Vedris and I believe I've been sent here to warn the city."

"We're already facing some attacking evil," snapped Mr. Pierce. "We'll worry about your ravings later!" Turning quickly, he gave Bex and Lindris a nod and the three of them sprinted off toward the battle.

"But don't you see?" Lord Gresk shouted as he watched them run off, "this attack was only the beginning, only half of the threat." If Mr. Pierce heard his warning, he gave no sign. Cleric Michaels, for some reason, had to hear this dwarf out.

"Tell me what you know, and tell me quickly."

The massive fists of Hsyriliath barely missed Heather. Suddenly free from her strange trance, the girl's training and nimble speed helped her dodge the crushing attack, but she was unprepared for the demon's unholy strength. So great was the strike that it jolted the ground with a tremor that knocked Heather off of her feet. In a mad panic, the girl tried to scramble away as Hsyriliath's claws stretched toward her.

An abrupt scream burst from the monster as its back stiffened in pain. "You will not touch her!" cried Tolund with a swipe of his black sword.

Hsyriliath grimaced through the dwindling white flames. "Are you so blind as to not see death standing before you?" Ignoring the dying white fire and the fresh cut along its back, the demon turned upon Tolund.

"Heather, run!" shouted Tolund. Though terrified at all of this, Heather would not run. She knew in her heart that she could not abandon Tolund. Still, her heart trembled inside of her as she saw the boy's defensive swipes do nothing to dissuade the advancing behemoth. She also saw that the cloud of unholy pestilence had returned and was swarming about the demon, trying to heal its wounds now that the magical fire had faded.

As Hsyriliath clawed at him Tolund countered with a quick slash of his blade. The creature howled in pain. Though not a deep cut upon its forearm, Tolund's sword seemed to cause it greater pain than it should have. "Keep at it, Tol!" Heather called out. "Your blade is hurting him."

Tolund would have answered her if he wasn't furiously dodging the monstrous claws that were ripping at him. In seconds, the boy's right arm and left leg were wet with his own blood where the talons slashed faster than he could move.

"Heh, heh," the demon laughed mockingly. "Is an infant with a needle enough to thwart the new Lord of this world? The answer came swiftly as Tolund's sword punched through the middle of Hsyriliath's left hand. Black blood poured forth as the monster squalled in pain.

Hsyriliath's swarm sought to heal their master, as they'd done in its battle with the Lockslayer, but a curious thing occurred. Something about the wounds that Tolund's blade had inflicted repelled the beetles and flies. Darting in again and again, they pressed in to fulfill their duty, but could not bear to touch any flesh that had been touched by Tolund's sword. The blessings of the White Council, promised long ago, were proving true.

Holding his bleeding hand with his other hand, Hsyriliath spat forth an order in the hellish tongue of the Fallen Ones. Instantly, the swarm ceased trying to heal their master and shot toward Tolund, Heather, and their advancing friends. The five comrades disappeared in a cloud of beetles and flies. The flies bit and stung them, but the beetles were the greater danger. Upon all of their foreheads a single beetle clawed into flesh and began to bore its way in. "Won't you enjoy becoming the thralls of Hsyriliath?" mocked the demon.

"No!" cried out Heather as her eyes and pendant burned bright with power once more. Again the demon was consumed by holy fire only this time it seemed to double in heat and intensity. This time, so great were these desperate flames that the Fallen One could not resist them. Wailing and tortured, Hsyriliath vaulted toward the ruined forest to escape from Heather's wrath. In a panic the swarming cloud, including the beetles upon all of their foreheads, all rushed after their master. All at once Mr. Pierce and his four charges found themselves free of the swarm.

Panting and reeling, they all tried to catch their breaths. "Heather, I've…I've never seen the like," gasped Mr. Pierce. "Where did all of this magic come from?"

"My gift finally came to life," answered Heather. "I don't know how, but I'm glad it did." Tolund noticed that her eyes had stopped glowing again.

"It isn't just with that creature," added Bex as he rubbed the blood from his forehead, "you used a water-spell of some kind to move us from the Coastlands to Ansalion in one moment. How did you do that?" Before Heather could reply a new voice called through the black fog behind them. It was Cleric Michaels.

"We can't rest," he called out urgently. "It's not over!" Bursting through the mist, both the Cleric and Lord Gresk were upon them. Both of them looked terrified.

"Can't you hear it?" asked the strange dwarf. "In the distance, do you hear the roaring?" Furrowing their brows and looking about, all of them did hear the faint roaring of great beasts. "Those are the dragons I was warning you about. They're here!"

CHAPTER 26

A PRAYER IN THE DARKNESS

Captain Nathanial Shaw shook and trembled. Try as he might, he could not steady his soul at this moment. All about him, scattered just before the great northern gate of Ansalion, were the lifeless bodies of his fellow soldiers…of his friends and brothers. Worse than their deaths, for the young captain understood well the risk of warfare, was knowing that many of these close friends had been cut down by his own hand in this field of madness.

"How do you prepare for this? Who could imagine a siege like this?" he wondered aloud. The only living things left to hear him were the few remaining flies and beetles that flitted about as if they were celebrating their dark master's victory. The battle between the Lockslayer and the demon-lord had ceased its raging a short while ago. Captain Shaw could only guess by the silence that the two titans ended one another. Blinded by the black fog that still clung to the countryside, he had no way of knowing one way or the other.

All he could do right now was give thanks to the High King that the helm his father gave him the day he joined the Protectorate had saved him from his comrades' fate. He also cursed the memories that he would re-live forever, memories of him striking down his possessed allies to save his own life. A voice inside seemed to whisper a gentle thought that there was mercy in those acts. Young Shaw knew this thought was right, he knew that their minds had been lost to the blasphemy of the demon spawns, but that brought him little peace now. Though he'd done the only thing he could have done, surrounded by a relentless horde that sought his blood, he still hated and raged at his own success.

Nathaniel's great strength and battle prowess won this night. Though the mob about him pressed from all sides, their mindlessness slowed their actions. Using this against them, he had moved swiftly and struck swiftly to great effect. Even so, his armor had many signs of sword or mace strikes. Fortunately, despite the many attempts, nowhere had his flesh been cut and no true wounds had been suffered. Bruised and tired, the defender of the city had more to do to fulfill his duty.

Stumbling through the corpses, the tall warrior wept openly. Had he the time he would have slumped to his knees and mourned, but desperation spurred him on. Even on this side of the thick walls he could hear the screams and see the glow and smoke from the fires.

The massive gate was still closed fast and no one responded to his calls. Fortunately, as a Protectorate soldier, he knew of an entrance that common folk were unaware of. Following the walls, he stalked forward in the direction of the Jorlavar. With his battered shield and sword in hand he moved as quickly as his heavy armor and tired legs would allow.

Soon the captain reached the shore where the enchanted river flowed into Ansalion. It was at this moment that his heart began to wither. Perhaps it was exhaustion, perhaps it was the crushing grief, but for reasons he wasn't even sure of Nathanial Shaw felt the overwhelming urge to throw down his weapons on the riverbank and run away. He wanted to run away from the dying city, from the field of his dead comrades, and the fire, smoke, and screams. He wanted to run until he could not run anymore and be rid of all this suffering and grief. So strong was this command that it did not even seem cowardly to the soldier—it just seemed to be the only course his heart would accept.

Dropping to his knees, gripping his hair with both hands, he shut his eyes tightly to fight off this dream of retreat. "No!" he snapped at his own thoughts. Now warmness like a soothing wave or a breeze in summer swept through him. He began to pray.

"High King," he began, "You've asked much of me tonight, perhaps too much. But what is my course? I know I must run…one way or the other, but my soul is demanding escape and safety. I thought I was better than this, stronger than this." His head slumped down, pressed down by the shame of these words. He continued, "Still, didn't I swear an oath to You, an oath of service and fealty? Were those empty words spoken only for others to hear or did I mean them?"

The young captain took a deep breath and lifted his head. "I did mean them, my King. I swore to defend and protect others at the risk of my own blood. I swore that I would walk straight into fire if that was what was required. Forgive me, but I suppose I never thought, deep down, that it would ever come to that, but now it has. I hear the cries of your subjects, I smell the smoke and the death. I cannot abandon Your people. Forgive my doubts and my cowardice…I choose Your path. My sword is still Yours." That was that. Standing, he squared his broad shoulders and set his jaw firmly. "Amen," he whispered. Decisively, he moved again toward the river's edge and to Ansalion.

Peering at the Jorlavar in the darkness, he spied his path. An arch in the huge stone wall was set with thick iron bars sunk deep into the riverbed. This allowed the water to flow in, but prevented any invader from gaining entrance into the city. However, the architects of Ansalion's defenses were wise and planned for many eventualities.

Quickly, Captain Shaw removed his armor and chain mail and boots. Wearing his helm, tunic, bracers, and breeches and carrying only his sword, he dove headfirst into the rushing current. Without daylight or moonlight the depths of the river were too dark to navigate. Fortunately, the young warrior knew exactly where to find the hidden entrance. Just to the left of the bars, where a large boulder had been set in the wall's foundation, Shaw's training told him he was in the right spot.

The captain sang a prayer that exalted the High King, a prayer known only to paladins, soldiers, and clerics. His singing sounded eerie underwater. Instantly, the image of a holy crown shone from the rock in a golden light. Touching the crown with his right hand, Shaw smiled as he saw the rock magically fade into nothingness. Swimming through quickly it was as if the boulder had never been inlaid into the wall. A shiver ran down the lad's spine as he passed through the hidden tunnel. All those entrusted with this secret knew that if any enemy or evil being sought to pass through using the secret hymn, the huge rock would reappear and entomb their corpse inside it forever. Once through, he looked back to see the boulder fade back into the wall, sealing it up as if Captain Shaw had never passed through.

Caution guided his resurfacing. The soldier had to assume that enemies would be lurking about inside the city walls. Gasping for air as quietly as he could, he surfaced behind a clump of reeds that concealed him. Wiping the water from his eyes, he was shocked at what he saw. Before he could even make sense of the horrors of Ansalion's desperate plight, Captain Shaw's head shot up toward the dark skies. Roars and the beating of great wings echoed above. Dragons were on the hunt.

CHAPTER 27

FLIGHT

The roaring was getting louder. From high overhead they heard the beasts coming closer. "We've got to find shelter!" barked Lord Gresk. "They'll be on us without warning and in this blasted mist we'd have no chance to defend ourselves or evade their attacks."

"Can dragons even see us through this fog?" asked Lindris.

"I don't know, Lass," answered the newcomer, "but for the sake of our skins we'd best assume that they can."

"Also, as the sun rises higher," added Mr. Pierce, "it will make us more visible, mist or no mist."

While the two dwarves and Cleric Michaels discussed a solution, the young fighters peered up at the dark sky nervously. Heather did not seem to notice any of this. All her attention was upon Eli's broken body.

"The forest is no good," exclaimed Mr. Pierce. The demon fled that way and there's no telling how fast it can recover from that last battle."

"Ansalion's too far over open ground," said Cleric Michaels. "We'd be picked off halfway to the gate and, by the sounds of things, the city isn't a sanctuary for anyone right now."

Tilting his head toward the sound of the river, Mr. Pierce had a thought. "The Jorlavar is our only chance."

"The river?" balked Cleric Michaels. "All that will do is rush us to a city that is under siege and where the dragons are heading as well. Also, the river is blocked by iron bars, iron bars that we can't get through."

Before anyone could reply the roars above echoed louder than before. To everyone's surprise, Tolund spoke up, "The river is the right path."

"How do you know that, Boy?" asked Lord Gresk.

"I just do," Tolund answered firmly. "It's just a feeling inside, but I trust it."

Mr. Pierce stepped closer and gave his charge a hard look in the eye. "Fair enough, Tolund. I think it's our best option as well for I've that same feeling." Turning about the gruff dwarf ordered everyone to make for the Jorlavar.

"No!" snapped Heather. "We're not leaving Eli to die here!"

Mr. Pierce responded with uncharacteristic gentleness. Placing his burly hands on the distraught girl's shoulders, he spoke softly and earnestly. "Heather, child, I know this is terrible and I know that he is your friend. But he's too big and heavy to carry quickly and we have to run for our lives right now. Do you understand, Girl? We have to run for our lives or we will all share his fate, which serves no one."

"But he's not dead, he's just wounded!" Heather looked about for any hope in the eyes of their gathering, but their faces just seemed to confirm Mr. Pierce's grim assessment. Nonetheless, Heather's back stiffened and she calmly wiped the tears from her eyes. Now she spoke in a resolute tone, "I don't care. I don't care about the sense of your words or how dangerous it is. I can't leave him and if you make me leave I'll just find a way to run back here anyway. You know I will."

Mr. Pierce looked to the cleric and his fellow dwarf for help, but he could tell that they all believed Heather's conviction even if they disagreed with it. Before a word could be spoken the black mist about them swirled and shifted and they could tell something huge was passing overhead. The grunt of a great beast sounded. Everyone froze and held their breath.

Cleric Michaels broke the silence after the dragon seemed to pass over and away from them. "If we remove his armor," he whispered, "we should be strong enough to drag him to the river. At least there we can float his weight."

Bex, saying nothing, moved quickly to the Lockslayer's form. Reading his intent, the rest of them joined the lad in the crater. In moments the ravaged armor was strewn about and they all marveled at the massive, broken form. Eli's skin was blending in with the dirt and blood from the fight. Wearing only his torn tunic, helm and faceplate, which Heather insisted be left on, and a necklace that bore small silver charms that resembled his weapons perfectly, the great Lockslayer was as light as they could make him.

Heather, though shocked at his bleeding and ruined condition, was relieved to see that he was still breathing. With the two dwarves on one arm and Cleric Michaels, Bex, and Tolund on the other, they began to drag the giant warrior as carefully as possible over the grasses and down the embankment to the river's edge. Lindris led the way with her eyes fixed on the sky above them while Heather followed behind.

Once at the water, Lindris and Heather went in first. Mr. Pierce ordered Bex to stand watch at the top of the embankment for any changes in the wind. The current in the middle of the Jorlavar was strong and swift, but near the shoreline it was manageable. The dwarves, Tolund, and Cleric Michaels pulled the Lockslayer into the river and held him up, floating him with his face up above the water. He was so injured that even the cool of the water did not stir him.

Tolund was on edge at this moment more than any other. When they pushed into the water he was certain that they were making too much noise. "Down!" cried Bex as he flattened to the ground. Everyone dropped as low into the river as they could as the huge form of an ebony dragon slipped across the night sky above them.

"That's the same kind of hatchling that slaughtered my kin in the Frostlands!" said Lord Gresk.

"That's awfully big for a hatchling, Gresk," answered Mr. Pierce.

"Aye, these are no ordinary dragons," snapped Gresk. Tolund shuddered at the force of its wingbeats over their heads and the way its presence ran a shiver up his own spine.

"Move quickly," ordered Cleric Michaels. "It knows we're here now!"

Everyone surrounded the Lockslayer's body and helped to keep him afloat. Bex was charging down the embankment with his axe in hand when Tolund spotted the mist parting behind him. "Bex, look out!" Tolund cried. Two great talons stretched out toward the lad and in an eyeblink Bex was snatched up and disappeared into the dark sky. Everyone called out to him as they heard Bex shriek once in pain and then grow silent. As if in triumph, dragon roars sounded all around them.

"Keep your heads down and swim," snapped Mr. Pierce. "Let the current take you!"

With one hand holding on to the Lockslayer's arm Tolund swam as fast as he could. He fought to keep from crying for, even in his panic, he could not believe Bex was gone so suddenly. All around him he heard the frantic breathing and furious swimming on his companions.

"Behind us!" called Lindris. Two more razored claws swooped down toward them. Moving at great speed, they cleaved the water and slashed toward them. The dragon's strike missed only by a few feet.

"They can't see us clearly through the mist," whispered Lord Gresk. "That brute was just guessing at our position."

"Still, we've a long way to go and that beast wasn't off by much," answered Cleric Michaels.

Tolund was terrified and feared that he'd led them all to their deaths on this river. The boy offered up a quick prayer to the High King. As if the Jorlavar itself heard and understood his prayer, the water suddenly slowed and then, impossibly, began to rush furiously in the opposite direction.

"What's going on?" cried Lindris.

"Our salvation, I hope!" shouted Cleric Michaels.

Moving back up towards its source the current doubled in speed. Tolund felt like a leaf being caught up in a flood. It almost felt like the river was carrying them in its arms and spiriting them away from the danger as fast as it could. Before the stunned swimmers could celebrate, the hideous snout and teeth of a full grown dragon broke through the misty veil on a course straight for them. A strange darkness steamed from this brute and, instantly, Tolund recognized it as the great black dragon that had served as the Tailor's protector.

The swimmers cried out in terror when the roar of the monster shook their bones. The dragon's jaws were wide open and closing upon them quickly. Tolund tried to swim away from those great teeth while pulling Heather with him, but the current overpowered their meager efforts. There were all at the mercy of the river and, fast as it was, the dragon streaking towards them was faster.

Tolund and Heather cried out in fear as the massive teeth were an arm's length from them. Suddenly, great branches appeared all about them as the behemoth's head crashed into the thick tree limbs. The sound of splintering wood mixed with the dragon's roar of pain. Now shadows engulfed them as the Jorlavar rushed them all beneath the cover of the forest canopy.

How long they hurtled up the river Tolund could not guess. It felt like a lifetime. Soon, however, the water slowed and swirled and gently pressed them all up onto a sandy bank. In the grayish light they found themselves sprawled out on a tiny beach amidst a mighty forest.

As they made sure that they were all safe and sound and that the Lockslayer was still breathing, their attention snapped to the churning of the river. Within only a few heartbeats the Jorlavar frothed and foamed and then returned to its ancient course and flowed back down in the direction of Ansalion and the lower lands. "It was a miracle, plain and simple," whispered Mr. Pierce.

"A miracle that saved our lives," added Cleric Michaels.

"Not all of us," said Lindris as she began to weep. No one spoke as the shock and horror of Bex's death suddenly struck them all.

After a while, Mr. Pierce asserted himself and began to organize the exhausted, broken party. He, Gresk, and Lindris set out to build a fire while Cleric Michaels and Heather saw to Eli's condition. Tolund heard his trainingmaster call his name, but he did not hear what the dwarf said because of a nagging from inside. Something was urging the boy to the darkness of the forest.

As if he were caught up in a deep sleep, Tolund staggered past the sandy shoreline, up an embankment, and into the thick foliage. The sound of his companions setting up their frantic camp seemed far off and unimportant. Tolund's hands quivered as he unsheathed his sword and held it tightly.

"We're not alone," he whispered to himself. Step by step he moved into the shadows of the woods as if he was entering an arena circle for battle. He no longer noticed that he was still cold and soaking wet from the river. His mouth dried up and his heart began to race. Six steps in, the hairs on the back of his neck and arms stood up. Tolund froze as something huge shifted the trees and bushes just before him.

In the eerie light, where the darkness of the thick forest still held sway, a macabre voice threatened, "Why have you come here to die?"

...To Be Continued.